LOVE
beyond
the
ILLUSION

Tangerine Sky Book 2

M.J. HUXLEY

M.J. Huxley

Cover Design © 2024 Lily Bear Design Co.

Editing and Proofread by: Melissa Smith Editing

First Edition: May 2024

This book is dedicated to women who are battling a little voice that tells them they're not good enough. Remember, you are beautifully strong and worthy of love.

Piper and Jack's story is for you.

A Note from the Author

Your mental health and personal triggers matter. Be advised that there are on-page descriptions of parental emotional abuse and off-page references to the death of a parent.

Love Beyond the Illusion is a slow burn but will pay off.

Playlist

"Save Tonight"— Eagle-Eye Cherry
"Lust for Life"— Lana del Rey
"Rock the Casbah"— Solar Twins
"Damaged"— Plumb
"Ocean Eyes"— Billie Eilish
"I Touch Myself"— Divinyls
"Circles"—Post Malone
"Iris"—Goo Goo Dolls
"Hurricane"—Cannons
"California Dreamin"—Freischimmer
"Crush"—Dave Matthews Band
"Electric"—Alina Baraz ft. Khalid
"Overexposed"—Song House
"Fading Like A Flower"—Roxette
"Days Go By"—Dirty Vegas
"Miss You"—Blink 182
"The Only Exception"—Paramore

Chapter One

Tucking my arm underneath the silk pillowcase, I roll over to the sound of my New York hookup snoring next to me. I stare at Landon's three-hundred-dollar haircut, square jaw, and alluring lips and wonder why I'm not more attracted to him.

The lack of moving air from a ceiling fan and the absence of the hum of an air conditioner leave a dense silence in the room. My overactive thoughts flip through the events of my childhood, how I grew up, and the choices I've made as an adult. It doesn't matter how old I get. They still seem to follow me.

Landon is getting married in a month. Despite knowing this, I showed up tonight as if nothing had changed. A guy engaged normally wouldn't bother me. I mean, it's his choice to continue sleeping with me, right? I'm not the one who's committed to someone else.

When we returned to the suite he booked, a wave of guilt rolled over me. I couldn't do it. And no matter how much of my mother is in me, I'm still part *me* as well.

I let my eyes trace the features of Landon's face while thinking about the wife he's about to have. She'll wake up to this view every morning. I'm not surprised when envy isn't the emotion that strikes, and that's because I also feel pity. My pity isn't only on her behalf because I doubt she's completely in the dark. It's for their future children and those who will come from his possible affairs. Landon mentioned his impending nuptials during a casual conversation over dinner. I sat across from him with my wine glass empty and my thoughts full, unsure how to answer his question.

Am I that person?

As a flight attendant, I fly in and out of New York City so often that Landon and I could easily keep this going like the last few months.

Suddenly, the thought of lying in bed next to him makes the hairs on the back of my neck stand up. Where is his fiancée? Where did he tell her he'd be tonight?

I've got to get the hell out of here.

I lift my phone from the floor next to the bed to text one of my best friends.

> **Me: I'm bored and need to get out of here. Meet me in the lobby in 15?**

Lina is with Landon's twin, Finn, in the suite next door, and I'm sure my text is interrupting the multiple orgasms she's receiving. I would be right there with her if not for my sudden melancholy lately. I wish I could say it began after Landon shared the news of him getting married, but it started well before then.

> **Lina: Same. I'll be right down.**

Lina and I met Landon and Finn a few months ago while they were on a flight from New York to Los Angeles. They're trust fund babies and live up to that title to the fullest. Each time we fly into New York City, they take us both out for dinner at impossible-to-get-into restaurants while putting us up in expensive hotel suites for a night of fucking on every single surface. Having a guaranteed hookup is nice, but I'm anxious and ready to move on.

Me: Thank goodness. Don't forget anything.

Pinching Landon's wrist between two fingers, I gingerly lift his arm draping across my torso. Resting it to the side, I slide off the bed and pull the comforter up in my place. I complained of a stomachache earlier this evening to get out of sleeping with him, but then he insisted on staying the night to care for me.

I guess that was sweet. I want to assume that he'll extend that same compassion to his future wife, but the realist in me knows better. The true reason that he stayed was horny hope that I'd suddenly feel better in the middle of the night and want a quick fuck.

With bare feet, I tiptoe over to my suitcase because I hate being without socks on hotel floors, and I don't want to wake up Landon. I shove the rest of my clothes inside, then hurry to the bathroom to swipe my toiletries bag from the white marble countertop. Being extremely quiet, I squish it into my suitcase.

Ugh. I wish there were a fucking air conditioner or some sort of sound.

I yank my hoodie off the back of an oversized chair, slip it over my head, and then carefully put on my athletics shoes. When I have everything packed, I glance around the room one more time before my eyes fall on Landon's sleeping body. It was fun while it lasted. But I can't be the other woman.

I'm sure he'll understand.

"Goodbye, Landon. Be faithful to your wife," I whisper before quietly slipping out the door.

My eyes are heavy with exhaustion on the elevator ride down to the lobby, but when I see my best friend's playful smile, I break out into a full belly laugh.

"Did we just ditch the twins in the middle of the night?" Lina calls out as I wheel my luggage across the mosaic-tiled floors.

"Yep!" I laugh.

"They're going to be pissed."

"Whatever." I shrug my shoulders. "Landon's getting married. Honestly, they're replaceable anyway."

"True. Did you get one last ride, though?" she teases, nudging my shoulder.

I sigh. "No, I felt guilty."

"She does have a conscience!" Lina smirks.

I'm the product of an affair and have been aware of that most of my life. My father was no more than a stranger to me. He was a simple man who paid his mistress to keep herself and his daughter a secret.

My father saw me as a burden—he'd already had his *real* family, so why did he need another? This was something that never bothered my mother as long as he kept the checks coming. Everything is about money with her. My mother has always been hyper-focused on how fast she can make a quick buck. She has freely discussed what she is entitled to from her lovers to our family. Will *this* relative die so she'd get her small windfall? When would *that* family member pass so she'd finally get the inheritance she thought she deserved?

The realization that my father paid my mother to keep me away became an unwanted passenger through every relationship I've had. It didn't help that my mother only looked at me as her potential income. My parents used me like traded goods. Growing up in that environment left me untrusting, hyper-independent, and unable to feel like I deserved love.

"Don't act so surprised." I roll my eyes. "What about you?"

"No, I wasn't in the mood." Lina frowns.

"You, not in the *mood*? Me, having *guilt*? What the hell is wrong with us?"

"I don't know. Maybe we're both tired of these lackluster men with their inability to use their penises properly?" The side of her mouth quirks up. "Just kidding. I'm flying into Boston next week, and you know what that means? I get to spend my overnight with Boston Jeff, and he's about a seven out of ten with his natural abilities."

"Mmm." I giggle. "Good in bed, but a little more emotional for your liking."

"Yes." She runs her tongue along the outside of her teeth. "Now he gets the job done well."

"He reminds me of Chris. You know, the one I met at the Pike Place Fish Market in Seattle last summer?" I ask.

Lina smiles. "Yes! I remember you were so disgusted by the fish smell everywhere."

"It was bad." I giggle. "We should grab a cab soon before Landon and Finn notice that we're gone," I interrupt her, suddenly realizing how long we'd been standing in the lobby.

Lina and I were dropped off at the hotel the airline booked

for us a short time later.

"I'm starving. Let's get some pancakes," I say, gesturing toward a small cafe to the left of the check-in counter.

She arches an eyebrow. "It's three in the morning."

"It's not like we're going to sleep anytime soon anyway."

She clicks her tongue. "Fine."

We walk over to the twenty-four-hour bistro to order pancakes to go. The woman behind the counter looks like a college student hopped up on too much coffee.

While we wait, I glance over at Lina. She's leaning against the pastry display case, letting out a wide yawn. My best friend is exhausted and should be in bed. We aren't required to report back to the airport until ten in the morning, which is plenty of time for me, but she's not a night owl like I am.

I lower my eyes, playfully glaring at her. "Don't act like you don't have fun with me whenever we're on the same flight crew."

"Oh, I have fun with you." She takes a finger and rubs the side of her eye. "I just always go home with less sleep than usual."

Unlike Lina, I'm not tired. My mind is restless at night, and if I were to give in to my urges entirely, I'd hit the hotel gym for a good workout preceding my sleep.

Chapter Two

As I travel up the long, windy driveway to our family property, a rush of fear strikes me that I will be moving back here for the first time in almost ten years. I head up the hill with the windows down, breathing in the scent of the fresh vineyards. I pass the tasting room and parking lot toward the base of the hill, then the wine cellars, barrel rooms, and the sorting and crushing stations. Further, I reach a second gate that leads onto our private property and directly to my parents' house.

I slow the car to a roll outside the double-swing security gate, punch in the code, and wait for what feels like an eternity to open. The pointed roof of the large rustic country house I grew up in peaks over the incline.

I pull around the circular driveway, park in front of the entrance, and then wave to the gardener, who's half into the branches of a tree he's trimming. I stroll around the car, removing the bags from the trunk. It's not that I don't want to be home, but I'd rather not be under these circumstances. The finality of everything has weighed on me for almost three months.

"Hello, is anyone home?" I call out, walking into the foyer. There's no answer. My mother is probably down in the tasting room. I glance at my watch and notice that it's almost closing time. She should be heading back to the main house any minute.

I make my way down the hallway, assuming that one of the staff members will be around somewhere, before I finally reach the downstairs guest bedroom. I look at the cream-colored wallpaper, extra-large bed, and Wine Country-themed wall decor and decide against it. I can't stay here. No fucking way.

I'm startled by the distant clunking sound of dishes in the kitchen. *I guess someone is home.*

I head back through the hallway toward the noise that ricochets off the vaulted ceilings. Rounding the corner, I see Gemma. She has her back to me as she's hanging pots and pans over one of the two islands.

"Hello, Gemma."

"Jack!" she yelps. "You scared me, honey!"

"Sorry, I didn't mean to." I laugh, extending my arm for a friendly hug.

Her eyes light up as she smiles at me. "It's so good to see you! When did you get in?"

Gemma manages the tasting room kitchen, creating a special menu of snacks and small plates for the guests who visit the winery. She is also my family's chef and has been with us since I was young.

"Just now." I scan the backyard and pool from the kitchen's panoramic windows. "Where's my mother?"

Gemma grabs a towel from one of the drawers and wipes a puddle of water on the counter. "She's down in the tasting room helping them clean up for the night."

"Okay, thanks." I grab an apple from the fruit bowl and bite

into it.

"How are you holding up? I feel like we haven't seen you since your dad's funeral."

"I'm just existing." I dismiss, not wanting to talk about my dad. I tuck my hand under my arm and lean against the marble countertops. "How are you doing?"

"Well, it's been hard on all of us, especially your mom."

My gaze lowers to the floor. "I know."

"But she is so strong and has an incredible support system here on the property. The entire staff has stepped up to help more," she adds. She's not trying to call me out for my absence after losing my father three months ago, but that's how it feels. I could have been here more often, I know that. I haven't been around much since I moved to Arizona for college.

"I'm sorry that I haven't been here more," I say.

"I know, but you've had a lot to take care of in Phoenix. You're wrapping up everything with the marketing firm and getting your condo on the market." She pats my shoulder with reassurance, but her eyes show disappointment.

My father unexpectedly passed away this summer. His loss was hard on my mom and me but also on the staff and community as well. It was easier to stay in Phoenix—far away from the stress and expectations—and away from the memories.

"Yeah, and I know she's grateful for that. As I am."

We're both silent for a beat before Gemma tenderly squeezes my hand. "It's about time for dusk. You should head to the west patio. I'll bring you a glass of red wine and a snack plate," she says before waving me off.

"Thank you."

As I roll my luggage to the couch and walk to the glass doors, I hear my mom's voice behind me when I reach out to clutch the handle.

"Jack!" she shouts before pulling me into a tight embrace. "I've missed you so much!"

I wrap my arms around my mother's petite frame. "I've missed you too."

Smiling, she draws her head back, holding my arms at a distance. "I'll grab something for us to eat, then meet you out there," she says before scurrying into the kitchen with Gemma.

I laugh to myself and these two women I've missed terribly, then settle into one of the chairs on the wooden patio. When my parents built this house, they added a balcony on all three stories to capture perfect views of the Wine Country sunset. The sky transforms from shades of coral to rose. Off to the side, the familiar rolling hills I've spent summer evenings running around as a child are lined with mature grape vines ready to be harvested.

A few minutes later, my mother joins me outside taking the seat to my left. She sets a snack plate and two glasses of red wine on the small table between our two chairs.

"How are you feeling?" she asks, grabbing a cracker.

I sigh. "The last couple of months have been a lot to process."

"I know. Things have been difficult without your father," she admits, patting the top of my hand. "But we're going to pull through."

"I still have a lot of reservations about stepping into this role," I admit.

"I understand, honey, but you were born to do this. You were always meant to run the winery," she lovingly reminds me.

"But I'm nowhere near ready to do this." I focus my eyes away from her. "I'm not dad."

"No one is expecting you to be exactly like your father. The whole operation is a lot for one person, I know that," she replies, lowering her sunglasses to cover her eyes. "Bradley Wines will only continue to be successful if someone can take on the things I can't. You know how this side of the business works."

"Yeah."

"I know this is hard for you because it was never your dream, but you would be amazing." She sighs.

"I guess I just figured I'd have more time to work on my career first."

"You've had six years in marketing. You've helped build so many successful restaurants. You have a degree in business. You have more knowledge and experience than your dad and I ever did."

Slumping against the back of the chair, I breathe a heavy sigh.

"Were you able to put an offer down for the house on Honeysuckle?"

I nod. That house is something that I'm looking forward to. The second I pulled into the driveway, I knew there was something different about it. It's a large, white, ranch-style home only about ten minutes from the winery.

I am excited about the house, but I still find myself clutching the rim of the wine glass with frustration. The winery was my father's dream, not mine. I'll never be able to live up to how this community saw him. He was an intricate part of this town and the close regions. I'll spend my whole life being scrutinized and compared to my father.

My entire life was planned out for me before I was even born. It's suffocating.

"You know your father always wanted you to take over the winery, Jack, and if this is something you're going to do, you'll have to establish yourself within the community again." My mom continues our previous conversation.

"I realize that," I say.

Living in a small community has its advantages and, unfortunately, disadvantages. One is that if I ever want to start a family, the assumption will be that I'll marry someone within the growers' community. We're tight-knit to a fault, work with our own, and pass down generational wealth like free candy on Halloween. Not to mention with an added side of pressure and privilege. *I can't fucking stand it.*

She lifts a glass of last year's red from the table, delicately pinching the stem and taking a sip. "I know you had a very tumultuous relationship with your father, but all he ever wanted was to give all of this to you," she says, gesturing toward the vineyard.

Dragging my eyes across the hand-planted crops that make up a hundred acres of my father's legacy, unease settles in my stomach. *Can I do this? Do I even want to do this?*

"I am aware of that too," I quip, sensing the weight of her words. The burden I've carried my entire life. The expectation has always been for me to run my family's business, and that's exactly why I needed to get away from here as soon as I had the chance.

Who was I without the Bradley name?

My father had no problem making it known how

disappointed he was with my lack of interest in the winery—a place he lovingly called his *life's purpose.*

"You were born into something great, and not everyone is as lucky as you are," she adds, resting her hands on the armrest of her garden chair. I ignore her attempt at a guilt trip.

I'm not some billionaire trust fund guy, but my family has made millions from wine. It began with my dad in the 1980s. He and my mom moved north from Los Angeles, searching for a quiet farm life to fulfill my dad's dream of owning a working winery and vineyard.

"You're not helping this situation by listing everything I already know." I square my shoulders. My hands clasped on top of my knees.

"The only other option is to let Steve's son Preston take over, and you can go back to Phoenix and continue to do what you've been doing."

I scoff at her apparent lack of providing a legitimate choice. "I can't do that to dad—or you."

"Preston is already a part of the community. He's been running Mountain Coast Winery for the last couple years, and I know his new fiancée is also interested in taking on a leadership role," she tells me.

Preston Rivers. My friend *slash* friendly rival since we were kids and the son of my dad's best friend. We grew up together and, at one point, were close. Then high school happened, and friendly competition became not so friendly. We both excelled on the swim team, fought over girls, and tried to one-up each other every chance we got.

But things took a turn when I caught him kissing my

girlfriend after a swim meet. I wasn't that into her, but it was a huge blow to my ego. When I confronted them about it, she said I wasn't "paying her enough attention" and that she wanted to "make me jealous." That plan backfired. It gave me an excuse to break up with her before graduation.

I've been disconnected for the last ten years, and I hadn't realized that Preston ended up taking the same path my father always wanted me to follow.

"That can't happen." My eyebrows snap together. "I didn't know Preston was getting married."

She grimaces. "Yes, I thought you knew. He's marrying Sophia Dennings."

My high school girlfriend. The same girlfriend who hooked up with one of my other friends our senior year. The one who wanted to marry me as soon as we graduated. The same girl who told me that college would be a waste since I'd already had a career and wealth. How we differed on so many fundamental beliefs and goals could not have been more apparent.

The last thing I wanted was to get married at eighteen and never experience anything for myself. An itch of unrest brewed inside my young mind as I knew I had to create my own path. When I left, I vowed never to return to my hometown, and in the years I've been gone, I've quietly returned only a handful of times.

When it was time to move back to Dupara after my college graduation, I stayed where I was and accepted a job at a marketing firm in Phoenix.

"Why am I not surprised that she went on to date another one of my friends," I condescendingly spit as if she didn't already know.

"Since Sophia comes from an old family of growers, it would have been a good match for you. I'm sure Steve was thinking the same thing about his son," she points out.

I try to hold back the obvious disgust with respect for my mom but fail miserably.

She shakes her head, grabs her glass from the table between us, and heads toward the maple wood French doors. "You have always been one to do things your own way—and with a slight chip on your shoulder, I might add. But one day, someone will come along and knock that chip right off."

"You never know," I kindly dismiss her.

"Alright. I love you, son," she says, stepping into the house.

Looking back toward the endless hills, I take the first drink of my red, which is now finally the temperature I prefer. "I love you too," I mutter into the empty air. I pull out my phone and scroll through my work emails.

When I handed in my official resignation letter to the marketing firm, they were heartbroken by my departure but asked that I stay on for sixty days to finish up with my clients who still have open projects. The rest are being dispersed among my colleagues.

I knew this day would come, but I never expected it so soon.

I stayed outside until the sun set and the automatic patio light turned on. I fly out to Vegas this weekend to finish up with my last client. Shortly after, I officially move out of my condo in Phoenix to relocate back up here to Dupara, giving up the last bit of freedom I'll ever know.

Chapter Three
Piper

I jiggle with the key to the front door while my phone vibrates in the pocket of my uniform. Sliding my phone out, I see who's calling—and like it always does when I see her name pop up on the screen, a dark, thick cloud rolls in, blanketing me with a heavy, dense pressure.

"Hello, Roxy," I answer.

"Why do you always insist on calling me by my first name, my little Piper Moon?" she asks. I never wanted to call my mother by her first name, but it hasn't felt natural to refer to her as *mom* since I was a child.

"What do you need?" I ask, wheeling my luggage into my small, one-bedroom, high-rise apartment in downtown Scottsdale.

"It seems I've gotten myself into a bit of a pickle again, sweetie. I'm going to need help with rent this month." My mother's voice lacks the typical shame or embarrassment that one would expect. It takes on a cheery tone like it always does because in her world, I'm a mere extension of her. Roxy has always felt entitled to anything I've had, and she eagerly takes what's hers.

I let my bag fall to the floor. I need to unpack my clothes from this last trip and switch them out for the next. "I thought Kurt was helping you with rent?"

"No, no, Kurt is out of the picture. He was not good for my aura. You know that's something I need to protect. And besides, you can afford it with your high-paying flight attendant salary anyway."

I huff at her comment regarding how much money I make. We've gone over it multiple times in the last four years, that I only make a living wage. But to her—someone who's had to rely on others for income, that seems like a lot.

"I've told you this many times. Flight attendants only make an average salary. That means I make enough money for myself and my lifestyle," I say, throwing my dirty uniform into the laundry basket. "I cannot keep supporting you."

The force knocks it to the ground with a loud thud, and it's all I need to grow more anxious for what's coming on this phone call. They all follow the same pattern. She asks for money, and I respond reluctantly. She makes me feel like a terrible daughter. I give in, and then she attempts to make me feel like it's my fault for even thinking about refusing her in the first place.

"That's not fair for you to say that. I am your mother, and I'm all by myself. You know that. And don't forget that I supported you while you were a child. The least you could do is pay your mother back by being there when I need *you* to support *me*," she replies with an edge to her words.

"I have been helping you since I was able to get a job." I weakly try to defend myself.

"As you should."

Roxy spits the same lines every time she needs something

from me—the ones I've heard since I got my first job as a waitress when I was fifteen. We needed help with rent since her boyfriend at the time had moved out. He left us with the apartment and the lease, which, conveniently, had my name on it. Roxy told me we'd be homeless if I didn't because her credit was bad.

With my name on the lease, she had even more power over me. Once, during finals week in my junior year of high school, I wanted to take some time off to focus on my studies, but Roxy threatened that if I didn't want my credit ruined, I had to figure out how to balance both.

I'm sure my mother would have pulled me out of school to work if it wasn't illegal. My mother is capable of working and providing for herself. She does not have any limitations preventing her from it. And the problem isn't *finding* employment. The problem is *keeping* it.

"How much do you need?" I ask, saving her from a full episode of gaslighting and manipulation at my expense.

"I knew you wouldn't leave your mother hanging." Her voice was tight like she was holding back a smile. Roxy knew I'd give in. I always do. She's emotionally ripped me apart my entire life, but she's still my mother. "Rent is due tomorrow, so I need you to send it through that little money app you always use. You know, the one that's on my phone?"

"Tomorrow?" I snap. "Nice to wait until the last minute."

"I'm not in the mood for a lecture. Just send it over."

I exhale with exasperation, hoping she hears. *Would she care anyway?* "Fine. Send me the request, and I'll transfer the funds tonight."

"I should be okay for next month. There's this guy I met

working the night shift, and he's super hung up on me. I'm almost positive he will start paying the rent on my apartment. He's setting it up so his wife doesn't find out."

"He's married!?" I shout.

She cackles. "If I'm lucky, maybe she'll find out anyway and leave him. Then he won't have to spend so much on her. He tells me she—" I remove the phone from my ear until her evil cackling is finished. Of course, he's married. Am I surprised? No. "You know, my little Piper Moon, you're becoming quite judgmental in your older years," she states condescendingly.

"Why does it have to be someone who's married? Don't you remember what happened with Paul? He was married. You guys had a fling. He said he would leave his wife and never did. And *my dad?*"

"The heart wants what it wants."

"Your heart always seems to want married, unavailable men."

"With bank accounts and cars, I might add." Her tone is cheery once again. She wears those words like a badge of honor.

"Have you ever thought about going on one of those dating apps? Maybe searching for someone who actually wants to be in a healthy, secure relationship?"

"The world is not as easy as your little brain makes it out to be," she replies. And there it is, another one of the many *kind* things that my mother likes to say to me. Her words do hurt, but only on the inside. On the outside, I've become numb to them over the years and have learned to accept the treatment as the norm.

I squeeze my eyelids shut, running through ways to change the subject. "How are you feeling?"

"Why do you always ask me that? It's not like you care. You barely see me. Since you went to college, nothing has been the same," she complains.

My mother's inability to regulate her emotions created an unstable environment for me growing up. We didn't talk about feelings. She's uncomfortable with them and shows anger instead of love. I'm expected to check in on her feelings and monitor her emotions. The constant worrying has made me believe I am only worthy when I can do something. It left little time for me to develop and monitor my own. I experienced my feelings being pushed aside and invalidated for much of my childhood and now as an adult.

When I started college, I got a small taste of freedom. I was able to get to know myself for the first time in my entire life. I was able to establish my inner voice and start putting myself first. I was punching holes in the dark veil I'd been living under, slowly gaining my vision. But no matter how I fought to open those holes, letting the light shine through, she was always there to cover them up again.

"I'm not in the mood to go back and forth with you. I just returned from flying the last two days, and I'd like to rest in my quiet apartment," I say, tucking the phone back into the crook of my neck.

She huffs. "Your life would be so much better if you found a man to take care of you."

"You mean a married man like you?" I'm losing my patience.

"Any man is better than no man at all. But you'll never understand because you choose to live your life alone. And don't think I didn't hear you bring up your father again. I'm not going to talk about him."

Maybe he was the only one who truly broke her heart. I barely remember my dad. My only memories are of him visiting me and Roxy when we lived in the apartment behind the grocery store where she worked. His visits were brief. The man, who I was told was my father, would saunter in but not further than the doorway. He would come around dinner time, usually in a navy suit. He'd hand Roxy a thick white envelope filled with cash before shooting me a quick look of acknowledgment and slinking away as quickly as he arrived.

I roll my eyes at her backhanded comment. "I don't *want* to spend my time alone, but I also don't want to make the same mistakes you do. I had a clear trajectory on that path until I decided I wanted different things."

A family. I've wanted one since I was a child. Sitting down together for dinner each night to talk about normal things like school or sports—simple and mundane, but it's something that I've never had. The only thing I think I've wanted more is stability. But I have accepted that it's not my path. I wouldn't even recognize a life like that anyway, since I've never seen it.

"You think you're so much better than me," she hisses. "At least I know how to use my beauty the way it should be used. Unlike you."

Roxy has always been beautiful and knows it. She's had a way with men that, as a child, I couldn't understand. Her natural allure allows her to seduce them into doing everything she wants, which is utterly fascinating. More so once I became an adult.

By my eighteenth birthday, my eyes had lightened to a vibrant shade of hazel with green more prominent, and with my strawberry blonde hair, I had become a dead ringer for my mother. By then, she'd taught me how to use guys for my benefit without getting attached. I don't want to be the wife who has to look the other way while my husband cheats. I don't want to fall completely in love with someone only for them to leave me one day. All men have affairs. All men will eventually leave. I don't get attached.

I add soap into the compartment on the left of the washing machine, then punch the button to turn it on. "Whatever. I'm getting off the phone with you. You'll have your money tonight." I hang up the phone before she has the chance to respond.

Chapter Four

Bailey and I are walking through the loud slot machine-filled airport to catch our new flight back to Phoenix. Yesterday, we should've arrived back home after working for three days, but our flight out of Las Vegas was canceled. We had to stay an extra night.

"You know how much I hate unexpected overnight layovers," Bailey says as we walk through the airport. "But at least I get to deal with it with my best friend."

Unexpected changes in travel plans have never bothered me. I roll with it because it's part of the excitement of the job. I feel the most comfortable on the go, spending most of my time traveling. I put more flight time in than any other flight attendant I know. Lina takes a close second.

I link my arm through Bailey's. "I do enjoy the unpredictability of it all. When you grow up in an unstable environment, I guess you get used to it." I shrug. "What would my world be without chaos and unstructuredness?"

She flashes me a lopsided grin. "You have to admit, it's so much better dealing with it with your three best friends." She nudges her shoulder into me as we walk.

I smile. "True. I don't know what I would do without you,

Lina, and Avery. You ladies are like my sisters."

"We are sisters, babe—" Her head quickly jerks in the opposite direction. "Jack?" Bailey stops and turns to a tall blond man briskly walking past us. It looks like he's headed to the second floor of the airport.

"Bailey, hello." The man in a black collared shirt and matching dress pants, with a strong jawline and windblown hair, pauses to greet my friend. *Damn.*

"How are you?" she asks.

"I'm doing well. You?"

"I'm great. Our flight was canceled last night, so we're finally flying out this afternoon," she tells him, then gestures toward me. "Oh, Jack, this is my friend Piper. Piper, this is Jack Bradley. He does restaurant concept marketing and works with Mason and my brother."

He shifts his focus to me. "Hello, Piper." When Jack's eyes meet mine, I blink several times.

"Hi. It's nice to meet you," I reply. My eyes locked with his, forcing me to hide a smile too wide. I get a flutter in my stomach.

His arm comes out to shake my sweaty palm, and thankfully, he doesn't seem to notice the damp feel of it. "I believe we met at Harry's wedding last spring."

"That's right," Bailey interjects, bouncing her eyes between Jack and me.

"I was there, but I don't believe we met." I don't look directly at him, trying to avoid embarrassing myself with my inability to keep a straight face.

Jack smiles. "I'm sure we did. You were one of the bridesmaids."

"Yes, but I would've remembered if we met."

"I remember *you,* Piper."

I blush. We're shaking hands longer than acceptable.

"Alright. Okay, so it was nice to run into you." With her best effort, Bailey attempts to break the tension between Jack and me.

He nods, letting his hand slip from mine and back to the top of the extended handle on his suitcase. "Yes, it was. Tell Mason and Harry I said hello," he tells her, but then his eyes end up back on me.

What the hell is going on? Why can't I look this man in the face? He probably thinks I'm so awkward. Yes, he's ridiculously attractive, but that does not explain the embarrassing physical reaction that I'm having.

Jack turns to me, grinning. "It was nice *formally* meeting you," he says before walking away.

I nod. "You too."

Bailey slowly turns to me with her eyes wide and a goofy smile. "Oh my god, Piper, you are so embarrassing." She laughs. "And your cheeks are red!"

"What?" Bailey picked up on my momentary brain lapse. Which means Jack did, too. *Great.*

"You had such an obvious grin on your face the whole time." She shoves my shoulder. With which that *said* grin comes right back. "See that one, and it's a mile long!"

Opening my mouth to speak, I'm unable to form the words—a waterfall of giggles bubbles from my chest. "I know. I don't know what came over me. The minute he looked at me, I froze. It was super weird."

The effect it had on me is similar to the energy pulling you into someone's gaze. The magnetism from a stare that almost feels as if there's a chain linking you and another person—but this was nothing like that. Jack's electric blue eyes have energy that could rival the sun. Where pulses emit with such intensity that looking directly at them is almost impossible.

"He's incredibly good-looking too. That square jawline—like Mason's. I want to bite it," she teases.

"Your brother's wedding was big, but how could I not remember someone that looks like that?" I tousle my hair in bewilderment.

"I have no idea."

"Tell me about him?" I demand, eager to learn more about this mystery man who gave me thousands of butterflies when I met him.

"Oh, so you're interested." Bailey nods her head while her eyebrows raise. "Jack was part of my brother's college fraternity and now works in marketing in Phoenix. I've only recently got to know him better after Harry and Mason asked him to partner with them on the restaurant concept and marketing for *The Poppy*."

"Alright," I say with a cheery voice, appreciating her spilling the tea about the tall, hot blond man who looks like he walked out of a 1990s Tiger Beat magazine. "B, he looks like a young Leo. I'm not going to lie. It made my knees weak."

"I can totally see that!" Bailey agrees, grabbing my hand to brace herself, laughing while we walk past the airport restaurants and bars. I can't shake the intense urge to head in the other direction. Hell, I always hook up with attractive guys, so why is my body itching to follow Jack? Maybe there's something different about him? I'm not sure, but I'm going to find out.

I abruptly stop, shifting toward my friend with a Cheshire smile on my face. "Do you know if he's single?"

She smiles with a large grin. "I believe so. I know which of Harry's friends from college are married, and I'm positive Jack is not."

My heart knocks on the back of my ribs. I nibble my bottom lip with excitement. "Should I go talk to him?"

Her eyes grow wide. "Yes! I saw the way you two had to pry your hands away from each other. I'd say he felt a little spark, too."

I swallow hard, my eyes bouncing from the restaurant that Jack looked like he walked into and my best friend. "Okay, I think I'm going to."

"I love how free-spirited you are. My stomach is literally flipping for you," she says.

I giggle. "Do I look okay?"

"Are you seriously asking me that?" Bailey cocks her head and lowers her eyes. "You are fucking gorgeous, and your hair looks all fluffy," she replies, leaning in to smell it. "And it smells good!

Chuckling, I bat her away. "Vegas was my last flight for the next few days. If we hit it off, I could jump on a later one tonight."

"You better text or call me later when you get home to tell me how it went."

My legs shake with excitement while I jump out of my skin. "I will. I promise!"

I lean in to give her a quick hug before turning on my heels to head into the restaurant. With my black carry-on wheeling behind me, I scan the small area until I see Jack's black shirt and immaculate side profile. He's sitting in the back corner with his face hidden behind a laptop. He looks deep in thought and typing away—presumably an email. After each step I take, I'm briefly hit with self-doubt but manage to push it away. My heart skips a few beats before I even fully enter the restaurant.

He sips from a glass of red wine when I approach the table. "Hello."

Jack glances up at me with a smile from where he's sitting. "Piper, hi."

"I was walking by and saw you sitting over here—"

Jack gestures to the seat on the opposite side of the corner table. "Would you like to join me?"

The chair rattles when I pull it out to sit down. I hadn't thought about what I would say to him or how I would explain why I followed him in here. "My flight doesn't leave for another two hours, and I figured you might want some company." *Alright, that makes sense.*

"I'd love some company." He grins warmly, gently closing his laptop. "Can I get you a drink?"

I zip my necklace back and forth, the sound only buzzing inside my ears. I'm suddenly more nervous than I expected to be. "Yes, um, a glass of wine would be great. I like chardonnay."

Jack waves the server over. "I know what to get you."

When she appears at our table, Jack orders a glass of wine by a name I know I've heard before, but my mind glosses over it. I'm distracted by the feeling of familiarity between us. *I know I haven't met him before.*

"I'm sure you'll like it. It's slightly buttery but still has those same elements that you'd find in a crisp, classic chardonnay," he explains. This man knows his wine.

"Do you drink a lot of vino?" I arch an eyebrow.

"You could say that," he says playfully. "So, you're a flight attendant?"

I continue to avoid his controlled gaze while trying to keep myself together. "I am. How did you know?"

The server brings over my glass. Pinching the stem, I gulp in a heavy drink of liquid courage. *Damn, I'm nervous.*

"Mason's girlfriend mentioned you were supposed to fly out last night, and I know she's a flight attendant," he says. "I assumed you were too." Hearing him say that Bailey is Mason's girlfriend is still a trip because she hasn't dated anyone since I've known her. Then, going from completely hating Mason to that romantic mess she turns into every time someone brings him up is surreal.

"Yeah, we met in flight attendant school and our two other close friends. You may have met them at the wedding. They were bridesmaids as well."

Jack crosses his arms on top of the table. "I don't remember them."

"But you remember me?"

"I do." He takes a drink. There's an awkward silence between us before he speaks. "You guys are flying home to Phoenix tonight?"

I set my glass on the table. "We are. We've been gone for the last two days."

"I bet that's a cool experience to travel so often."

I smile, thinking about the freedom I get from Roxy and how

lonely it can be. "It is. I've definitely gotten to know people from all over, which is pretty awesome."

Jack's eyebrow raises from over the rim of his wineglass as he takes a sip. "Like men in different states?" He smirks. *He's flirting with me.*

"Not often." I rub my lips together, biting back a smile again.

"Someone who looks like you and whose energy is as infectious as yours, I find that hard to believe."

I melt under his unapologetic flattery. My cheeks reddening, I take another sip. "Are you trying to make me blush already?"

"I'm not trying to. But if I am, I wouldn't be mad about it," he replies.

I laugh nervously, tearing my paper napkin into shreds on the table.

"I'm kind of hurt you don't remember me from the wedding." He twists the stem of his glass.

"I don't, I'm sorry. I guess you didn't make much of an impression." I tease.

His eyes pin me from across the table. "That's fine. You can be sure I'm not going to let that happen again."

I pull my mouth to one side. "Are you flirting with me?"

He rests back in his chair while folding his arms across his chest. "Absolutely not. I don't flirt with women I've never met."

"I thought you said we've already met?" I challenge him, finishing off the glass. Before the rim leaves my lips, he is already gesturing to our server to bring us another.

"We have. But you said we hadn't, which means we're still strangers," he says, picking up one of the two drinks that were placed in front of us.

"Fair enough." I sit straighter in my chair, feeling more confident after the two glasses of wine.

"Let's not be strangers then." Jack clasps his hands together and rests them with bent elbows on the table. "I already know your name and what you do for a living. The next logical thing for me is to ask what your favorite color is."

I suck in air through my teeth. "I don't know, I feel like my favorite color is a little too personal."

His eyebrows raise. "Can I guess?"

"Sure."

He bites his bottom lip before speaking. "Blue."

I scrunch my nose. "Obvious choice, that's everyone's favorite color."

"Red?"

"Nope." I sit back against the chair, crossing my arms at my chest to match his. Just then, the waitress comes over. Jack and I decide to order dinner, then another glass of wine each.

When our waitress brought the check, we'd been talking about the most random things for the last few hours. If someone asks me what we spoke about tomorrow, I won't be able to tell them because it's been utter nonsense.

"What time is your flight out?" I ask, suddenly becoming aware of the time.

"It was at 6:05."

I straighten in shock. "Oh my god, Jack, it's 6:41! You missed your flight."

"I'll catch another one." He calmly bends forward with a slight smirk. "What about your flight? What time was yours leaving?"

My ears burn. "My flight left two and a half hours ago," I bashfully admit, folding my arms on the table in front of me and forcing us closer together.

"It looks like we're both going to stay in Vegas for the night." Jack loosens the thin silk tie that hangs tight around his neck. "What should we do?"

Fuck yes! I'm infused with a surge of adrenaline. I'll enjoy a fun night with a tall, sexy man with blue eyes and an energy I feel in my bones.

My weekend just got a hell of a lot better. I can't say that skipping my flight to spontaneously stay in a random city with a man I've just met—or, according to him, who I've already met isn't out of character. But this is the most fun adventure I've had in a long time.

I polish off the rest of my drink. Dipping my head forward, I meet Jack's eyes—which is much simpler now that I've had a few glasses of wine. "Let's go have some fun, Jack Bradley."

"Check!" He calls out to our server. A satisfied smile moves across the perfect bone structure of his chin and face.

Chapter Five

"**I**'ve never met anyone like you before! You know wine, and you're good at the slot machines," I say in my high-pitched voice that increases in elevation with each passing alcoholic beverage. "No one is good on the slots!"

Jack laughs, slipping another player card into one of the penny machines we can't seem to leave. "Trust me, I'm not. You're just good luck."

I flush. "Maybe."

Foggy-eyed, I grab the light green martini from the side of my Jurassic Park-themed game. And to think I loved dinosaurs as a kid? I've only played on it twice since I've had myself shoved into Jack's space while he plays on his. He's not bothered by my lack of personal space and has even wrapped an arm around me a few times to nudge me closer.

My eyes fall closed as I take a sip from the oddly shaped glass that holds an apple-flavored beverage. Wait. *How did I get this drink? Is this what I ordered?* It tastes like shit. "Why is this green?" I ask, haphazardly pushing it less than an inch from his face.

Chuckling, Jack draws his head back. "It's a green apple martini. I told you not to get it. You hate green apples."

I pull my mouth to the side, creasing my forehead. "How do you know I don't like green apples?"

Jack wraps his hand around the back of mine, drifting the glass away from the front of his face. "When we were talking about the fruits we don't like, you gave me an extremely passionate speech about how green apples are the worst fruit and should be removed from every grocery store permanently." His hand wraps around mine, placing the martini back down on the side of his game. "You even listed three reasons why."

I nod. "Oh yes, I forgot that. And yours are blackberries."

"You remembered." He smirks, pressing the *BET* button, and the game starts spinning.

"I'm bored with these stupid machines and this nasty drink." I hold up one unstable finger into the air. "And my experience in this hotel *slash* casino would be greatly enhanced if I was to win something."

"I think I can find you a different drink. I'll take another one too." Jack slips a hand into mine and tugs me into a standing position. "Let's get you something you'll like and find a game where your odds will be better."

"You are my hero. Do you know that, Jack Bravley?" I say, quickly falling behind him as he gently pulls me through the dense crowd on the casino floor.

Jack stops and turns to me. "What's my last name?"

"Bravley? Bradley!" I excitedly scream, proud of myself.

The corners of his eyes crinkle as he chuckles. "It's Bradley, Piper. Bradley."

"My bad." I rub my lips together, ashamed at how my drunken words are coming out.

"I'll let it pass." His thumb rubs the inside of my palm. "You're adorable. Which you have going for you."

If my hand wasn't so numb, I could feel his light touch. I don't need another drink, but I'm having so much fun with him. I don't want the night to end. Jack leads me over to the independent roulette tables. I fall into the seat to his left as he quickly rattles off the rules and strategies of the game.

I know how to play roulette. It's my favorite table. I humor him, smiling and nodding. Instead of paying attention to what he's explaining, I study the small scar on his forehead right above his right eyebrow.

I suddenly find myself only a half an inch from his face—once again. "Where did you get that scar from?" I boldly ask.

Jack finishes making his selection on the roulette screen, then waves down one of the cocktail servers before answering me. He doesn't back away, letting his breath dust over my lips. They tingle. "I fell into a grapevine when I was seven."

I try not to crack a smile because I expected him to say a bicycle accident or a fight with a kid at school, but falling into a *grapevine* was the last thing I would have thought.

"Interesting," I say, lifting my hand to let my index finger gently glide across the scar. Jack doesn't back away or even flinch.

"What can I get you guys?" A large black tray with empty glasses appears between us.

"What would you like?" he asks me.

I shrug. "I don't care, something fruity but not apple."

"She'll take a pineapple martini, and I'll have a vodka soda," Jack tells the woman before she briskly walks toward the bar to fill our order.

My eyes fall to his lips. "That was a good choice."

"I knew you'd like it." He runs his tongue along his bottom lip, sensing my stare.

It's almost one in the morning when Jack and I find ourselves in the middle of a rowdy craps table. We're shoulder to shoulder with various groups of people that line the oval perimeter. Each time someone rolls the dice, the entire table screams and hollers—including myself and Jack. The energy level in this spot is unmatched compared to other games on the casino floor.

As a text message comes through, I fumble to get my phone. Bailey is messaging me from our group chat.

> Bailey: Just checking on you, Piper. How was Jack?

> Me: Still in Vegas. He's a fucking catch. Tell you about it in the AM.

> Lina: Who's Jack?

> Avery: Who the hell, Jack? TELL ME NOW!

I giggle.

> Bailey: We ran into him at the airport. He went to college with Mason and Harry.

> Me: We hit it off, and now we're in Vegas together.

> Bailey: You're still in Vegas?

> Avery: Shut up! Why are we just now

hearing about this?

Lina: Piper! Why didn't you tell us?

Me: I will tell you ladies all about him later.

Before I have a chance to get distracted from more of their responses, I shove my phone back into my cross bag. "I have to go to the bathroom," I whisper yell into Jack's ear, fighting the urge to bring my lips to his earlobe.

He shoots me a mischievous grin. "Is that an invitation?"

My lashes flutter. "Funny."

"I am, aren't I?"

"I'll be right back." I toss over my shoulder, heading off the casino floor.

I palm the double doors right as my phone vibrates once again. I might as well give my friends the scoop, or they won't leave me alone for the rest of the night. With slightly wobbly legs, I sit on the pink couch next to a full-length mirror in the ladies' room.

"Spill it." I hear Bailey's voice on the other end. "And you're three-wayed in with Avery and Lina too."

I giggle. "Hello, my lovely friends."

"You missed your flight home?" Lina asks in a lively tone.

Avery laughs. "That must have been some good conversation."

I rub my lips together, thinking about Jack. "Oh, it was! And a pair of the most perfect electric blue eyes to stare into." My words come out with a subtle drawl, but I still smile into the mirror with satisfaction for keeping myself together.

Lina laughs. "How drunk are you?"

"Yeah, you sound plastered!" Avery adds.

"A lot. I'm a lot drunk. But I'm still standing, and you three know I've been worse off than this before." My voice comes out rushed and breathy.

"Oh my god. I love you so much!" Bailey exclaims. "Jack is safe, so I'm sure you'll be fine."

"That's good." Avery comments with a sigh of relief.

"Stop it, ladies," Lina scolds them both. "Like you don't know Piper? She's a goddess at handling stuff like this. She's good. Let her have fun." She's not wrong.

"I have not a care in the world."

"Of course you don't," Avery says playfully.

We all share a laugh.

"Enjoy, babe. Be safe and update us tomorrow," Lina says before I end the call.

After using the bathroom, with wild butterflies in my stomach, I realize I'm in store for the best hookup of my life. My reflection is a little blurry, but I can't help winking at myself in the mirror. Jack is a catch. He's completely out of my league, and that's why I'm going to enjoy every single minute of our drunk Vegas fun.

By the time I'm back at the craps table, it's Jack's turn. He quickly glances down at me. "I missed you."

I gaze up at him through my lashes. From this angle, his eyes sparkle, and his lips look more plump than usual. "I missed *you*."

He holds out his hand in front of me with black and white dice in the center of his palm. "Will you blow on my dice?" *So cliché, but I fucking eat it up.*

"I'd love to," I tell him, puckering my lips together and lightly blowing into his hand.

His focus bounces between my lips and my eyes. I don't mind blowing on Jack's dice, and at this point in the night, I'd probably blow on other things if he asked me.

"I'd blow on other things if you asked me to." *Oh my god. Did I say that out loud?*

I did. But I don't care.

Jack's eyebrows snap together, and he licks his lips. "I think I can arrange that."

Chapter Six

Jack

At two in the morning and another alcoholic beverage later, we now find ourselves in a small yet funky lounge off to the side of the madness that has surrounded us all evening. The sound of high bells of the lucky or unlucky slot machines chime in the background.

"I'm surprised you haven't stayed with your first choice of wine this evening because you sure know more about wine than the average man," she teases, with a little smirk lifting the corners of her mouth.

I lean in, with bent knees touching the small black circle table between us. "My family owns a winery," I tell her, stroking the top of her thigh. A bold move for me because I'm not usually the one making the moves.

"That explains it." Piper raises her eyes to me. "I'm assuming you aren't part of the family business since you work in marketing."

My body automatically stiffens. I'm thrust back into the unfortunate reality of the loss of my dad and how my whole life is being turned upside down. The sinking feeling in the pit of my stomach returns after a brief reprieve the last few hours.

"Yeah. I moved away to attend college in Arizona, then started working for a marketing company out there after graduation." I take a generous swig from my drink. It burns going down, but I take another anyway.

Piper rests her chin in her palm. "So, do you have any plans on ever being a part of your family's winery?"

"That's where things get a little complicated." I feel my face fall. I should probably talk about this, and who better than a girl I barely know? I laugh internally at the irony, then clear my throat. "I unexpectedly lost my dad over the summer, and since he basically ran the entire operation by himself—with the help of my mom and our winemaker Rob, everyone expects me to step into my dad's place."

Piper's eyebrows raise while she brings her drink to her lips. "That's a heavy load," she says before sipping it.

"It is, isn't it? And to make matters even more fucked up, my dad's best friend, who is part owner, wants his son to take over instead of me," I explain, removing my hand from her thigh. I haven't spoken to anyone outside the people involved about what's going on with my family's business. It feels freeing.

"That sounds like some shady shit. How do you feel about it? Do you even want to take over though—" All of a sudden, she stops mid-sentence and looks down at the floor between us. "Wait. Where is our luggage?"

I tilt my head to the side and rub my lips together, stifling a laugh.

"Why does it look like you're trying to keep from laughing?" She snickers, batting her eyes at me. "If I may add, you're not doing an excellent job with it."

She is adorable, and I can't hold it in anymore. *Did she truly forget what we did with our stuff?*

I finally explode, letting out a full belly laugh. "We left our suitcases with the concierge."

"Oh, yes. I knew that." Piper nods vigorously, probably convincing herself as much as she's trying to convince me. *She forgot.* Piper glances up at me through her long eyelashes with her cheeks the color of crimson. When our eyes meet, electricity flows through my veins, causing the hairs on both arms to stand straight up. She's embarrassed by being so drunk, but I find her effervescent energy charming.

For a moment, our eyes lock. My heart hammers the back of my chest. The energy with this woman is off the charts. She pulls her bottom lip between her teeth and feeling bolder than I typically do, I'm overcome with a desire to taste that bottom lip of hers.

I slowly lean in until I can see the specks of green in her hazel eyes. To my pleasant surprise, she doesn't back away. We share a breath for a moment before her eyes fall closed. But suddenly, she jerks her head away and scrambles to grab something from her purse that hangs across her body. Piper clumsily pulls out her phone.

My is still racing from how close I got to touching her lips when I notice the color draining from her face as she stares at the screen.

"Do you need to take that?" I'm unsure how to respond to the sudden change in her expression.

Blinking a few times, Piper shoves her phone back into her purse. "No, I don't." A heavy cloud has appeared over her. It's a contrast to everything I've seen until this point. My mind reels with who could have called. Judging by the look on her face, it wasn't someone good.

Fuck, was it a boyfriend? An ex-boyfriend?

I feel my jaw tighten.

Piper looks over at me, a half-smile on her face. "No, I don't have a boyfriend."

I love her attitude.

"That's not what I was thinking," I quip. Before Piper can reply, a cocktail server walks over to us with a tray carrying two shots of what looks to be vodka.

"These are from the older couple at the end of the bar," she says, bending between us. "They said you two look like how they did when they first fell in love fifty years ago."

Piper and I both glance over to the left. The man and woman hold up their martinis in the air with sweet smiles on both their faces.

"Wow. Okay, thank you." I hand Piper a shot glass, then take one for myself.

"They're still staring," she says through a tight grin.

It feels so good to let loose and be free. I smile at her, then raise my glass toward the couple. "Bottoms up."

Piper and I take both shots together, quickly followed by a light, distant clap.

She grimaces. "Damn, that burns."

I slam my glass on the table and rise, knowing that this shot will heighten my buzz. I'm having fun with you," I admit, gently lifting Piper from her chair and into my arms. She immediately falls into me with a giggle. The smell of lavender hits my nostrils. It's powerful yet subtle at the same time and causes my body to flush with warmth and my dick to flex.

"Me too. It's bizarre, right? That we're here in Vegas together after both of us skipped our fights—*flights*, I meant flights." She curls into me, giggling once again.

"It's definitely not where I imagined I'd be spending my Friday night."

She tucks into my shoulder with my arm around her. I look down, her round eyes blaze into me. My heart skips a beat when she lifts her chin, bringing her glossy lips upward with a confident smile.

"Piper?"

"Yes?" she answers with a raspy voice.

I've never been one to hit on a lot of women. My experience in life has mostly been them coming on to me. An old roommate once told me that women find silent, reserved guys more attractive than those who try too hard. Up until that point, I haven't thought about it that way. It's always how I've been. But with Piper, I'm compelled to pursue her. "Can I kiss you?"

Her eyes flicker while she breathes out a confident, "Yes."

My eyes take in the landscape of her mouth before lowering my lips to hers in a gentle kiss. The instant we connect, my world comes to a complete standstill. She's soft and warm—and kissing her feels as natural as taking in oxygen.

I involuntarily squeeze her tighter, tugging her deeper into my mouth. She opens slowly, letting my tongue slip in to caress hers. It moves deliberately inside my mouth, exploring and tasting.

Her shoulders sink into me as she curves further into my chest. Piper slips her arms around me back. Every single care I've had in the world dissipates, and I'm powerless to stop it. I submit to the weightless feeling of existing only with her. This is a new sensation for me.

I cautiously pull back but continue to lightly kiss the different areas around her mouth. "I don't want to be without you. I've never felt such an instant connection with someone before," I whisper into her sweet skin.

"I feel the same," she mumbles as the noise of clanging chimes from the gamblers increases once again.

A quick movement from the corner of my eye startles me, and then both Piper and I are hit with a downpour of ice-cold liquid. I gasp as the shock in temperature cuts off my air. I quickly noticed that Piper got most of whatever spilled on us and was drenched.

"Oh my god, I'm so sorry!" says the young, anxious man standing beside us.

"What the hell, man?" I snap, stepping between Piper and this clumsy asshole.

"It's okay!" She laughs, clutching my blazer. "It's fine. I'm completely fine."

"Are you sure? Are you alright?" I start to laugh as well. Swiping some cocktail napkins off the table next to us, I hand them to her first, then grab a few more for myself.

"I'm fine. It's only water, that's all," she reassures me again, shaking the leftover ice cubes from her shirt.

My eyes fall to her hard nipples peeking through her thin, cream dress. All I can think of is circling my tongue around their raised peaks. "Are you cold?"

She glances down at her chest, biting her bottom lip. "Yes.

Can you tell?"

"Yep." I let her notice me staring before my eyes darted back up. Piper's chest raises as she sucks in a deep breath.

After wiping the side of my face, which is mostly where the water hit, I turn to Piper and, without thinking, run the napkin along the bare skin of her neck and down to the dampness of her collarbone.

"If I take it off, you'll get a better look," she taunts.

My dick twitches inside my pants as my fingertips lightly dust her skin. The warmth raises my pulse. "I don't want this night to end."

She looks up at me with vibrant hazel eyes and giggles. "Neither do I."

I feel unrestrained and more free than I ever have. Who gives a fuck about what's going on with the outside world? My whole existence is here in this moment. I've fought for control over my life since I was a child. For a brief time, I had it, but I should have known that it would be taken away. I have to live in someone else's dream. Someone else's life. My freedom and independence will be gone. My identity as *just* Jack Bradley will be gone.

I'm an introvert, quiet and would rather keep to myself. Soon enough, I won't have the luxury of being any of those things anymore. But tonight, in this moment with Piper, I can hang on to just being *Jack*.

"Let's get married," I blurt out, not hearing the words in my head before they hit the air.

Fuuuuuck.

Piper's eyebrow snaps together. Her pupils dilate even under these bright fluorescent lights. They bounce back and forth for only a brief moment before she answers, "Okay."

Oh my fucking god. She said yes! This is unbelievable. As if fate was somehow involved, another cocktail server walks by with a shot on her tray. Without hesitation, I snag a glass and down the vodka. Piper does the same.

"Charge it to the card on file?" the server confirms.

"Yes, then close us out," I respond, not letting my eyes break from Piper's. Her face is glowing. "Yeah, you want to?" A smile beams across my face.

"Yes!"

"That's awesome. Let's do it!" I pull out my phone, and even though my eyes are a little blurry, I can still find the search bar to locate the nearest wedding chapel. Another twist of fucking fate, the closest one is only a short walk down the strip.

Piper grabs my hand as we exit the smoke-filled casino onto the bustling street. The guttering, flashing lights, and warmth of the desert air are a small reprieve from inside. I wish I could say that I'm shocked that at close to three in the morning, the sidewalk is packed with people, but I've been here enough to know this is typical.

Walking hand in hand, Piper and I make our way through the crowds of people venturing out at this hour. Or have been out all night, like us. I keep a strong grip on Piper, ensuring not to lose her while we're back and forth along the crowded sidewalk.

We finally make it to the *Tiny White Wedding House,* and it's exactly how I pictured it. I laugh as I lead us through a small opening in the white fence surrounding an even brighter white building. We pass fake grass to the side while we walk under the drive-through area. *For people in need of a speedier wedding, I guess?*

When the door opens, I'm hit with a unique smell that can only be described as old and musty.

"Did we step into a time machine? Because this place looks like it's from the wrong decade," she comments.

"I've always wanted to travel back to the 1950s," I add, scanning my eyes across the small waiting space. "And now that I have, I think I'm good staying in our time."

She laughs.

I see the chapel, and I'm stunned by how cool it is. The decade jokes aside, it's surprisingly unique in here. There's an aisle with a bubblegum-colored carpet and three rows of short white pews on either side. Taking in the simplicity of it, I find a small arch at the top of the aisle decorated in fully bloomed white roses. *I wonder if Piper likes flowers? And if she does—I wonder what kind?*

"Hello, can I help you?" a woman with a squeaky voice asks from behind a low counter.

My eyes dart to hers for approval. She nods, showing me she hasn't changed her mind. I haven't changed my mind either. My thoughts and actions take over, and I hear myself begin speaking with the woman. I've always been calm and collected, but right now, I'm doing something rash and out of my comfort zone. It feels fitting that I do something for myself before I give my independence away.

Chapter Seven

PIPER

The man I met earlier today stands directly before me. I face him with apprehension—yet simultaneously, I feel alive, exhilarated, and powerful. *Or that could also be the three martinis, countless shots of vodka, and multiple glasses of wine talking.*

It's not like this is what I imagined my first marriage would be like, but here I am. And yes, I expect to have multiple marriages. Isn't that what happens to everyone? I'm not sure what I'd imagined my first marriage would be. Maybe a man that I've at least slept with first? But I do not doubt that Jack knows what he's doing in the bedroom. I'd bet he's good with buttons, zippers, leggings—I quietly giggle and blush.

I'm only twenty-six, have had way too much fun tonight, and feel on top of the world. I am fighting to keep my eyes from wandering up and down the length of his body. My ambitions are nonexistent now, but I'm still a classy lady. *Or am I?* I crack a smile. My personality is one with class, but I also do what I want.

Jack doesn't take his eyes off me. One side of his mouth quirks up into a smirk that makes my knees weak. "Are you ready?" Jack's voice is tight as he holds back his laughter. His arms are down, and his hands are clasped in front of him. His longer-on-top dirty blond hair is parted to the side with one piece curving into his right eye. *Fucking sexy.*

"I am. Are you?

"Yes." His blue eyes pierce me from less than a foot away. I struggle to keep mine from roaming around the features of his face, desperately trying to learn more about this man who will become my husband in a matter of minutes.

The bell on top of the large white door to the right of us dings as a broader-shouldered man in an Elvis costume enters the room. "How about we get you two love birds married!" he excitedly exclaims like he didn't do this less than fifteen minutes ago. The couple before us clearly could not wait to leave the chapel to start their wedding night as they pawed at each other out the door.

My eyes circle back to the tall blond man standing in front of me, letting him answer our colorful officiant.

"Sounds great!" Jack says, looking relaxed and at ease, maybe even a little happy?

I'm buzzing.

"Didn't dress up for the occasion?" Our Elvis officiant directs his question toward me. "I like that. It is about love here in the *Tiny White Wedding House.*"

Slightly embarrassed, I glance down at my choice of clothing. I bubble with laughter at what I'm getting married to. I lightly tug on the cream-colored dress with random drops of red wine stained along the bottom hem. I've had it on all night.

I thread my hands through my hair, pulling it over one shoulder. "I'm a simple girl. I don't need the flashy things that come with weddings." I push back at his condescending yet well-intentioned comments.

The officiant's eyebrows raise while he turns toward my husband-to-be. "She's a fiery one, my man."

"Seems to be." Jack grins at me.

I tap one of my white slip-on high-heeled sandals in annoyance at how long this is taking. "Is it part of your job to comment on the bride's outfits?"

His eyes shoot over to Jack again as if I'm not here. "I like her."

Jack laughs nervously, dipping his head down and quickly rubbing his chin.

"Well then, let's get started," the Elvis impersonator states before jumping right into reciting the opening to the marriage vows. As he speaks, I feel my eyes gloss over. His voice sounds as if he's speaking in slow motion, and I see Jack nod his head and blink a few times every so often. *Don't pass out. The room is not really spinning.*

As a little girl, I watched my mother flex herself in and out of doomed relationships with less-than-stellar men. She moved on from one to another, staying as long as they could provide her with what she needed at that given time. I'd be lying if I said I didn't learn how to make rash, unhinged decisions with men from the best. Blinking a few times to clear the blur that is now my permanent vision, I try to focus back on Jack.

As if we're the only two people in the room, Jack slowly pulls something from his pants pocket. I look down as he reaches over and takes my left hand in his.

"I made this for you," he says, slipping a curled-up piece of white paper into the shape of a circle onto my ring finger.

I examine what he's placing on my finger and where he got it. My lips part in shock at what I think it is. "What's this?"

"It's the paper wrapper from a straw. I thought you needed a ring."

"We're almost at the part with the rings—" the officiant tries to interject, but Jack and I ignore his protests.

I lift my hand, letting my thumb run over it. *This is so sweet. Why am I still giggling?* "That's so thoughtful. I can't believe you made this."

He smiles, running the back of his knuckles along my cheek.

"I guess you two are going to do this your way. Make sure you sign the license on your way out. Viva Las Vegas!" he exclaims. "Oh, and you may kiss the bride," he adds before retreating into the back.

I stare up at Jack from under my eyelashes. He cups my face with both hands, then brings his soft lips to mine, running his tongue along the seam before I open for him. My heart flutters. I'm bathed in utter euphoria. I've only just met him, but there's a bond and comfort in his kiss that makes me believe there's so much more to him.

Jack and I are married in what feels like a blink of an eye.

Chapter Eight

A pounding in my skull jolts me awake. My eyes frantically bounce around a pitch-black room. I wipe the wetness from my forehead and notice I'm still wearing my clothes from yesterday. I only have my black collared shirt and pants, but my shoes are off. I hear a light snoring sound on the other side of the room. Someone is in here with me—*wait, Piper*! It's Piper.

I sigh in relief and reach behind me on the bed, pawing for my phone. When I find it, I click on the flashlight, rise to my feet, and carefully walk across the room to the floor-to-ceiling windows. Tapping the button on the remote to open the thick, heavy, blackout curtains, I'm blinded by the direct sunlight blasting into the dark room.

I leave the curtains partly open and look down at the busy Las Vegas strip below. When I hear Piper move around on the other side of the oversized bed, I walk over to her side.

"Jack?" she mutters.

I sit on the bed next to her head, which is halfway off the edge. Piper's dress rides high on her legs, with the top half of her body rolled in the white hotel sheet.

"Hi." I smile warmly.

Her long strawberry blonde hair is fanned out across two

pillows before she lifts her head. "I feel like shit. What the hell happened last night?"

I shake my head with confusion. "I'm not quite sure. I remember some of it, but not all," I answer, but my voice is still shaky with uncertainty. "The last thing I remember is coming back to the penthouse extremely excited, but I don't remember what for."

"To hook up?" Piper stills. Her eyes are wide while panic crosses her face. "Did we sleep together?"

I fold my arms at my chest. "I'm sure we didn't sleep together."

"How do you know? I mean, I don't *feel* like we did, but you never know."

If I fucked her last night, she would definitely feel it this morning, especially with the way I'm attracted to her. I tilt my head to the side, looking directly into her eyes. "Trust me, if we slept together, you'd remember it."

Her face reddens, but her eyes narrow. "So sure of yourself?"

"Without a doubt," I say firmly. Piper's lashes bat a few times before she looks away. I smile with the satisfaction of making her blush.

I lift off the bed to search for our luggage. I quickly realize that we are in the same suite I'd booked for myself at the beginning of the night. Heading into the main living area, I spot two black roller carry-ons in the corner by the door. I wheel them both back into the bedroom to see that Piper is now sitting up.

"I need a shower." Her voice is raspy.

"Here's your bag. You know, the one that you thought you lost?"

She gives me a side-eye. "Thanks."

"Are you okay? Besides the obvious splitting headache and death-like hangover," I joke, making light of the situation.

Piper runs a hand through her tousled hair, flipping it to the side of her head. "I'm alright. I wish I remembered more this morning."

My face softens, understanding how she feels. All joking aside, last night was fun, and I'm surprised by how fast I felt comfortable with her. That doesn't happen to me very often, with or without alcohol. There's a thick awkwardness around us, and now, I'm unsure how to act around her. To say that I'm grateful that we didn't have sex is an understatement because I have a feeling she's not one that I'll easily forget. "We had fun. It's alright."

"I know. I had a lot of fun with you. More fun than I've had in a long time."

I smile, feeling the same. "At least I'm a nice guy and didn't take advantage of you."

"You wouldn't have needed to take advantage of me." *I wouldn't have?*

"Interesting."

She heads toward the bathroom with her clothes and a small bag clutched in her arms. "With how drunk we both were, I'm glad we didn't end up doing something stupid."

Pursing my lips together, I nod with shared relief.

While Piper is in the shower, memories of last night slowly start rolling in. Thinking about it makes my head spin. Both of us need some food, water, and definitely an aspirin—*or two.* I head into the kitchen, searching for complimentary bottles of water, and luckily, I find a dozen of them stocked in the fridge.

I grab three to take back into the bedroom, but on my way, I pass a large wooden dining table and a bouquet of white roses, but something catches my eye. I look closer and notice a yellow-tinted piece of paper nestled underneath the stems. I tuck all three water bottles into one of my arms and then remove the paper with the fancy calligraphy from the top of the table.

My heart stops.

I blink a few times to make sure I'm reading this document correctly. With my eyes still blurry, I can only make out a few words: *State of Nevada, Marriage Certificate*, and my signature: *Jack Bradley*. Directly across from my name, written in my very own handwriting, is that of Piper Harris, and right below hers is one that shoots an electric shock up my spine, *Piper Bradley*.

The bottles of water fall from my grasp as my arm goes limp, quickly rolling in separate directions across the floor.

Fuuuck.

"What's wrong?" I see Piper appear fully dressed and standing in the door frame to the bedroom.

"We got married last night!" I yell, pinching the terrifying piece of paper in the air in front of us.

"*What?*"

"We. Got. Married. Last. Night," I repeat, emphasizing each word. Still in disbelief, I take a few steps closer to hand her the certificate. With her pupils dilating, Piper reluctantly takes the paper from me and holds it up to read.

"*Piper Bradley!* Oh my god. I took your last name?" she shouts.

Is that what stuck out to her? Not that we got married in

Las Vegas while completely intoxicated and that the witness signature is from someone who I am fairly confident we both don't know. That was not the reaction I expected.

"Of course you took my last name. Why wouldn't you?" I quip, somewhat offended.

She shrugs her shoulders. "I don't know. I guess I never thought about it before."

"I always knew I'd give my future wife my last name." *Why the hell am I upset?*

Piper raises her arms in the air with her palms up in front of us. "It's shocking seeing my name—but written differently, I guess. Why do you care?"

"I have no idea. I don't care." Flustered, I rake my hand down the front of my face, feeling the small beads of sweat that have appeared. "But what I do care about is the fact that this is insane. How could this have happened?"

My mind spins with the stress and pressure that I have going on with my father passing and staring down a narrow tunnel that my life will soon become. Not to mention that the community thinks I abandoned them and doesn't want me back in it. *This is fucking insane.*

Piper rubs her temples with a forced grin on her face. "Look, it was a mistake, but I'm sure this happens in Vegas all the time. Let's do some research to figure out how we can get it annulled. That's all."

"Yeah, you're right."

"I guess the marriage certificate explains where this came from." She hands me what looks like a tiny rolled-up piece of paper in the shape of a ring.

I hold it between my index finger and thumb to get a better look. "It looks like a rolled-up wrapper from a straw," I say.

"I had it on my ring finger when I woke up this morning."

My body flushes with warmth. "I grabbed the wrapper off the table in the wedding chapel lobby. I vaguely remember making that for you."

"It was a very sweet gesture," she says, slipping it back on her finger. *Is she keeping it?*

"I hope you don't like it too much because I'm sure it won't last long."

Piper rolls her eyes. "Probably as long as our marriage."

"That's true." We stand in silence for a minute, quietly smiling. Both of us stare at the floor while tension swirls between us. This situation is so fucking awkward. "I'm going to hop in the shower, too, and then we should probably make our way downstairs to get something to eat. Or we can call for room service if you prefer?"

"Grabbing breakfast sounds great." Piper kneels to retrieve one of the water bottles from off the floor.

Before I shut the door to the bathroom, I turn to her. "I intended to bring one of those to you."

She grins before screwing off the cap. "It's the thought that counts." I watch as she brings it to her lips, and I remember our intimate kiss last night.

A few minutes later, I stand alone in the shower, surrounded by the tiled walls. The hot water falls like thick raindrops pelting the stiff muscles of my back. On the bright side, if I was going to get married in Vegas to a woman who I barely know, at least it ended up being a fun, sexy, and adorable one.

I'm unsure of what came over me when I asked Piper to marry me. It may have been another attempt at making my own choices in life, or it might have been the fact that something inside of her speaks to something inside of me, and I didn't know what the hell to do with that information. But here we are.

I feel only semi-normal when I get out of the shower, but I still need breakfast. Coming from the bedroom, I see the back of Piper's long hair as she sits with her knees up in one of the tufted chairs in front of the large window overlooking the strip. I want to spend more time with her, and I hope that our drunken choices don't ruin that for us.

"Hungry?" I ask, circling the small sitting area to stand in front of her.

She looks up at me with her beautiful hazel-green eyes. "Starving."

Piper and I leave the suite and walk down the long hallway toward the elevator. The intensity between us is so thick that I can almost feel it suffocating me between the four walls of this confined space. I shift a couple of times in place, then shove my hands into the front pockets of my jeans. Based on how Piper is fidgeting with the strings of her hoodie, she's also unsure how to act around me.

A few uncomfortable minutes later, we're seated at a small cafe on the lobby floor of the resort and casino.

"After all the fun we had last night, I now fully understand why there are no windows in casinos," she tells me after placing her order.

I hand my menu to the server and smile at Piper, anxiously waiting for another off-the-wall comment about something completely random.

"And why is that?"

"Because it causes people to lose track of time. The lack of awareness from the light of day to the darkness of night confuses people, making them think that the night can never end, and it will simply keep going," she shares with me in a single breath.

I laugh. "That's exactly what got us into this mess in the first place. We didn't want the night to end, and by what we did last night, it technically didn't." I take a sip of my hot cup of coffee.

"That's right." She smiles, tucking her loose hair behind her ear.

When our food arrives, Piper and I sit silently, trying to put the pieces together from the last twelve hours. But then, unexpectedly, an idea forms in my head. She'll think I'm crazy as hell, or she'll be interested. I straighten my shoulders and suck in a deep breath. "What if this little situation we got ourselves into could benefit us both?"

Piper stops mid-bite, her fork suspended in the air. "What do you mean?"

Resting my elbows on the table, I clasp my hands under my chin. "Remember last night when I told you about how I'm being ousted from my family's winery by my dad's long-time friend and business partner?"

Piper's expression quickly changes from interest to confusion. "Um, I don't think so. Sorry," she says, glancing down at the rolled paper straw around her ring finger. "Clearly, I don't remember much."

Holding back a smile, I rub my lips together because she's still wearing the paper ring. It's unbelievable what we did, but based on our *love document*, it did, in fact, happen. "I understand. Everything is a bit fuzzy. It is for me, too, but I vaguely remember discussing this with you." I pause, watching as her expression changes.

Piper nods. "A little bit, I do."

"Okay, awesome. What if we pretended to be together to make me look more stable? I'm also in the process of putting an offer on a house, and this would make it so much better."

"You want to stay married to me so it can help you look better while taking over your family's winery?"

My eyes grow wide. "Yes. That's exactly right."

"I'm sorry, but that sounds ridiculous. You're a good-looking, successful guy. Don't you have any female friends that would love to be your *fake girlfriend*?"

I have other options, but Piper and I are already married. We'll have to be together until we get this figured out anyway, and I'm sure it will take at least a few weeks to get our marriage annulled. Our family lawyer could easily handle it with discretion when the time comes, so why not see if we could use it to our advantage?

I set my cup of coffee down on the table before answering. "Thank you—and yes, I do, but I think this could only work if it's strictly professional. *A business deal.* I don't want any headaches or confusion about feelings to be involved. As long as we go into it knowing that this agreement is only for business, then we'll both be able to go our separate ways when it's over."

"You're *actually* serious?" She stares at me from across the table with her eyes the size of saucers.

"I know it sounds insane, but I think this could work

for me. Look at it from a marketing standpoint," I continue, "People love families and young couples, and without getting you pregnant, I think this is the next best thing."

She coughs and blinks a few times. "Did you say getting me pregnant like it was an actual thought?"

Oops. "Okay, maybe that was a bad example, and I'm not actually meaning us, like you and I—I'm only stating the obvious, and this small community is all about families."

"You are a special guy, you know that?" She sneers.

I return with an exaggerated smile. "I am, aren't I?"

"Let's say hypothetically, I consider what you're proposing—how long would this last, and how would we make it work? I live in Phoenix, and you said you're moving back to Northern California." She points out valid concerns, but she's considering my offer. *Yes.*

"I would only need one to two months max. I think that should be enough time to re-establish myself in the community and around the winery before we can simply break up. We can get a divorce, and I'll even pay for it. We have a family lawyer that would take care of it for us." Piper still has a look of disbelief on her face, but I continue hoping she doesn't change her mind. "As far as our living arrangement, you can be long distance, but I will need you to be around for big events like harvest season that's coming up. Then we'll go from there," I explain, trying my best to close this deal. Maybe not the ideal approach.

"Wow, you do have this planned out, don't you?"

"No, actually, it just came to me."

Piper clasps her hands together on top of the table. "How can you casually ask me to do something like this? You have to know how it sounds?"

I think for a second before responding, but it seems pretty clear-cut to me. "It's transactional. That's all."

"Are you sure you don't want to annul this marriage and then find someone you already know well?" she presses, still unsure.

I'm confident that she's considering it, but I can see the expression on her face as she filters through all the ways this plan won't work. "It's convenient that we're already married. We're stuck together for the foreseeable future and have already done something completely rash together. We both felt comfortable enough to do that, so why not this?" I arch a brow. "And honestly, it sort of feels like this just fell into my lap."

Piper glances around the room before breathing out a heavy sigh. "I barely know you, Jack Bradley. What if you're some psycho?"

"I'm not. You married me, didn't you—*Mrs. Bradley*? That wasn't your concern last night," I reply.

Piper tosses a mini muffin at me from the other side of the table. "Funny."

"I am funny. See, you already know that about me," I say, after catching the muffin.

She blushes and rolls her eyes.

"Besides, I went to college with Harry and Mason. I've known them for years, and I'm sure they'd vouch for my lack of serial killer tendencies."

"Are you going to expect me to perform girlfriend duties?" she taunts.

Of course, she'd think that. But doing those things would only make things complicated. "Absolutely not."

Her shoulders relax. "Okay. That's good to know."

"Unless you wanted to." I wink.

Piper tosses a crumpled-up napkin at me from across the table. "Stop it."

I catch it with one hand and chuckle.

She threads her fingers through her hair, then leans in. "If I agree to this, it's going to cost you."

"You want me to pay you to be my fake girlfriend even though you're already my real wife?" I admire how her hazel eyes have hints of green under the dim light in this booth.

"Obviously. I need to get something out of this because, under the current terms, you're the only one I see benefiting from it," she retorts.

I guess I didn't think of how she'd be compensated. "Fair enough."

"I want a lifetime supply of plants. I love plants."

I draw my head back in disbelief that she asked for plants instead of money, as anyone else would. "You don't want me to pay you?"

She shrugs her shoulders. "Sure. That works, too."

"How much do you want?"

Piper clicks her tongue. "How much is the winery worth?"

"You cannot be serious."

"I'm ." She pulls her lips to one side and sits back against the black rubber booth. "Make me an offer."

Now that she's married to me, she could take a hell of a lot more than I'd ever willingly offer. I need to be fair so she doesn't get any ideas about other ways of benefiting from our twenty-four hours of mistaken judgment. I have no idea what to offer her. What's too much? What's too little?

I suck in a breath and throw out the first number that comes to mind. "Ten thousand dollars."

"That's peanuts. No way," she responds.

"You asked for plants?"

She pouts.

"Fifteen thousand dollars."

I feel her leg bouncing underneath the table. She's nervous but not letting on that she is. "Higher."

My hands fly up. "Seriously?"

"How bad do you want it?" Piper challenges, but it sounds like she's taunting me rather than negotiating. And I fucking love it.

"Twenty thousand dollars and not a penny more," I playfully say, folding my arms at my chest.

She is gorgeous, and there's an obvious attraction between us, but I need to remain focused on the future of my family's winery. This is an entirely ridiculous idea, but something inside tells me to trust it.

"It's not like I'm doing anything else at the moment." Her face lights up. "You've got yourself a deal."

Chapter Nine

How the hell did I end up marrying someone that I had just met?

I fall to my bed and glance over at the luggage that needs unpacking, then drag my eyes across the hall and into the kitchen, where the remainder of my groceries still need to be put away. They're both going to have to wait. I'm exhausted, hung over, and still in shock.

Waking up in his hotel room this morning was a surreal experience. Not only did we not have sex, but he was a perfect gentleman about it. I can't say that it didn't sting when both his body language and actions made it clear that he wasn't at all interested in me—a stark contrast from the vibes I was getting the night before. Maybe he was nervous? Perhaps he wasn't sure how to act around me. I know I felt that way.

The thought of Jack makes my stomach flip. I can't believe he's going to pay me to be his fake girlfriend for the next two months. When he brought it up this morning at breakfast, my initial thought was *absolutely not*. The whole idea sounded completely strange and wild. But the more I saw the color of his eyes change and the way his mouth quirked up when he spoke, the more his idea didn't sound all that bad—getting paid to be some rich, gorgeous guy's fake girlfriend with some added time in Wine Country? I could make it work.

There's a buzzing sound next to my ear.

Jack: Hello, Piper, this is your husband.

My husband? What the fuck. A blush at his cheeky comment.

Me: Hi, how are you?

Jack: Just checking in to make sure you made it home safely.

Me: I did. I just got back not too long ago. I'm assuming you made it home safely as well?

I roll over onto my stomach and let my feet float.

Jack: Yeah. I sent you an email with the dates you'll need to be in Northern California. Did you get it?

Me: I haven't yet. I'll take a look later.

I fire off that text, thinking he will continue his flirty small talk.

Jack: Let me know, and we can lock it down. The important events of the harvest season start as early as the end of next week. I'd like you to accompany me to most of them.

Maybe he is the same stiff Jack from this morning? His tone is dry. Or maybe mine is dry? *Who the hell knows at this point?*

> Me: Let me look at my work schedule, and I'll get back to you.

> Jack: Great. Can you get back to me by tomorrow night?

My upper lip lifts, and I arch an eyebrow at the continued formality of our exchange. He's treating me like a coworker. I guess I am. He *is* paying me to do a job.

> Me: Sure, that's fine.

> Jack: Okay, talk to you then.

I roll my eyes, slide my phone into my pocket, and head into the kitchen. I start putting away the groceries I picked up when my phone vibrates once again, but it's not a text. I swipe it off the counter and answer.

"Hi, babe." I tuck the phone into the crook of my neck and continue to put the food away.

"You never called me when you got home?" Bailey complains in a whiny voice.

I'm quiet briefly while my brain slams itself into overtime to think of what I should tell her—or better yet, what I *can* tell her. I don't even know what she'd say if I gave her a play-by-play of my *alcohol-induced, accidental-marriage, paid-girlfriend weekend.* She'd never believe it.

I squeeze the unopened salad dressing bottle. It's funny that out of our friend group, Lina, Bailey, Avery, and myself—they'd all say I'm most likely to get tangled up in something like this.

"It was an interesting time, actually."

"Hmm, how so?"

"Well,"—I lean against the kitchen counter—"we ended up missing our flights and hanging out all night in Vegas."

Silence.

"How did that even happen?"

"Yeah, we spent hours in that restaurant bar just talking. Once we figured out what time it was and missed our flights, we had to stay in Vegas for the night," I continue.

"Yeah. Let's talk about that good conversation," she teases.

I grin, my cheeks burning. "It really was."

"Keep going!" Her words are fast and breathless. "What happened next? Did you hook up with him? Why am I even asking you that? Of course, you did!"

I giggle. "We didn't hook up. Surprisingly, I'm glad I didn't."

"Am I hearing you right? You gave up the chance to sleep with a guy you have overwhelming chemistry with?" she clarifies in playful disbelief.

"We got drunk and ended up falling asleep in his suite—and in the same bed. But I'm glad that I didn't. Jack was—*is* different." Roxy's voice pops into my head as soon as my words hit the air. *"Everyone will hurt you and eventually leave. No one will be around for you except for me."* I stifle my joy about the connection with a great guy and bury it under a shell I've created to hide.

I hear her in a full belly laugh over the phone. "Wow, only you." She laughs again. "Are you going to see him again then?"

"Maybe. Honestly, the next morning was so awkward that we left it with a simple *call you if I'm in town* thing."

"But doesn't he live out here?"

"He's moving back to California. His parents own a winery, and his dad just passed away over the summer, so he's moving back to take over," I tell her.

I know what I'm doing. If I've learned anything from Roxy, it's how to manipulate people into thinking you're giving them something they want. I'm giving my best friend what she wants, which is the details from my twenty-four-hour Vegas escapade, without elaborating on the more questionable events of the story.

"Damn, that sucks. But clearly, you two have a little something between you. You're not going to explore it even a little bit?" she presses.

I suck in my lip, then take my phone in my hand. I feel guilty about lying to her, and it makes sense that she'll figure out I'm with him in California at some point. Bailey, Lina, Avery, and I talk almost daily. "I think we'll see each other again. Who knows, maybe I'll visit Northern California to see him," I say, making sure she hears the optimism in my voice.

"There you go, now we're talking."

I laugh. "I have to let you go. I need a shower, and I haven't even unpacked yet."

"Okay, I'll see you Thursday. Oh, and Avery is on our flight crew heading out too!" she rushes out before we have the chance to hang up.

"I know. I saw that in our group chat. See you in a few days!"

After the shower, I start unpacking. Halfway through a pile of dirty clothes, I remember that Jack said he'd sent an email about when I need to go to California. I grab a quick snack, flop onto my bed again, and open my laptop.

From: jack.bradley@email.com
Subject: Harvest Season Events
Hello Piper,

The following events will occur close together, so you'll need to come out for at least ten days to two weeks. It would be best if you could be here by the end of next week.

1. Meet with my mother (yes, you will have to formally meet my mother since we are "dating")

2. Wine Growers Kick-Off Event

3. Harvest Dinner

4. Bradley Family Wines Crush

5. Any other small event that comes up during this time frame.

Let me know if that works with your flight schedule. We'll talk soon.
Thanks,
Jack Bradley

My eyes scan every word of his email, looking for any sign of emotion or flirtatious nature, but there isn't. *Is he my boss now?* I don't recall mentioning that I would be working *for* him during our initial conversation. He even signed his first and last name at the bottom of the email, like I don't know his last name is Bradley. *What the hell?* Technically, it is mine now, too, which is so fucking strange. And even more, it's not a premade email signature, and he had to have consciously typed that out.

I rub circles into my temples, then flip my hair to the side and remind myself that he is *paying* me twenty thousand dollars to basically boss me around.

Maybe I do work for him? Fuck.

Luckily for Jack, this week is when I'm putting in my scheduling bids for next month, and it happens to be that my current schedule aligns, so I can take two weeks off starting next week. But I'm not going to make it easy on him.

From: moonsoverpiper@email.com
Re: Subject: Harvest Season Events
Hello Jack,
Thank you for the email. I will need to move a few things around, but I should be able to make room for you in my schedule.
Your new beck-and-call girl,
Piper Harris-Bradley

I hit send, then flip onto my back, satisfied with my response. Smiling up at the rotating ceiling fan, I hear the chime indicating another email. Rolling back over, I see Jack has already replied. Damn.

From: jack.bradley@email.com

```
Re: Re: Subject: Harvest Season Events
Good. See you next week.
Your   boss,   who   is   definitely   not
rethinking his hiring choices,
Jack Bradley
```

Staring at his email, I run through a series of smart-ass comments and comebacks, but I'm too tired. I smile to myself, then finish unpacking.

Bailey, Avery, and I are on our first flight of the day, conducting the preflight checks of the emergency and medical equipment before the passengers start boarding.

"Piper, how's everything going with Roxy?" Avery asks, resting her arms on top of the seat. Bailey takes a few steps over, occupying the small space in the aisle.

Only Bailey, Avery, and Lina know about the complicated relationship with my mother. I can't even recall how often they have been my shoulders to cry on after a fight or disagreement.

Sometimes, those fights were from guilt trips for not seeing her as much as I should. Other times, they consisted of Roxy blaming me for her inability to find a good job—which, in her words, is because she had to lovingly sacrifice her education or well-off boyfriends to support me as a child. This particular time, I was trying to stand my ground about paying another month of her rent. She'd quit a job she had as a bank teller because the manager was, in Roxy's words, on *"a high horse."* Whatever the hell that means.

I let out a heavy breath. "It is what it is. She's never going to change."

"Did you send her the money like she wanted?" Bailey asks.

"I didn't want to, but I did. She told me if I didn't send her rent money, she'd be homeless. When I hesitated, she mentioned all the times she supported me as a child." I frown. "She's my mom. I had to do it."

"Damn. That's got to be tough to hear from your mom. It's not like it's your fault when you're like, I don't know—seven?" Avery hisses.

"It's a mind fuck, that's for sure." I wish her eclectic personality came with a warning label for manipulation and emotional immaturity.

Avery frowns and puts an arm around me. "I'm sorry, babe. I know that must be so hard. You know the three of us are always here for you."

"Yes, I love you all for that, but we all have problems. I can handle Roxy. You lost your parents so young, Avery. I should be grateful that I still have my mom, right?"

Both of my best friends shake their heads in unison.

"No, not at the expense of being treated like she's always treated you," Avery snaps back.

"Avery is right. You don't deserve it," Bailey adds, her eyes soft as she looks at me.

"I love you both, you know that?" I reach my arms out, hooking them around my friends. The three of us hold each other tightly.

"Wait, make room for invisible Lina!" Avery exclaims.

"Oh yes!" Bailey rounds Avery, extending a side hug into the empty space between them.

"Lina gives the best advice in situations like this." I smile.

Chapter Ten

That fucking saying about *what happens in Vegas stays in Vegas*—it's bullshit. I arrived there as a single man with enough problems on my plate—and left there a married man with potentially more problems. And what Piper and I did wasn't a random hook-up on a drunk night—we got fucking *married*.

It's a real legal marriage. It's crazy what desire will make foolish people like us do.

I hope having Piper around will make my situation with the community go smoother. But who the fuck knows? It could all just blow up in my face.

After Piper and I went our separate ways this morning, I took an afternoon flight to San Diego for our annual guys' trip. Since some of my fraternity brothers from college now live in different places around the country, we plan a yearly guys' weekend to reminisce about college and update each other on careers, marriages, and growing families.

While waiting to board my flight, I remembered that Piper and I hadn't spoken about the logistics of her coming out here or when that might happen. There was zero planning, and it made me anxious.

I cycled through three email drafts, each from informal to formal, with one in the middle.

I did marry her, and yes, there is something about Piper that feels familiar, but I still don't *know* her. I decided formal would be best at this point.

After another ten minutes of drafting and deleting, I finally sent one off. Expecting to hear a response by the time the plane landed in San Diego, I was worried when I hadn't seen an email from her come through yet. *Who doesn't get email notifications? I'm sure she has it linked to her phone. Right?*

My heart pounded in my chest as I scrolled through my phone, preparing to text the woman who had come barreling into my life at full speed. Why was I so nervous?

Our conversation was brief, but she eventually checked her email, and now I finally have a date for when we'll officially start *fake dating*.

What the actual fuck did I get myself into? I walk up to the small dive bar in downtown San Diego near the hotel where we'll all be staying. As I head up the stairs and approach the rooftop bar, I see Harry and Mason talking with our fraternity brothers. Mason is now dating Harry's sister Bailey-who also happens to be one of Piper's best friends.

Piper.

My mind floods with images of her long strawberry blonde hair and the way her nose scrunches when she says something sarcastic.

"Jack!" Mason calls out from one of the two couches that my friends are occupying.

I'm not the type of guy you'd imagine seeing in a fraternity since I'm more reserved, but this group has become like brothers to me over the years. Each year, we choose a different location. Last year, I was golfing in Cabo San Lucas. It was a more tropical romantic destination, so most brought wives and girlfriends. I was dating the daughter of a previous client of mine at the time, and she wanted to go, but I didn't want to spend three days with her in my space.

I wave and head over. It looks like the three of us are the first out of the five to arrive.

"I thought you weren't coming in until tomorrow?" Mason asks as I approach the table.

"Change of plans. I ended up staying in Vegas an extra day, so I decided to come straight here instead of flying back to Dupara first," I say.

"Good to see you, man. I think the others should be getting here soon too," Harry replies, taking a sip from his drink.

"Chris won't be coming because his wife is in labor," I tell them, referring to the sixth guy in our group who will miss this year's trip.

"I saw that on our email chain. Good for him," Harry says.

Mason leans back, resting an arm on the back of the couch. "I plan to knock Bailey up as soon as she lets me."

Harry stiffens. "Dude, that's my fucking sister."

"I know." Mason flashes Harry a sly smile. "I keep forgetting."

I laugh, glancing at the menu.

Mason turns to me. "What about you, Jack? How are you doing since your dad passed away?"

I let out a sigh. I hate talking about this. "I'm doing alright.

It sucks, but I'm getting through."

"I know I've told you this before, but I'm so sorry," Harry says sympathetically.

"Yeah, man, I'm sorry." Mason pats my shoulder. "You're officially back in Northern California now, right?"

I nod.

"Oh, and Bailey told me that you and Piper hit it off in Vegas? How'd that happen?" Mason asks. He found that out fast. I wonder if Piper said something to Bailey. Something tells me that she didn't tell her friend everything.

So, what am I supposed to say to mine? *I married your girlfriend's best friend in Vegas, and now I'm paying her to help me look good in the small town where I grew up, so it will be easier when I take over my family's winery. Oh, and on top of that, I'd love to handcuff her to my bed and fuck her the entire night.*

They wouldn't even bat an eye at the last part. These guys are more vocal about their hookups and women than I am.

"That's, uh, true. Yes." My throat briefly runs dry. *Should I tell them?* No, I can't.

The mention of her name weaves through my mind, and she's threaded back once again. Piper is like a gust of lavender wind that's whipped its way into my life. I thought this guys' weekend would make me feel better, keeping my mind off the winery. But I've only arrived, and I'm consumed with those thoughts—and of her.

Harry swirls the ice around in his glass. "You guys are like into each other then?"

"I'm not sure," I say vaguely. "We're just hanging out."

"Bailey and I were *just* hanging out at first too." Mason grins.

Harry slaps his knees. "Again, my fucking sister. It's hard enough watching you guys together. I don't need to hear about it all the time too."

Mason laughs off Harry's comment.

The dynamic between the two is a helpful distraction as I dodge their line of questioning about Piper. They know I've never been one to talk about the women I've been with. I'm more private than that.

"I've known Piper for a while, and she is, without a doubt, the more livelier one out of my sister's friends," Harry adds.

I rub my chin, thinking about her little attitude. "I can see that."

I'd be lying to myself if I didn't acknowledge being instantly infatuated with her. When I first saw Piper at Harry and Jess's wedding last March, it took me a month for her to get out of my mind. When I ran into her and Bailey at the airport, I was even more intrigued when she followed me into the restaurant.

"Are you nervous about taking over your parents' winery?" Mason asks.

Rubbing the back of my neck with my hand, I let my other rest on the back of the outdoor couch. "I am apprehensive. It's always been my dad's dream. I hope I can bring something of benefit."

Harry bends his elbows on his knees. "Dude, you are a marketing genius. That skill alone will elevate you."

Mason nods and sets his Jack and Coke on the table. "You have a business head. You'll be extremely successful. But the question is, do you want it?"

"I don't know, man." I shrug.

"It sucks that as soon as I move back to Phoenix, you're going back to Northern California," Mason adds.

"I know. I'm going to miss it out here," I say, popping an appetizer into my mouth. "I was in the process of buying a place too."

Over the next few hours, the rest of the guys arrive, and by later on in the night, we're all back into our rooms.

Chapter Eleven

JACK

I'll be renting a villa in Dupara while my house is in escrow. While lifting my suitcase from the trunk of my car, my phone vibrates in my pocket. The call is from Jacob, the new marketing strategist. He will take over the two accounts I've signed contracts with while I finish the one with a few loose ends.

"Hi, man, what's going on?" I answer, shoving the phone into the corner of my neck.

"Sorry to bother you, Jack, but Amy with *Spark,* you know that new vegan restaurant downtown?"

"Yes?" I answer, remembering the high-maintenance, indecisive divorcée who specifically requested to work with me after stalking my LinkedIn profile for weeks before we had our first formal meeting.

"Well, she wasn't too fond of the live plants in the concept art."

My jaw flexes in response as I walk up to the front door. "Alright, does she want them swapped out for fake ones?"

"She said she wants to scrap the idea of the greenery altogether and go with something sleeker and monochrome."

"But it's a vegan restaurant," I quip. "Natural tones, plants, different types of foliage. It will help orchestrate the guest experience."

Jacob lets out an audible sigh, hearing that she's giving him as hard of a time as she gave me. Thank god that account is all his now. "Yeah, I know, Jack, but you know what it's like to work with her."

I glance around the room briefly before responding. This place is beautiful. It looks so different from when we had our after-prom party here in my junior year of high school. They've definitely updated it since then.

"That's fine. Touch base with the designers about her new ideas and make sure she knows that larger changes may accrue additional costs."

"Okay, thanks. I appreciate it."

"Also, make sure to send her the itemized list of each element she currently has in her contract with the newly proposed ones as well. Then, she can get a side-by-side comparison. Call me if you need my assistance once you've acquired the updated contract."

"Good call. Thanks, man," he says, "Oh, and how was Vegas?"

Piper's lips and beautiful long hair flash in my mind before I have a chance to speak. "It was, uh, interesting," I stammer.

"It always is out there, isn't it?" He chuckles.

"You have no idea."

"A few years ago, I was dating this chick—super hot with great legs. We joined a group of my friends out there for a birthday weekend. Well, she and I got super wasted the second night we were there, and she tried to convince me that we should get married. I was like, what the fuck? Who *actually* does that?" he states with a confident inflection.

I'm sure many people have drunken almost-married-in-Vegas stories, but I would bet Piper and I are one of the few who were dumb enough to go through with it. Annoyed by my actions, I ignore the sweat pooling under my arms and quickly get off the phone. "I'd love to hear more about your Vegas weekends, but I've got to let you go, Jacob."

"Of course. Thanks. I'll be in touch."

As soon as I hang up with Jacob, I stroll around the villa, checking out where I'll be staying for the next few weeks. The owner, Faye Hopper, and her husband have been close friends with my family for many years. They ered me a heavily discounted rate for one of the two villas on the property that are typically reserved for when their family comes into town. I'm grateful, considering it's harvest season, one of Dupara's busiest times of the year for tourists.

Walking into the living space, my heart sinks. Piper and I will be staying here together. The villas are smaller than I remember. They're nice and nothing to complain about, but for two people who barely know each other, things will get tight real fast. Fuck. I wish Faye's two-bedroom villa hadn't already been booked.

Hell, we didn't even share a cab on the way to the airport. I offered, but she turned me down. Maybe embarrassed about what happened the night before? Maybe she wants to make sure we keep everything professional. That makes sense. I did hire her to do a job—a strange one, but still a *job*.

I head into the bedroom to start unpacking my things into the closet and dresser. Should I leave room for her? I hang my clothes on the left, keeping one entire side empty. This whole situation feels so odd. It reminds me of being in college again.

Moving into the cramped dorm rooms with someone I didn't know.

I wonder if she thinks we'll have different hotel rooms? Nothing will be available during this time of the year with such short notice—unless she's willing to stay in a questionable motel downtown. And if that were the case, I wouldn't let her do that even if she wanted to. It's not safe.

Okay, no more thinking about Piper, back to unpacking. I've been so wrapped up in her that I completely forgot I had some of my stuff delivered to my mother's house.

I could have stayed with her on the property, but that's going to be a hard fucking no. Not with the memories of my dad and absolutely no privacy. And with Piper coming to stay, that would be worse because then we'd have to pretend around the clock. I can't do that to her. At least here in the villa, we only have to fake in public. Then, we can come back here and be ourselves.

I sit in this quiet room, contemplating how my life will change when I take over the winery. I wipe my hands along the tops of my legs. A nauseous feeling hits me in the gut as a reminder that my life in Phoenix will be gone. The independence I've protected so furiously since I was eighteen will be gone.

How am I even supposed to meet women out here? I've only dated a few women in Phoenix, but none I could see myself marrying. My love life as an adult has been similar to how it was back in college. I dated, slept around, and partied—like most people do at that age. I've always been shy, which often comes across as cold or arrogant. Surprisingly, girls were drawn to that. I rarely had to work for attention.

Many of my friends are married now. Marriage hasn't even

been a priority to me. I haven't even considered dating anyone seriously because I've been having fun dating whomever I want while maintaining my freedom. But now that's all been ripped away. I realize I might have wasted time because now my options will be nonexistent.

I swipe my phone off the dresser and call my mother.

She answers on the first ring. "Hi, Jack, are you back?"

"Hey, yes, I just got to The Vintage Inn."

"That's great. I'm so happy that Faye was able to help you out."

I glance over to the empty side of the closet that I saved for Piper. "Yeah, I know, especially during this time of year."

"But you can always stay here at home too."

"Thanks, but no thanks."

"Well, you do what you want, but know that the downstairs room is there if you need it," she offers again.

"I know, Mom. I'm going to go work out for a while. Then, I'll head over for dinner. Can we spend some time on the operational stuff?" I like my space. I want to be able to come and go as I please, as I have done in the past.

"Yes, of course, honey. I'll see you soon."

It still makes my blood boil that Preston thinks he can do it. The audacity of him and his father, assuming they're taking this from me. It's one of the only things driving me right now. I need to get my ass to the gym.

After changing, I head down to the small on-site workout room to burn off the tension that's been building inside me for some time. When I get down to the gym, a text comes through from Piper.

Piper: Hi, Jack, it's your wife.

I smile at her charming wit. *My wife.*

Piper: I'm good to fly out next Thursday. Is
six days enough for the first trip?

My heart flies from my chest. *Shit.* She is coming. *This is
happening.* Of course, it's happening. We're going to be living
together in less than five days.

Me: That sounds great. Email me your
flight information so I know when to pick
you up at the airport.

What if we hate each other? What if she leaves her products
out all over the bathroom? How am I supposed to jack off in
peace? *What the fuck am I doing?*

Piper: I'll send it over right now. Should I
book a room?

I knew this question would come up at some point. I don't
want her to get freaked out by the one-room situation. I'll check
with Faye about possible cancellations one more time before
Piper flies in.

Me: I'm staying at a family friend's inn
while my house goes into escrow. You'll be
staying here with me if you don't mind.

After I click send, my breath halts as I anticipate her backing
out.

Piper: Okay, that's fine. You don't mind?

That's a loaded question. Do I mind if a sexy woman who I'm obviously attracted to stays in the same villa as me? Yes—and no.

> Jack: You're coming out here for me. It's the least I can do. And it would look strange if we were supposed to be dating and staying separately.

> Piper: Yeah, for sure. We'll be fine. You're not messy, are you?

I crack an unwanted smile.

> Jack: I don't think so. Are you?

> Piper: No.

> Jack: Well, alright then. I guess I'll see you next week.

> Piper: See you then. Good night.

And with that, we make no plans to speak again before we prepare to spend all day and night with only each other and in extremely close quarters.

Chapter Twelve

Piper

"There's only one bed," I gasp. "We should check to see if they have anything else available so we can have privacy."

Jack squeezes between me and the narrow hallway leading into the villa's main living space, carrying two of my bags and wheeling another behind him. "We're going to have to make it work because there's no way we'll be able to get anything else for a whole week during harvest season. I've already checked." He brings the luggage into the large primary bedroom. "And although my mom has two extra rooms, her place is out of the question. I'm not staying in that house."

I sigh, scanning my eyes around the romantic Mediterranean-themed villa. It's been awkward between us since he picked me up from the airport. He barely said two words during the almost thirty-minute drive out here. It's hard to believe he's the same fun and charismatic guy I rashly married in Vegas.

That still sounds weird, even in the safety of my head.

Walking over to the window, I open the curtains to a small cobblestone patio, a personal pool, and vibrant rolling hills covered in full grapevines.

"We're having dinner with my mother tonight. We should come up with a story about us and how we met," he suggests, sitting in one of the three chairs surrounding a small wooden dining table.

"Alright. What did you have in mind?"

"On the way here, I was thinking that it would make sense if we'd met at Harry and Jess's wedding back in March—which is technically not untrue." He arches a brow. "Piper."

A smile slips. "Seriously, when are you going to let that go? And yes, since I'm friends with Bailey, and her brother was one of your clients. That's easy." I let my hands fall from the thick curtains, turning to face him. "Then, we can say we fell madly in love?"

Jack shakes his head. "My mom knows me too well. She'll never believe that I magically fell in love with someone that fast."

Jack doesn't realize it, but that one sentence tells me everything I need to know about him and his past. He probably hasn't had many serious girlfriends. "Why? Have you not dated many women?" I press, taking a seat on the edge of the couch.

He avoids my eye contact before answering. "I have dated only a handful of women that one might assume to be more *serious*. None of them have met my mother, except my high school girlfriend, and that's only because I was still living at home."

Another very transparent comment that gives me a window into Jack Bradley. "Interesting. Well, how about we say we've been dating casually, and since you're moving up here, you thought you'd bring me to visit? We can mention that we'll be doing long distance and all. Seems simple enough."

"That works. Completely painless and surprisingly normal." He smiles.

I rub my palms along the length of my thighs. "What time are we going? Should I change soon?"

"Sure, whatever you want to wear will be fine, and we'll leave here in about thirty minutes," Jack tells me before lifting off the chair. "I have to step outside to make a few phone calls." He tosses over his shoulder before shutting the door behind him.

"I guess I'll go change and freshen up." I point toward the bedroom, throwing him a cheeky comment. But it's no use. He can't hear me anyway.

I sift through my luggage, looking for something to wear. I had no idea what to bring since I'm sure we'll be involved in a wide range of activities. Lina came over to help me pack, and she basically threw my entire closet into one massive suitcase, one medium-sized carry-on, and an extra-large brown tote. It worked to my benefit that we both travel frequently because our expert packing skills came in handy.

I take out a pair of black pants, a white sweater, a denim jacket, and cut-off booties with a slight heel that I never get to wear back home. I brought a couple of fall dresses, but I need to feel comfortable and like myself tonight before things get trickier as the week goes on.

I shut and locked the bathroom door behind me, feeling relief to be alone. Jack's energy is intense and hard to read, which is both unsettling and exhilarating at the same time. And that says a lot, coming from me. I had to constantly read my mother's emotions my entire life. I never knew whether each day would be a good one or a bad one for her. When I was a child, I had to be on guard, always anticipating her emotional needs and how to help her work through them.

Taking my time in the bathroom, I change my clothes and freshen up my hair and makeup before walking out. Jack's sitting on the side of the bed with his chin in his hand. He looks up as soon as he hears the bathroom door open.

"Is this okay? You didn't mention what type of restaurant we're going to, so I figured I'd go with something nice but casual."

Jack's eyes roam my body, and it causes a shiver to move through me. "You look fine." That intense look for a *you look fine*?

"Okay, thanks." I aggressively pick at one of the buttons on my denim jacket.

"Everything will be alright. Stop fidgeting."

I drop my fingers, suddenly self-conscious. "I'm not fidgeting."

Jack puts on his coat. "Look, it's not like you're my real girlfriend. It doesn't matter if my mom likes you. I just need you to make me look good around other people." He gently rubs the side of my arm. "Meeting my mom is only to make things more believable."

His words surprisingly sting and my expression falls. "That was harsh." I sneer.

Jack's shoulder drops and his face softens. "That did come out sharp. I'm sorry." I give him a side-eye, folding my arms across my chest. He steps closer to me and gently brings his other hand to my arm so he's standing in front of me. It's a subtle gesture, but it fills me with comfort. "I meant that I didn't want you to have to worry about it, that's all. And if it's any consolation, I like you."

A smile breaks through my small pout.

"Beautiful," he says, running his tender hands down my arms.

"Thanks."

When he notices that I'm not bothered anymore, he releases me and turns around to grab his keys from the counter in the small kitchen. "Ready?"

"Yeah. Let's go meet your mother."

Once again, Jack and I take the ride over to the restaurant in silence. Every so often, I'll hear him clear his throat over the music. But when a certain track comes on, I catch the corner of Jack's mouth curve upward. "This is one of my favorite songs." Maybe that can break the tension? "I love "Rock the Casbah" by The Clash," I blurt out, looking over at him. Jack rubs his lips together, holding back a smile. I stare at him for a moment, trying to get a read. My eyebrows pinch together. "I sure hope you aren't smirking at this song."

With his hands on the wheel, he glances over at me. "It's not that, I love this track—"

"I do like the remix by Solar Twins a lot more," I add, cutting him off.

Jack's half-smile turns into a full smile that covers his entire face. "Oh, I know you do."

I sit straighter in my seat, planting my palms on my waist. "What's that supposed to mean?"

"You don't remember dancing on that tiny side table while we were having a drink at that lounge in Vegas?"

My face slowly turns red as the memory instantly comes back. "Oh my god. Yes, I did do that, didn't I?"

"Fun times." He briefly laughs before his face quickly turns stoic once again.

As we pull into the small parking lot, I stare out the window at this quaint, old-town shopping area filled with restaurants and wine bars.

Jack turns the car off and twists in his seat to face me. "Are you ready?"

"As ready as I'll ever be," I reply, continuing to take in the shops. Across the street is a bicycle shop that looks like it rents bikes to people to take on wine tours. *Because getting plastered while riding a bike in the sun sounds like a fabulously safe idea.*

Jack's face softens, sensing my uneasiness. "My mother is warm and friendly. I'm sure she will love you just as much as you will love her."

"Thanks." I force a smile.

He gets out of the car and comes around to my side to open the door. I step out and sling my purse across my body, ready to put on a show.

"We should probably hold hands," he suggests, slipping his hand into mine. It's a little stiff at first, but then they slowly mold together. My heart beats fast in my chest from nerves—or our closeness. I'm not sure which one it is.

"There's my mom." Jack gestures to a woman with short blonde hair walking toward us from the other end of the parking lot.

With my free hand, I start to pick at the button on my jacket again.

"Stop fidgeting." He quietly chuckles.

"Okay, okay." I smile at Jack's mom as she takes the last few steps toward us.

Up close, Heidi looks a lot like Jack. She has his electric blue eyes and perfect bone structure. She looks young for having a son in his mid-twenties, but I can also tell she has spent a lot of time outside in the vineyards based on her sun-kissed skin. She's beautiful.

"Piper! It's so good to meet you, sweetie," she exclaims, extending her arms to me for a full-body hug.

"It's great to meet you as well," I return, smiling.

She turns to her son, giving him the same deep embrace. "Good to see you."

"I'm glad Piper was able to come out." He squeezes my hand.

"Yes, it's lovely." Heidi turns to me, scrunching her nose. "My son has never brought a woman home. All the what—ten years you lived in Arizona? Not once did he let me or his dad meet someone he was dating."

Jack clears his throat. "Okay, Mom."

Heidi continues, ignoring his gentle warning, "But I knew when we had dinner last week that something was different about him. He has this sparkle in his eyes that I've never seen before. I knew he had finally met someone special."

My hands sweat. I'm speechless. It's going to break her heart when she finds out we're going to *break up* in less than two months. Jack and I were in Vegas last week—did he come home with that sparkle in his eye because he met me? No, that can't be true. Our connection wasn't real. It was simply having too much to drink. I'm sure we would have had the same connection with a lamp with how that night played out. I laugh on the inside.

Jack flashes me a lopsided grin. "Thanks, Mom, for embarrassing me the one time I do bring someone home."

"Oh, Jack. It's true." She hooks an arm around both of us, then gestures to the entrance. "Let's head inside, shall we?"

Jack steps in front of us, holding the door open as his mom and I enter the restaurant's lively atmosphere. The server seats the three of us at a high pub-style table.

"We can drink our wine anytime. Let's help some other small businesses tonight. What do you say?" Heidi beams, staring at the menu in front of her.

Jack turns to me, his elbow grazing mine on the table. "Does that sound alright?"

"Yes, that's perfect. I'm looking forward to trying all of them."

"Fabulous," Heidi replies and twists in her chair to wave down our server. She orders two wine flights to share, choosing only local, smaller wineries.

After our flights arrive, we all grab different glasses to taste. Jack's mother crosses her arms on the table and leans in. "Okay, so I would love to talk to you, Jack, but I want to get to know this beautiful woman."

I glance to my side at Jack.

He smiles at her. "It's okay. I'm sure you have a million questions."

"Of course I do!" She turns to me with her face lit up. "My son says you're a flight attendant, but he would only tell me that you both met in Phoenix. As you probably know, he's a man of little words, so I'd love to hear all about it from you."

I swallow hard, trying to hide any obvious signs of being nervous. "We met at a friend's wedding last March. One of my friends was marrying the brother of another friend in our group, who happens to have also attended college with Jack."

"That's so sweet. You both run in the same circle of friends?"

Jack nods, setting his glass on the table. "Yes, you could say that."

"That's so important. Jack's father and I were good friends before we fell in love, and it enhanced everything in our relationship," she adds.

The tips of my ears burn at her mentioning being in love, and at the same time, I feel Jack shift in his seat next to me.

When the appetizers arrive, we spend a few minutes nibbling on the food before Heidi speaks again. "How long have you been a flight attendant?"

"Since I graduated from college," I answer. I hope she doesn't ask me questions about Roxy or my childhood. People don't typically understand the unconventional way I grew up. Especially those people who weren't raised by emotionally immature parents. I grow nervous about having to rattle off the bullshit line about my family to a genuinely kind person. The same line plays in my head like a skipped record. I've rehearsed and practiced many times over throughout my life.

Without realizing it, my right leg bounces. Suddenly, I feel Jack's firm hand slip over my knee. He applies just enough pressure to calm my nerves and bring my leg to a still. It relaxes me instantly. "So, that's about five years," I continue as Jack's thumb moves back and forth, caressing the top of my knee. It's distracting but also pleasant.

"Do you enjoy it?" she asks.

"Yes, I love it. I get to have all these incredible experiences every time I go to work. Things are always changing and moving fast, but I take it all in and enjoy the ride."

As the night progresses, we continue with light conversations. Jack's mom tells me little things about his dad and how they met. She shares stories of Wine Country and how much she enjoys living here.

"Did Jack ever tell you that he wanted to be a professional roulette player when he was younger?" She laughs, clutching my hand from across the table.

Jack cocks his head to the side as his laugh comes out strained. "Oh, Mother."

"He didn't tell me that, but I find it completely believable," I smirk. Jack's eyes flicker in my direction, and I know exactly what he's thinking. Memories of our night in Vegas when he took a few roulette games a little too seriously. He got bothered while trying to teach me his strategies, and I showed no interest.

"Alright, I think we're good on the stories for tonight. Piper will be in town for the whole week, and I'm sure you'll have another opportunity," Jack says, flagging down our server to get the check.

"You're right. I'm sure you both want to get some rest. How do you like The Vintage Inn and Villas?" Heidi's face lights up.

"It's beautiful." I take the last sip of my wine.

Her eyes are now wide. "It's one of the most romantic boutique hotels in the area."

Jack pauses in the middle of his signature, keeps his eyes low, and darts them in my direction. I feel a flush creep up my face.

"Yes, it is." His mom is right. The place where we're staying is cozy and dreamy. It's a perfect spot for a couple who's madly in love.

As the three of us stand in front of the restaurant saying our goodbyes, Heidi pulls me in for another hug filled with warmth. I had to creatively maneuver around some potentially awkward conversations, but it was a nice time. It was endearing when she peppered me with questions, craving to get to know the woman whom her son had finally brought home to meet her.

Jack intertwines his fingers through mine as we walk back to the car.

"Oh, wait!" she yells to us.

Heidi jogs over with a wide smile. "A few of the ladies from our women's group are having a pool and spa day tomorrow. I'd love for you to join us." She shoots a look at Jack. "Unless my son has something planned for the two of you."

"She'd love to," Jack responds for me, then squeezes my hand. I take that as my cue to play along, so I smile and nod like he's paying me to do.

"Wonderful. I'll text you the details," she says.

Our second attempt at leaving was successful this time.

Jack and I walk in separately after another deafening car ride back to the villa. His shoulders are square as he takes off directly into the bedroom. My mind is panicking about how we're going to pull this off. It's uncomfortable. I feel like I'm doing an awful job. I breathe out a heavy sigh, then drag my feet into the bedroom behind him.

Chapter Thirteen

Rolling over a few times in the king-sized bed, I try to fall back asleep, but my brain refuses to shut off. It's like a continuous carousel of things I've done and the decisions I could have made differently. I flip over onto my back and stare at the white ceiling. My body is restless, and my mind is active. Now that I'm in Dupara, the weight of what Jack and I agreed to do is beginning to settle.

What type of person agrees to be the fake girlfriend of a guy she barely knows? People who are damaged, that's who. People who know what "normal" people would do but always end up doing the complete opposite.

I squeeze my eyes shut, blocking out reality. But soon, I hear the echo of Roxy's voice in my head from when I was a child. She has repeatedly told me I'll never be good enough for anyone because I am an extension of her. We'd always have to be together since every man I'd ever tried to love would eventually leave me like they've all done to her. My mother's words are now my internal dialogue. When I was a child, and now as an adult, it's hard to distinguish her words from my thoughts.

I need to get out of this damn room to clear my head.

I throw off the covers and swing my legs over the side, letting my feet touch the soft pile of carpet. Grabbing a white robe from behind the bathroom door, I creep down the hallway as quietly as I can. The lights are off in the villa, making it pitch-black around me. Jack is sleeping only a short distance away on the couch, so turning on any lights is out of the question.

I map the kitchen from memory and feel my way to the refrigerator. The low light from the open door will let me grab a quick snack and return to the bedroom without being noticed. Guided by the edge of the counter, I run my hand across the smooth, cold surface of the tile. I move quickly when suddenly fingertips glide over smooth fabric and a warm, firm bump.

"Can I help you?" A soft voice emerges from the darkness.

Jack? Oh my god! The heavy vibration from my heart echoes in my ears. Jack is directly in front of me. The light flips on, illuminating the kitchen and exposing where I'm standing. Our bodies are almost flush, and my palm comfortably rests on top of his length. *Which is semi-hard.*

"Oh my god!" I scream, instantly jerking my hand away and stumbling back.

Jack chuckles. He's leaning against the counter with a half-eaten apple in one hand while the other is folded under his bent arm. "If you wanted to know what my cock feels like, all you had to do is ask."

Heat burns the back of my neck. My throat constricts with horror. Shoving my face into my hands, I try to pretend that this did not happen. "I'm so sorry! This is humiliating." One side of his mouth is quirked up while his broad shoulders bounce with laughter. "What are you doing up anyway?" I snap, slightly annoyed at what I just did.

"I was looking for a good time." He chews through a smile. "And I seem to have found one."

"Ha. Ha." I snicker, then peer over at the stiff-looking sofa. "You really don't have to stay on the couch." I feel guilty in the larger bed while he's clearly having trouble on the couch. "I realize our current situation is making things—uh, a bit tricky, but I really don't mind."

"That's not why I couldn't sleep. I'm not always a sound sleeper and wouldn't want to disturb you." He leans back and crosses his ankles together.

I lower my eyes, shuffling my feet in place. "I understand that."

"Why are you up?" he asks.

"I couldn't sleep either."

He smiles, and I'm sucked back into the energy from his blue eyes. I quickly look away. My chest feels light and airy. I decide to drag my focus back to him, locking my eyes with his. Breathing in his energy once again before pulling away. "Looks like we have something in common."

The more I get to know Jack, the more I'm drawn to him. We both battle sleep. I'm not sure yet what deprives him—whether it's demons or his own insecurities, but I'm craving to know. "The nights don't just plague you. They come for me too," I admit, pressing my lips together.

"Is that why you decided to come out here to feel me up?"

I turn toward the refrigerator, rolling my eyes. "Yes, that's exactly why."

"At least you admit it," he retorts.

Nothing looks good, so I shut the refrigerator door behind me. "What's your story? Why are you eating an apple in the dark at three in the morning?"

Jack hands it to me, but not before stealing another bite. I briefly pause before taking it from him. *Is he giving it to me to hold?* No. He wants to share it with me. Now, this looks good enough to eat. With a smile on my face, I bring it to my lips and take a small bite.

Following the movements of my mouth, he clears his throat. "I had all these new marketing ideas running through my mind, and I wanted to get them flushed out before I forget all of them." He shrugs. "Then, I got hungry."

"Ideas for the winery?" I hand it back to him, half assuming he wouldn't want it anymore.

Jack circles it with his fingers a few times, keeping his eyes trained on me. When he finds the spot I bit, he opens his mouth and sinks his teeth into it. Purposefully avoiding the peel's obvious unbitten areas like a typical person would. "Yeah." He holds his hand out again. "There are so many moving parts with this whole thing that my brain just doesn't stop."

It's three in the morning. I'm stuck with him for the next week and a half—I guess I can play. I lean forward and sink my teeth into the apple. It's even more delicious after his lips and tongue have been all over it. *That's right, I can play too.*

Jack's eyes fall to my mouth.

"Those ideas must have been good if they woke you up in the middle of sleep." I pretend to be unbothered by how his eyes flare. I see movement from underneath my bottom lashes. Jack brings a gentle thumb to my lower lip and wipes a drop of juice that I didn't realize was there. My lips tingle and unintentionally part under the heat of his touch.

"My brain likes to work overdrive while I'm trying to sleep. Some of my best ideas have come to me between the hours of one and four in the morning." He wipes it away but takes care in going slow until he reaches the corner of my mouth. A bolt of electricity surges down my back and settles between my legs when he takes his finger and brings it to his mouth to lick it off.

I pull in as much air as possible through my nostrils, trying to keep myself from passing out. *Fuck, that was hot.*

He casually takes another bite. "So, what plagues your nights?"

I pause for a moment, diving into myself and contemplating a response to his question. We've developed a unique relationship, but I still don't know him well enough to fully commit to sharing my emotional baggage—*my mother.* I've kept the complex layers of my childhood and the details of Roxy hidden from most people for as long as I can remember. And I don't plan on letting anyone else in.

But I do feel safe enough to give him something. "I have a complicated relationship with my mother."

Jack adjusts himself against the granite counter. "Sorry to hear that. I didn't have the best relationship with my father either."

"I wish things were different."

"Don't we all? The emotional toll of a strained relationship with a parent is a heavy feeling." His voice is low, and his words sound sincere.

I feel my shoulders relax a little. I want to believe that Jack would fully understand Roxy, but it's impossible. He might think he's relating to me, but no one truly knows unless you lived it. I let out a deep sigh. "Anxiety, my own demons, thoughts of inadequacy. They all play in a never-ending loop as well."

Jack lifts the apple to his mouth one more time, making sure I see him run his tongue along the sweet flesh. Everything comes to a halt. I hungrily watch as his lips push out. I startle when my panties dampen, imagining his mouth buried inside the wet heat between my legs. He takes that last bite and then tosses it into the trash.

"We all have our own demons. They just visit us in different ways," he breaks the silence.

I'm shaking myself out of it—we're still engaged in a conversation. "Yes, I deeply feel that statement. The mind of an overthinker is a black hole of what-ifs."

"I'm sure."

I instinctively fold my arms across my chest. "I think it's because the distractions of the day are gone, and all that's left are me and my thoughts. Most of the time, I'm either alone in a hotel room or in my apartment. You'd think that becoming a flight attendant would put me with people constantly, but it's actually quite the opposite. I've found that I'm sometimes even lonelier than I was before."

That's all he needs to know right now. Jack and I both have things that keep us staring into the darkness behind our eyelids as the hours drag on. Worry constantly knocks on our door, threatening to rob us of our peace.

"Right now, we have each other, so at this point, neither of us is alone." Jack's voice is smooth and reassuring. He pushes off the counter and takes a small step forward, but it's enough to invade my space.

The air becomes dense around us. "Yeah, I guess you're right."

My eyes track his movements with uncertainty as he raises a hand toward my face. The hammering in my chest is so loud, and I bet he can hear it too. The smoothness of his skin on my temple is all I feel when my eyes fall closed. Jack subtly leans forward, his breath brushing the corner of my mouth. "I'll be right out here if you wake up again looking for another late-night snack." He tucks a loose strand of hair behind my ear.

"Okay." I swallow hard. "Thank you."

His eyes bore into mine as he backs away. "Goodnight, Piper."

I dash out of the kitchen before he can fold himself into the makeshift bed on the couch. I fear that if I look his way again, there will be no stopping me from crawling in with him.

Fuck. *Why does he have to be so fucking hot?*

What is stopping me from making the first move? We acted solely on our urges by getting married in Vegas, but that doesn't explain why I feel like he's deeper than quick hookups that would come and go.

I need sleep.

Chapter Fourteen

Jack was up at six thirty this morning. I wasn't, but I know he was because I heard the front door open and close. After some time, he walked in carrying a breakfast burrito and coffee. Both were for me. When I asked him if he was going to eat, too, he said he had already eaten down at the restaurant. It was a kind gesture but a big reminder that Jack and I weren't even friends. It is like I'm working for him. We act separately.

I thanked him for the food and the three different types of creamers before heading outside to eat on the patio while he stayed inside, working on his laptop at the small dining table.

I wish I could say eating alone bothered me, but it didn't. I was enjoying peace. Even though there are multiple villas around us, the seclusion and serenity of these lands make you feel like you're cut off from everyone else. I haven't felt a peace that deep in a long time.

After breakfast, I get ready to meet Heidi and the other ladies for a pool and spa day.

"Take my keys," Jack calls out over his laptop screen. "The hotel is only about two miles down the road."

Jack has black square-frame glasses on. It's the first time I've seen him wear them. I blink several times, utterly taken aback by how sexy it is. It's almost shocking. The same loose hair that's always out of place on the right side of his forehead partly hangs over the lens in front of his eye. He has a black T-shirt on and gray basketball shorts. *Gray fucking shorts. I wish he'd stand up so I could get a little outline.*

"I didn't know you wore glasses?"

"I do." He gives me an awkward grin. "Only when my contacts start to bother me."

"Yes—of course," I stammer—a *stupid thing to say.* "And thank you, but I can put it into the GPS on my phone. I'm sure I'll find it." I grab my pool bag, slip my sandals on, and head toward the door.

"Wait." Jack removes his wallet from his back pocket and slides out a silver American Express card. "Take my credit card if you need it for anything." He holds it out in front of us, pinched between two fingers.

I stare at the piece of plastic in his hands, then shake my head. "No, Jack, I don't need your money."

"I want you to take it. You're here for me, and I will pay for everything," he insists, flashing me with that bright smile. "Plus, I'm a gentleman."

What is it with those glasses?

"Fine, if you insist," I say, snatching the card from him. He probably would have offered to pay for my flights if I hadn't gotten free flights from the airline. "What are you going to do while I'm off winning over your mother and the other influential ladies of the town?"

Jack grins and then clasps his hands together under his chin.

"The ladies of the *Ton* will happily invite you into their inner circle, Miss Piper. I'm sure your afternoon will be spent chatting about all the gossip that Dupara County has to offer."

"Funny."

"I thought so."

My hands hang off the side of my beach bag. "Seriously, what are you up to today?"

"I have a call with our ops manager to run through some changes we'll be making with marketing and some daily functions as well," he replies, leaning back in his chair.

"Cool. Well, go get 'em tiger." I wink.

"What?"

"Isn't that what girlfriends are supposed to say?"

"Maybe," he quips. "But what would *Piper* say?"

"I would say—" I pause for a brief moment, then glance around the room a few times, searching for an authentic answer and not what would be expected of me. "Good luck, and tell me about it later."

Jack's eyes light up. "Thank you. I'll tell you how it went when you get *home.*"

I laugh. "I'll see you when I get home, dear!"

"Can't wait. Goodbye," he calls out.

Holding back a snicker, I walk down the entryway toward the front door. Jack's car is parked in the first space right outside the villa. I hop in, plug the hotel's address into my GPS, and get on my way.

While on the drive over, I thought of what I would talk about with these women. What if they ask me questions about Jack, and I can't answer them? We talked about so much during our short time in Vegas, and I wish I could remember all of it. Some things have come back here and there, but not much. I'm hoping I can pull this off.

The GPS alerts me that I've already made it to my destination. Jack was right. It's literally down the street. I pull his black BMW into the small parking lot of a rustic boutique hotel. Reaching into the back seat, I grab my bag and water bottle. Placing the bag in my lap and suck in a heavy breath. "I can do this," I whisper to myself while gripping the rubber padding on the steering wheel.

I walk into an airy and naturally charming lobby. I catch a glimpse of the pool through the large windows and see a group of about eight to ten women chatting between two covered cabanas.

"Welcome to *The Grey House*. How can I help you?" a woman behind the counter with short brown hair and wearing what looks like a horse-riding vest greets me.

"Hello, I'm here for—"

"Noreen, she's with us. That's Jack's girlfriend," a woman's voice interjects.

"Oh, hello!" the woman behind the counter says in a cheerier tone.

"Hi, Piper." Heidi is suddenly standing on my left in a one-piece bathing suit and a floral cover-up. "Noreen, this is Piper."

"Hello, it's great to meet you", I say, smiling at Noreen.

"It's so good to meet you, Piper. I can't believe Jack brought a woman home," Noreen says, bringing her eyes back to Heidi. I guess she knows Jack well enough to comment on his love life. Has he *really* never brought anyone around his family? I've always been reluctant to bring guys that I've dated around Roxy, but that's for obvious reasons. But Jack's mom is warm and kind.

"I know, isn't she beautiful—and so sweet? I invited her with us today. Can you send out Paul in a few minutes to grab her order?" Heidi asks.

"Of course. It was great meeting you, Piper, and if you need anything at all, give me a holler." Noreen reaches over the counter to touch my arm.

"It was wonderful to meet you as well and thank you so much." I smile.

"Let's head out and introduce you to the ladies in our women's group." Heidi hooks a loose arm around me and leads me to the pool area.

As we approached the other women, I noticed that not one of them was swimming, which I was relieved to discover. When Heidi first mentioned a spa—and *pool*, I was nervous about it being too cold for me. This Phoenix girl is not about to swim in seventy-nine-degree weather—unless the pool is heated, of course.

Heidi begins my introductions. "This is Adeline. She's the CEO of the Chamber of Commerce."

Stretched out on the lounge chair, wearing a cream-colored wrap dress, she tips her oversized sun hat to look in my direction. "Nice to meet you. Love to see our Jack finally settling down."

I beam with pride playing the part of Jack's girlfriend, and I find myself wishing it was real. When he does find someone to marry for real, she will be lucky and adored. "It's great to meet you, Adeline."

"And this is Heather. She owns Helena Wines," Heidi

continues, ushering me over to the next chair.

Heather sips a tropical cocktail with an umbrella on the top. She looks slightly younger than Jack's mom and Adeline. "Great to meet you, love."

As Heidi and I make our way to each small group of women, my head is spinning by the time we finish with two brunettes that look about my age.

When we approach them, Heidi looks caught off guard. "Piper, this is Sophia and Misty. They both work for Mountain Coast Winery here in town."

Sophia rises from the chair, flips her wavy chestnut hair around, and looks me directly in the eyes. "Jack's girlfriend. It's nice to meet you." She's smiling, but there's something misleading about it.

Misty raises her sunglasses and waves at me comfortably from her seat.

"Hello," I say to them both.

Heidi turns to the brunette, lowering her eyes. "Sophia, I thought you and Preston were out of town this week?"

"We were supposed to be, but it was more important to stay here for the beginning of harvest season," she says, shooting me side glances—or are they *daggers*? *What is her problem?*

"Oops," Heidi squeaks, pulling her phone from her cross bag. "It's the winery. I have to get this."

While Jack's mom steps away to answer the call, I'm left alone with two women who clearly already don't like me. I open my mouth to break the uncomfortable silence when Sophia speaks first.

"So, how long have you and Jack been dating?" she asks with

her nose slightly angled up.

A cool breeze whips through the air, eliciting goosebumps and a shiver. "Since March."

"That's not very long. And he already brought you home to meet his mom?" she says condescendingly.

Sophia knows Jack in a way that the other women don't, making me uncomfortable and territorial. "Yes, I guess." I stare at her caked-on makeup. "We're very close."

"Interesting."

"How do you know Jack?" I hold my breath for fear of the answer I'll get.

"Jack and I were high school sweethearts. Some say he never returned here because he couldn't get over me. But I'm engaged to Preston, his best friend now. I'm sure that's probably hard for him."

My heart freefalls inside my chest. *His high school sweetheart? What the hell?* He never mentioned this or *her.* Maybe he thought she wouldn't be around? That bad energy and evil side-eyes with those snarky comments make so much sense now. Frustration whips at my back as I grow increasingly pissed off with this shitty situation that I've been put into.

The vibration from my phone breaks my initial shock, only for a second. It's a text from Jack, but I'm in a stand-off with his ex-girlfriend, so I don't bother answering him. "Oh, that's interesting because I heard he moved away to get away from you." That's probably a lie, but I can't let her win.

Sophia's fake, exaggerated laugh sends another cold chill up my body. "I'm sure that's what he likes to tell people, but I don't care. I'm engaged to a very wealthy man who spoils me and who also happens to be part owner of Jack's winery."

Why is she telling me all this? Does she think I fucking care? I'm expecting her to pin me into an argument over whose boyfriend's dick is larger—which, in that case, she'd know since I have yet to see Jack's.

Now I'm pissed. He's my husband. I should know what his dick looks like—*feels like.* The slickness from my sweaty palms causes the bag to start slipping from my hands.

"Sorry, Piper, I didn't mean to leave you!" Heidi cries out, sprinting back over to us. "I have to run back to the winery. There are some shipment issues. Please stay and have fun."

"Bummer. Wish you could stay, Heidi, it's always so nice seeing you," Sophia says sweetly. *Wow.* I roll my eyes. This day couldn't have gotten any worse.

I adjust the bag in my hands, gripping it tightly. "No problem. I think I'll stay for a bit."

"You can hang out with us." Sophia sneers, plastering that same fake smile on her face. *Bitch.*

"I think I'll go hang with Adeline and Heather. Thanks anyway."

Heidi and I are shoulder to shoulder, walking over to the other side of the pool. "Jack and Sophia dated in high school. She was so infatuated with him, but don't worry, honey. That ship sailed a long time ago," she whispered.

I do like his mom. "I'm not. Jack and I have a great relationship." *Another lie.*

Before we reach the opposite side of the pool, she turns to face me fully. "I can tell by the way my son looks at you that you're something special. I've never seen him look at anyone like that before."

My breath comes to a screeching halt. *The way he looks at me?* It's all a facade, and I feel guilty for misleading her. "Thank you, Heidi."

"Also, it's better not to hang out with Sophia. She can be a little bitchy," she adds.

"You don't say?"

She laughs, giving me a quick hug. "I'll see you soon. And tell my elusive son that I say hello."

"I will."

Chapter Fifteen
JACK

It's a little past two in the afternoon when I hear the front door open. Piper is back, and I'm anxious to know how her day went. I texted her earlier to check in but didn't get a response back. I was expecting to see her enter the living room, but instead, I hear the bathroom door slam shut. The wooden door colliding with the side of the wall cannot be a good sign, and the sound makes my heart pace. I'm tempted to go in after her, but I shouldn't invade her space.

I quietly walk up to the closed door and gently knock on it. "Piper? Is everything alright?"

"It's just fucking peachy! Thank you for being so thoughtful and checking on me." Her voice is muffled, but its sharp inflection is hard to miss.

What the hell happened?

"Are you upset about something?" I bring my ear to the wooden door.

The door suddenly swings open, and I almost fall forward from the force. Piper is standing in the bathroom with one hand on the handle and the other on her hip. She pushes her lips to the side of her mouth and raises her eyebrows. I can feel the tension radiating off her shiny body—massage *oil*. My dick jumps.

I shake it off, ignoring the inappropriate thoughts rushing my brain. "You look pissed. Tell me what's wrong."

"Sure, I'll tell you all about the pleasant surprise I got today during the *little* ladies' spa day. Your fucking ex-girlfriend," Piper spits, then shoves past me, leaving the bathroom, and stomps right into the living room.

Shit. I rub the back of my neck. I completely forgot about Sophia. I should have warned Piper about her. I'm an asshole for not realizing she could have been there today too. "I am so sorry. I completely forgot that there'd be a possibility that Sophia would be there."

"Clearly."

She is pissed. I take a few steps toward her. "We dated in high school and haven't been together since. That was a long time ago," I try to explain. Piper and I aren't a real couple, and it shouldn't be a big deal about Sophia other than communication. But it doesn't stop me from needing her to know that there is nothing with Sophia. "Look, I'm sorry I didn't mention it to you, but why should it matter?" I ask. "I broke things off with her years ago."

"Oh, I'm going to tell you why." Piper's hands fly up to her hips. "It is very obvious she is not over you."

I'm not surprised to hear this. It's been no secret that Sophia had trouble with our breakup. She even tried to follow me to Arizona for college. Thank god, it didn't work out for her. "I can't say I'm shocked. Sophia has been trying to get back together with me for years."

"It would have been nice to know this. She is a wicked bitch and tried to make my day as uncomfortable as she possibly could." Piper sits on the bed, angling her head away from me and toward the window. I feel like such a jerk.

I shake my head in frustration with myself, then slowly walk toward her. As I bend to sit down next to her, my leg rubs against the warmth of her skin. She flinches but doesn't move. I let my eyes scan up and down her slick skin that's still covered in the remnants of lavender massage oil, the same scent as her shampoo. I came over here to comfort her, but now all I want to do is let my tongue lick up the inside of her thighs.

I adjust my shoulders and sit up straighter. "Yes, she is. Would you like to tell me what happened?"

"I don't think it's worth getting into the details, but in a nutshell, she basically dragged me into a who-knows-Jack-best competition. This was so strange because then she kept finding ways to insert that she's engaged to someone who is perfect and treats her *like no man has ever before*—which I know was a subtle dig at you. And to make matters even more aggravating, she said all these things when your mom wasn't around. Like she was trying to get a rise out of me, so I'd lose my cool or something." Piper fidgets with the strings on the dress that covers her bathing suit.

I lay my palm on top of her agitated hand, squeezing lightly. "I'm sorry that you had a rough time with her, and I'm sorry for not giving you a heads up first, but please don't let Sophia get to you. She's a horrible person, and she knows it. She's probably jealous about how beautiful you are," I say, slipping out the beautiful part. Piper is gorgeous, and I've mentioned it before, but this time it comes out more sincere.

Piper's head whips around. Her eyes flicker to mine briefly

before falling to my lips. I'm tempted to suck that puffy bottom lip of hers into my mouth. We both blink away at the same time. I casually hook my arm around her shoulders, and I feel her muscles relax and release into me.

"How does takeout for dinner tonight sound?" This is the first time I've had her in my arms since the night we got married in Vegas. It feels good.

Piper tucks her head under my chin with her ear resting on my chest. "Don't we have to attend that new restaurant opening tonight?"

"We should be going, but honestly, I don't think it's that big of a deal if we don't. There will only be a few influential community members there anyway." I try to sound convincing even though we should be going. But tonight, I need to spend some time with Piper. I've been a little distant since she arrived yesterday morning, and I should make up for that. It was never my intention, but I've been struggling with how to act around her.

"We're going to have dinner and actually hang out together?" she asks with slight sarcasm in her soft voice.

"Yeah. Do you want to have dinner with me tonight, Mrs. Bradley?"

"I would love to have dinner with you." She snuggles a little closer.

"What do you feel like?"

"Pizza and wine."

I laugh. "That was quick."

"I had to eat cucumber sandwiches and drink fruit-infused water all day with that damn woman. I think I deserve an entire medium cheese pizza to myself."

I draw my head back and release my arm from around her shoulders to look her in the face. "Why are you so cool?"

"It's hard work, but between the two of us, someone has to do it."

I look down, grinning. "*Sassy Piper* might be my favorite."

She giggles, slips out of my arms, and flips onto her stomach. "Hmm, let's see what we can find," she mumbles and grabs her phone from the other side of the bed, leaving her cute, round ass in the air. The sheer fabric of her coverup is riding higher than where her toned legs meet her bottom. My mouth waters at the thought of the only thing that's separating me from her delicious skin being that thin, hot pink bikini.

I quietly bite my fist.

"According to Google, the closest pizza place is right down the street. It looks like they have great reviews, and we could walk there to pick one up?" she suggests, crossing her legs behind her back. Now, her bright pink-polished toes are in the air, taunting me as her feet pump up and down on the bed.

Sweat beads form on my forehead. "Perfect. Let's go," I say, popping up eager to get my mind out of imagining my face inside of her ass.

Piper twists her body around, propping herself on one elbow. "Yeah? We're walking?"

"Yep. Let's go," I say again before grabbing my jacket and heading toward the door.

"Wait, let me change first!" she says, crawling off the bed.

I only have to wait by the door for a few minutes before Piper emerges with tight jeans on, a hoodie, and a pair of bright pink

Converse. I can't take my eyes off her as she slings her purse across her body and walks toward me.

"What?"

"Nothing." I blink a few times. "I've just never seen you in such casual clothes."

"Is that weird?"

"No."

"Then, why do you have that strange look on your face?" she presses, twisting the strings on her hoodie.

She looks adorable, yet sexy at the same time. I warm at the thought of her jumping on me for a piggyback ride while her arms are wrapped around my neck. She brings this playful and carefree spirit out of me. I can almost feel her heartbeat against my skin.

"It's nothing." I open the door for her to step out first.

We walk the short distance down the narrow restaurant and hotel-lined street. Our arms and shoulders brush against each other here and there, but she keeps her hands securely tucked into her hoodie pocket, and I do the same, hiding mine in the front pockets of my jeans.

"What was it like growing up out here?" We cross the empty street.

I shrug my shoulders. "I don't know. It's a small town, so everything you could imagine living in a small town would be—plus tourists."

Piper glances up at me from the corner of her eye. "And you came all the way to Arizona for college? Aren't there great colleges here in California?"

"Yeah, but I wanted to get away. I needed something different.

I wanted to live in a place where I could be myself. I was tired of being 'Bradley Wines.'"

"I can understand that. You wanted to get away—to breathe," she continues as we approach the red doors to the pizzeria. "To just be yourself."

"Exactly." I smile.

The delicious smell of crisp pepperoni pizza hits us when we walk through the doors. The packed small restaurant buzzes with people dining at red and white checkered tables, and the sounds of arcade games fill the air. Piper and I take our spot in line behind a couple and a young boy.

We both stare up at the illuminated menu on the wall behind the order counter.

"We've already established that you're going to be eating an entire medium cheese pizza by yourself," I tease her, bumping her shoulder with mine.

"That's right." She giggles and nudges me back. "You better order your own because I'm not sharing."

"I would expect nothing less. Besides, I need more flavor in my life. Cheese is boring. I like mushrooms, pepperoni, bell—"

"Jack Bradley?" The man with the family in front of us turns around. He looks familiar, but I struggle to place him.

With my eyebrows knitted together, studying his face. "Cole Hopper?" I ask, still a little unsure.

"Yes! How the hell are you, man?" he greets me enthusiastically before sticking his arm out to shake my hand.

I haven't seen this guy since high school. I would love to say I'm surprised to run into him here many years later, but I'm not. Most people who grow up in Dupara County never leave

Dupara County.

"I'm doing well. It's nice to see you."

"This is my wife, Annie, and my son, Levi." Cole gestures toward his family. "Jack and I went to high school together," he tells his wife.

"Hello." His wife glances at Piper and me.

"Nice to meet you both," I say, then dip my head down to Piper and wrap my arm around her. "This is my girlfriend, Piper." The fact that Piper's face flushes when I introduce her as my girlfriend doesn't go unnoticed. Heat prods at my cheeks and stings my ears after I see her reaction, and now I bet I look red too.

Piper smiles. "It's so nice to meet you both." Then she bends down to Cole's son, Levi. "It's good to meet you, Levi. How old are you?"

"I'm five and in kindergarten," he answers Piper and flashes us a smile with his two bottom teeth missing.

"How exciting." Piper stands and slides back under my arm. My muscles flex, tightening around her. Thank god this interaction is slightly more natural between us.

"Are you up here visiting? Last I heard, you were still living in Arizona," Cole asks, lifting his son into his arms.

"You know my dad passed away over the summer, and with that sudden loss, I've decided to move back to run the winery," I explain.

"I heard about your dad, and I'm so sorry I couldn't make the services." I open my mouth to thank him, but he continues, "But I thought Preston was going to take over?"

My jaw clenches, followed by irritation flying up my back at the mention of Preston or that people think he might take over my dad's business.

Cole's wife takes his son. "It was so nice to meet you both, but it's our turn to order," she says, shifting her focus back to Cole.

"Alright, you guys order, and I'll meet you at the table," he says as she and his son head to the counter to place their dinner order.

"What would make you think that?" I ask in an accusatory tone.

Cole crosses his arms at his chest. "That's what the word around the town is."

As if sensing my frustration, I feel Piper's tiny hand slip into mine. She calmly intertwines our fingers and gives them a gentle squeeze.

Adrenaline starts coursing through my veins. "Interesting."

"I think because everyone thought you weren't going to come back. You've been gone for so long," Cole tries to explain his admission.

"Yeah, well, I am back. I have every intention of taking over." I hope my old buddy Cole takes it upon himself to spread more accuracy among the community—one which I still feel bitter toward.

"I think it's our turn," Piper sweetly interrupts.

"Yes, we should order." I force a smile. "It was great seeing you, Cole. Your family is beautiful."

"You too. I hope I didn't upset you. Hell, I bet people would rather have you as a leader in the community than Preston, anyway. But that's my opinion."

I pat him on the back. "Don't worry about it, man. We'll see you around."

Piper's hand stays locked in mine until we leave. It wasn't until I started carrying out two medium that she released her grip.

"Who is Preston?" she asks as we walk through the parking lot of the villa's property.

I pause before speaking, "Preston is one of the reasons why you're here. I knew he and his dad wanted to take over the winery, but I didn't know that they were sharing that information with other people."

"Wait." She stops abruptly on the flower-lined path. "Sophia mentioned being engaged to a man named Preston today. It's the same guy, isn't it?"

I blink slowly. "Yeah, that's Preston Waters. He's the son of my dad's best friend and business partner. Someone who also used to be one of my closest childhood friends and now is engaged to my high school girlfriend."

Piper's bright green eyes dilate, giving me a clear view of the little brown specks that dot the rim. "What the actual fuck? This is some crazy drama. What did you drag me into?"

I start walking again, and she picks up pace right beside me. "I guess I didn't realize how complex it actually was." I turn to her when we reach the front door of the villa. "But in my defense, I did tell you that my dad's partner and his son were trying to take over the winery." I give her a playful wink.

"Yeah, you did say that, but you happened to leave out that this is clearly personal and not just about business," she says, lifting the two pizza boxes from my hand so I can unlock the door.

She's complaining, but her body language is telling a different story. She wants to be here as much as I need her to be.

"I didn't even think of it that way. Are you upset with me?"

Piper grabs a cold bottle of white wine from the fridge. "I'm not upset, but if we're going to be partners in this, I need you to communicate with me like a partner."

"You're right, and I haven't been," I say, completely understanding where she's coming from. This whole thing was my creative idea, and yes, I may be wasting twenty thousand dollars if it doesn't work, and yes, I may have been able to pull this off by myself, but I'm starting to realize how much better this could be with her. I need to stop viewing this as my problem to tackle alone—I need to utilize her more because she's clearly willing to help.

"No more surprises. I'm here to help you—yes, you are paying me, but regardless of that—I'm here for you." She pops open the bottle.

"I know. No more surprises." I head out to the patio and set both boxes on the table. Is she really going to eat this entire pizza herself?

She soon joins me, carrying two glasses of chilled white wine in her hands. Piper hands one to me before settling into the seat on the other side of the table. As she takes her first bite, I get caught by how tiny her nose is. The bottom has a more prominent button shape to it, with a few freckles scattered on top.

I stare at her with a smirk on my face.

"Why are you looking at me like that?" she asks.

'I'm looking forward to seeing you demolish that whole thing by yourself," I say as my eyes scan the features of her delicate face. The orange hue from the dusk sky shines off her strawberry blonde hair, making it look like a deeper shade of red.

Piper cocks her head. "You have no idea what I'm capable of. Just sit back, watch, and be amazed."

Chapter Sixteen

"**A**re you nervous about the harvest dinner coming up in two weeks?" I ask, washing out our wine glasses after dinner.

Jack slides the back door shut and flips up the lock. "A little. It's all the same pressure that I wanted to escape from to begin with."

"Is there anything I need to know before we go? There isn't some random, distant cousin hell-bent on taking down Jack Bradley, right?" I say, partly sarcastic but slightly serious, considering the recent events that have unfolded.

"I hope not."

"Are you sure about that?"

"Actually, I'm not." He laughs. "I wouldn't be surprised if there were."

After drying off the glasses, I put them back into the cupboard. "If there is, lucky for you, I'm here to defend your honor." I bend in a playful curtsey.

"Oh really?" Jack leans back on the counter next to me, boxing me into the space between the refrigerator and his body. He crosses his arms and dips his head, turning it toward me.

"Yes." My heart is pounding in my chest. He's only wearing

a black T-shirt, but the heat radiating from him is almost unbearable.

"And how do you plan on doing that?" he challenges in a soft whisper.

Oh god. What am I supposed to say? I can't tell him all the things I'd like to do to him that have nothing to do with defending his honor. "I'm your girlfriend. That's what I'm supposed to do." Deciding to dodge the question entirely.

Jack's jaw flexes. He quickly glances at me, then looks away before meeting my eyes once again. "Technically, you're my wife."

My lungs constrict hearing him call me that. "I guess that's true."

"I'd love to hear your take on what wives are supposed to do."

I start to sweat, unsure of what to say. "I'm not sure. I've never been married before."

"I guess I'm lucky to be your first then. Can't wait for the day when we start acting like it."

I suck in a sharp breath. "Acting like what?"

"Do you need me to explain to you all the things that married couples get to do with each other?"

"Are you tempting me?" I back away, creating space between us to breathe effectively.

"Maybe."

"I thought you didn't want any distractions?" My eyes scour the room for a quick escape from the tension.

"A distraction—or two might not hurt." Jack arches an eyebrow.

I can slip into the bathroom—which has been my only relief

since I've arrived here. "I'm going to get ready for bed. It's getting late."

Hearing wife at first sounded strange, almost an empty random word without connection to me. But this time, the word fell from his mouth with intention and purpose. Like a reminder of who I belong to. I wipe my sweaty palms on my pants while Jack smiles, giving me a quick nod.

I slide between him and the counter in the shoebox-sized kitchen, sprinting right for the bathroom. Closing the door behind me, I let my back mold into it. One hand grips my stomach while I bring the other to my chest to soothe the frantic and erratic beats of my heart.

Things would be much easier if he weren't a tall, blond heartthrob who jumped out of a teenage poster. I run a damp hand along my face. *Gross.* I need a shower.

I cautiously open the door, peeking around the corner to make sure Jack isn't in the bedroom. When I don't see him, I tiptoe to the dresser to grab my pajamas, then slink back into the bathroom.

I take a long, hot shower. It's been almost thirty minutes by the time I'm ready to face him again. I change, brush my teeth, throw my hair up, and head out. It's quiet. I wonder where that tall blonde could be. I creep into the living room, scanning my eyes from the back door all the way around to the kitchen. "Jack?" I call out.

No answer.

Maybe he went out for a run. I grab a glass of water, then head back into the bedroom to check my phone. Lifting it, I immediately see a message from him.

Jack: Went on a run, be back shortly.

I turn around to sit on the edge of the bed and message him back, but then I catch a glimpse of a figure coming toward me. Jerking my head up, I see Jack strutting through the doorway.

"Hey, I'm glad you're out. I was hoping to hop in once I got back." He briskly heads toward the bathroom.

Speechless, my eyes drink in the mouth-watering sight of him from head to toe. He's got on gray joggers that hang low on his waist and a black hoodie. I watch on bated breath as Jack walks toward the bathroom, pulling off his hoodie to expose a thin white T-shirt that's now completely transparent from sweat. *He's taunting me.* His baseball hat is on backward, and he's out of breath. I'm completely fucking frozen, so I simply nod in acknowledgment.

Once the door closes behind him, the air forces itself from my lungs. *What the actual fuck?* I need my own villa, or hotel, or even a different goddamn town. I don't know how I'm supposed to live with him in such a confined space when all he does is suck the energy out of every room.

I shake my head back and forth, clearing my thoughts. I just have to get through the rest of the week, and then I'll be home and away from his ... *heat.*

Until he beckons me out here once again.

Falling into the mound of a fluffy comforter, I clamp my eyes shut, hoping that when I open them, he'll be fully dressed and out of my sight. But soon, they fly back open, realizing it's highly unlikely.

I turn off the dim light from the small lamp on the

nightstand, then cover myself up. Pulling the blankets to my chin, I sink into the soft mattress of the large king-sized bed. I curl into a fetal position and wish for the solitude of sleep.

Only a few minutes later, I hear Jack's slow footsteps on the carpet next to the bed. A clean, refreshing scent, hits my nose. My mouth waters, imagining tasting his slick skin. Without opening my eyes, I know that he's standing right next to my face.

"Piper," he whispers.

"Hmm?" I crack my eyelids open. Jack's eyes and parted lips are mere inches from my face. My gaze immediately falls to his bare chest. Then, to the small white towel wrapped loosely around his waist. I wonder what else he's hiding under there besides the ripped abs on his stomach.

"I'm going to sleep on the couch. I'll see you in the morning." His smooth, sultry voice liquifies my insides. Everything melts, pooling between my legs. My thighs twitch. I push them together, dulling the ache. It's been a long time since I've used one of my battery-operated friends. I brought one with me, but how the hell am I going to use it with him here?

I rub my lips together, unable to look at anything else but that light piece of cotton that's separating me from what's underneath it. I wonder how mad he'd be if I gently yanked it off. "Are you sure?"

"Yeah."

"Okay, see you in the morning," I grit out before rolling over. I'll spend another night craving to know what it would be like to have his strong arms around me while I sleep. I toss and turn, unable to slow my racing pulse. This is infuriating. How can he smell so fucking delicious and look so effortlessly sexy without even trying? I flip over on my back, cover my face with the pillow, and wait for my nerves to settle or for sleep to come.

I wake up the next morning to the sound of my cell phone buzzing next to my ear. The warmth from the sun gingerly escapes through the thin slats of the closed shutters. Jack is probably up—like always. I roll over and pull my phone from the charger.

Roxy: I need your advice.

Roxy: Where are you?

Roxy: Hello?

Roxy: I need you.

Roxy: Why aren't you answering?

Roxy: I haven't seen or spoken to you in a
couple of days. You know you can't do this
to me.

Roxy: Fine. I figured you wouldn't be there
for me. You never are. Do you need space
again? Whatever. But when I need space
from you, you never check on me to see if
I'm okay.

I read through these familiar messages first thing in the morning, which effectively kills the buzz I had from dreaming about what Jack was hiding under his white towel. I rub the sides of my temples in a circular motion. Roxy is spiraling again. She goes through these manic-like episodes every few months or so. She'll become erratic, emotional, and, at times, even hateful. They've worsened in the last few years since she moved closer to me again.

I decide to call her back instead of text and, to no surprise, she picks up on the first ring. "Oh, you finally decided to call your mother back," she snaps.

Rolling my eyes, I sit up straight in bed. "Sorry, I've been in Northern California. I told you I was going to be here for a week."

"I know that. I wasn't worried. I just needed to talk to you about Rick," she says.

"Who's Rick?"

"That older gentleman I met at the exotic car show over the summer."

"Yeah, okay. What's up?"

"Now, I kind of don't want to tell you. I needed you last night. If you would have answered, then you'd get to know," she whines. This is also something she does. Roxy likes to give me the silent treatment as a form of punishment. This time, she's threatening to withhold her communication like I need to earn it.

I hear some light banging in the kitchen, followed by the sound of water. Jack is up. I get a little flutter in my stomach and the urge to get off the phone to see him.

"Stop playing games. Just tell me."

"Fine, if you really want to know, his son and his grandkids want to go to Cabo San Lucas with us next month, but I don't want them to. I'd like it to be only me and him. We got into an argument about that, and he said that if I'm going to be in his life, then I need to get used to spending time with his kids and their families," she complains.

Seriously, she is such a child.

"Roxy, there is nothing wrong with that. If anything, you should feel grateful that he has a close relationship with his kids and especially his grandkids. Not everyone does," I tell her.

"Oh, here we go. Another dig about what a horrible mom I was." Her voice is pinched, and I can tell she's getting defensive.

I throw the comforter off and swing my legs over the side of the bed. Sitting up, I hold up my phone with one hand, already mentally drained from such a brief conversation with my mother. "I'm not going to get into this with you. You know that's not what I meant."

"That's how it always goes with you, Piper. You act so ungrateful like you had such a horrible childhood."

I need to save what's left of my emotional energy and end this call. "I'm back in town on Sunday, and we can talk then if you're still upset." I stand in front of a rectangular mirror that hangs behind the dresser, fluffing my hair and wiping the sleep from my eyes.

"Oh, I'm sorry for inconveniencing your life. Don't bother calling me when you get back!" she shouts before hanging up.

I wish I understood how to talk to her. I replay my own words multiple times in my head before saying them out loud, but it's no use. And it's exhausting.

Looking at my reflection, I watch a single tear fall from my eye. Even after all these years of feeling numb to them, her words still hurt parts of me. Jack in the other room is the only thing preventing me from crawling back into bed and wallowing in my own sadness. The promise of laughter and awkward banter lightens my chest. I quickly wipe away the tears, apply a small amount of mascara, and head out of the bedroom.

"Good morning," Jack greets me with a cup of coffee in his hands. The patio door opens, allowing a crisp, cool breeze to blow through the villa. It's refreshing. I feel the clean air in my bones as it bathes in calmness. A stark contrast to what I woke up to.

I smile. "How did you sleep?"

"Adequately." His smile is upside down. "I must say, the couch is getting more comfortable with each passing night."

I nod, tucking a hair behind my ear. I feel Jack watching me as I open the cupboard, take a cup, and pour myself some coffee. I feel my cheeks burn, and I grow self-conscious about how I look this early in the morning. "Thanks for making coffee."

"Of course," he says.

I cup both my hands around the warm mug. "So, Mr. Bradley, you wake up early and go to bed late. Do you ever sleep?"

Jack's thumb and index finger rub his chin. "Sometimes." His gaze shifts to my legs. "Is that what you sleep in?"

I glance down, giving my tight button-down pink and white plaid shirt and matching drawstring shorts a once-over. "Yes?"

"It's a good thing that I slept on the couch last night," he replies, raising an eyebrow over the top of his coffee cup while it touches his lips. The same lips that mine burn to feel again.

"Why do you say that?"

"Those pajamas look like they come off easily."

I feel a flush creep up my neck and face. "Who says I would have worn anything to bed?"

"What's that supposed to mean?" he asks with a straight face.

"Since you have no plans on sleeping next to me or even in the same room—I guess you'll never know," I quip.

He steps into me. "I never said I had no plans on sleeping in the same bed with you."

"So, you do plan on it then?" I look up at his sharp jawline and perfectly tousled, fresh-out-of-bed hair.

Jack's eyes lower while a mischievous smile pulls at his lips. "Are you inviting me into your bed?"

"It really depends on if you can behave yourself," I say, clutching my coffee mug with two hands. I bring it to my mouth, taking a slow sip.

"Based on what you're wearing right now, I doubt that's a promise I'd be able to keep," he says.

I have absolutely no response. "That's good to know. I'll keep that in mind."

"Fair enough." He flexes the muscle on his arm. "Do you want to grab breakfast with me at the cafe on the property?"

My heart leaps into my chest. "Sure. Do you mind if I put on something more appropriate to leave the house in?"

"I think that's a good idea. Take your time."

I flash him a quick little smile, then head back into the bedroom to change.

After we get back from breakfast, Jack works at his computer for the rest of the morning while I lay by the pool. We make small talk here and there, but he mostly keeps to himself. He'll step out the front door every so often to take a private phone call.

I take a quick break after lunch to hit the gym and spend much longer here than I intended. It feels fucking amazing to relieve some of the pent-up sexual tension that's raging between me and Jack. A little cardio also helps me feel better about Roxy's guilt trip.

I quickly finish and make my way back up the hill to our villa. When I walk in, I find Jack still sitting at the desk, typing away on his computer. I would love to see his marketing ideas for the winery, but it's not my place to ask.

"Hey." He closes his laptop when he sees me come in. "How was your workout?"

Walking over to the sink, I rinse out my water bottle. "It was great. I didn't realize how long I was down there for."

His eyebrows pinch together. "Yeah, I almost came down there to check on you."

"Aww, that's sweet. You do like me around." I snicker.

"A little." Jack shrugs and walks toward me. "I was thinking we could head over to the winery today. It would be nice to introduce you to everyone and show you the property."

I can't help my joy or the smile that slips after hearing his suggestion. "Yes, I would love that!"

Seeing where Jack grew up lets me get to know him more. He's reserved and slightly mysterious, and I'm jumping at the chance to uncover a new layer of this man that sends my nerves into overdrive. I'm craving more of him, and since I can't have him in the way I most desire—buried deep inside me, I'll take seeing the place he's rooted to.

"If we want to make this believable, it would make sense that I'd bring my girlfriend there to meet everyone," he adds.

"Definitely. You grew up on the property, didn't you?"

"I sure did. And most of the people who work there have known me most of my life as well," he says, grabbing his black-framed glasses from beside his laptop.

Don't put them on. Don't put them on.

Fuck. He put them on.

I thread my fingers through my hair. *Damn, he's sexy.* "That sounds great. I'm excited. Let me rinse off in the shower, then we can leave."

"I'll be out here working until you're ready to go," he says, returning to his work.

Chapter Seventeen

J ack and I drive down the long rural highway to Bradley Wines for only a short time. I stare out the window, captivated by the vast open farmland surrounding us on either side. I can't guess how many large homes are tucked away behind privacy gates and long, twisting driveways.

Jack veers the car off to the right at the base of a paved road. It's a long drive up as we approach his family's property.

"This is the best part," he says, rolling down the windows. I close my eyes and breathe in the sweet smell of the ripe vines. I turn to Jack, and his eyes dart between me and the narrow hill we're climbing.

The cool breeze brushes past my skin and blows my hair around in front of my face. "It's beautiful!"

"I know, isn't it?" his voice vibrates over the sound of the wind whirling through the inside of the car.

"This is the tasting room." He extends his arm out the window and points toward a small stone structure with a burgundy roof. "Those are the wine cellars, barrel rooms, sorting and crushing stations," he continues as we get further up the hill.

"This looks like a little slice of paradise out here." I smile at him, taking it all in.

"It's where I grew up." He reaches over the center console to grab my hand. "I'm glad you like it."

Jack slows in front of a double-swing security gate. He punches in the code, and it opens. Making our way up what seems to be the last hill, a pointed red roof comes into view. A rustic country house peaks over an incline of the roughly paved driveway. As we pull up, I'm overcome by this property's sheer size and magnitude.

Jack circles the looped driveway before stopping in front of the entrance.

We remain in the car for a few minutes. "The first person you're going to meet is Gemma. She is the absolute best. She's my mom's assistant, best friend, godmother, and chef, among many other things."

"Alright, so she's kind of a big deal." I chuckle nervously, fidgeting with one of my earrings.

"Gemma is going to love you. She's just like my mom." He wraps his fingers around my wrist and lowers my hand from my ear. "Ready?"

"I am. I'm excited to see this place."

Jack quickly squeezes my hand before stepping out and walking around the car to open my door.

As soon as I step out, a strong gust of wind blows up my dress, exposing the tops of my thighs and panties. Panicking, I scramble to keep it down, locking my arms at my sides.

"That was a nice view." Jack's laugh rumbles through my chest.

My cheeks redden. "That wasn't funny."

"It kinda was. I hope that doesn't happen in front of all the employees you're about to meet."

"Now you've unlocked a new fear. Thank you for that," I say.

Jack hooks his arm around me. "Don't worry, I'll be here to enjoy the view—and keep you covered."

"It's not funny!" Still laughing, he nudges me through the front door to the house.

"Piper!" my name is screamed from across the room by a short and cute older woman with curly brown hair. She sprints over, grabs me by the shoulders, and I'm deep into a full-body hug before I realize it.

"This is Gemma, Piper," Jack says.

"It's so good to meet you!" she exclaims.

I smile, completely bathed in her effervescent energy. "You too, Gemma. Jack cannot stop telling me how wonderful you are."

Holding my hands in front of her, she turns to Jack. "He says that now, but I wasn't his favorite at one point," she teases. "Someone had to keep you in line when you were a kid, huh? He was such a little troublemaker."

"That's true. Now I appreciate it, though."

Gemma turns her focus back to me. "Okay, Piper, I'm going to whip up whatever you want for dinner. Is there anything you don't like?"

"Thank you so much." I quickly think about how honest I should be. Do I tell her I am probably the pickiest person she'll ever meet? Or do I suck it up for the sake of making a good impression instead of giving her the laundry list of my food aversions? "I like just about anything."

Jack draws his head back. "You should make those chicken pesto flatbreads you just added to the tasting room menu. Piper will love those."

I tighten my mouth, holding back a smile, proud that Jack knows what I'd like. Glancing over to him, butterflies fill my stomach as those feelings of familiarity return. "I think that sounds really good," I say, bouncing my eyes between them both.

Gemma brings her hands together under her chin. "Fabulous."

"I'm going to continue to show Piper around. We'll see you for dinner," he says, sliding his hand back into mine.

Jack showed me around the entire five-bedroom home, including the two balconies and one lower deck. He saved his favorite spot for last. We reach the third story, which consists of a large open room with a skylight, an oversized bedroom, and a bathroom. He leads me straight toward two French doors.

He pauses, stepping in front of me before he opens them. "Close your eyes."

I stare at his stoic expression for a moment, unsure of what I'll see when I open them again. "Okay." Seeing only black, I feel Jack's warm hands on mine, leading me down a shallow step onto what feels like a wooden balcony. The bright sun blazes through my eyes even though they're squeezed shut.

"Alright, you can open them." He drops his hands right as I take in the surroundings. "This is one of my favorite places on the whole property."

We're standing on a small balcony that barely fits two chairs with a circle table in the middle. The views from this height provide an unobstructed show of rolling hills covered with grapevines, green grass, and a bright blue sky. "It's mesmerizing. Everything about this place is perfect."

"I'm glad you like it." Jack glances over the balcony to the left. "You want to check out the tasting room?"

I excitedly nod my head. "I'd love that."

"Yeah? Okay, let's go." He leads me down the stairs and through the house while giving me a quick rundown of the behind-the-scenes operations of the whole business.

"You'll get to meet the whole gang today. Most of them have been with my parents for years. Rob, the winemaker, and Marybeth, director of marketing, have been around since I was a kid," he goes on as we walk out the front door.

"That seems like a lot of people to impress." I'm picking at the button on my denim jacket when I feel Jack's gentle grasp on top of my hand.

"I told you in the car, you don't have to worry about that. These people are like family, and they'll all love you."

I force a smile, then fall into step behind Jack. We both make our way down the gravel dirt road toward the tasting room. The sun is out today, but the heavy wind is crisp and blowing my hair around my face.

"It's very windy out here in the country." I giggle, pushing my hair aside, but it doesn't help. A heavy gust whips another couple of strands in front of my face, blocking my view. I roll the bottom of my foot on a large rock, and without control, my legs quickly slip from underneath me. From the side, I see a flash of darkness. It's Jack's hand shooting out to grab my arm, preventing me from sliding down the shallow incline.

"Oh my god!" I shriek, grabbing his shoulder tightly with my other hand to brace myself.

"Shit, that was close." His firm grasp holding me upright.

I'm twisted toward him, with my feet planted into the ground. "That would be my luck today, to fall on my face right before I meet some of the most important people in your life."

He turns to face me, and our bodies flush. "First, your dress flew up, and now you almost slipped. I'm starting to get a little worried."

"You?"

He lowers his eyes, turning them into slits. "Were you fidgeting again?"

"No, a very aggressive wind slammed into me. My hair blocked my view, and I couldn't see." I grip his arm until we reach the bottom of the hill.

Jack leads me. "Sure."

"That's what happened!" I argue.

His chest vibrates as he laughs through his words. "I believe you."

Once I'm safely away from the rocks, Jack brings an arm around my shoulder. The sweet smell of grapes and fresh air isn't enough to mask the overpowering, clean scent of him that hits me when I curl into his body.

We approach the tasting room from the side. The parking lot is full of cars—tourists, I'm assuming. Jack and I step onto a small, paved pathway with little flower beds on either side and a tiny sign poking out of the grass in the shape of a wine glass that reads *Offices*. He reaches to touch the ornate brass doorknob but pauses before turning it.

"This is where everyone's office is located. Edward, who runs all wine-making production, Marybeth, and both my parents' offices."

I nod, keeping my hand securely in his.

Jack dips his head to make eye contact with me. His blues are light. He's excited—which makes me feel more confident. "You are beautiful, kind, and authentic. You're going to be fine."

"You're just trying to stroke my ego."

"Obviously. But seriously, don't trip on anything, and keep your dress down. If anyone gets to see what's under your skirt, it will be me."

"Jack!" I playfully hit his shoulder. "You're such a jerk."

"Sorry. I'm kidding," he says, opening the door to a long hallway with rooms on either side. The walls are lined with large black and white portraits of what look to be various stages of the development of the winery.

Jack stops in front of a photo of two men and Heidi, who I recognize. She looks a lot younger and has a baby in her arms. "This is my dad, Steve, my mom, and me when they bought the second half of the vineyard. I think I was only about a year old in this picture.

"The three of them look so happy. What has happened between you, your mom, and Steve in the last year is unfortunate. That's got to be difficult for her." I analyze the facial features of Jack's dad. Their bone structure, square jaw, and light hair are so similar, although Jack inherited Heidi's beautiful blue eyes.

"I know, right? I've never liked Steve, but my parents were close with him, and now it fucking sucks for my mom."

I squint to get a clear look at his dad. "You look so much like your dad."

"I've been told," he mutters as we round the corner into the first office space.

"Jack!" An older man in blue jeans and a flannel button-up shirt rises from behind a large maple desk.

"Hi, Edward." Jack pulls him in for a side hug before turning to me. "This is my girlfriend, Piper."

"Well, hello there, Piper. How the hell are ya?"

I smile. "I'm good, thank you. It's nice to meet you."

"We're all so excited to see Jack with a woman. We were getting a little worried he'd never settle down," he says, patting Jack on the shoulder.

Jack shifts on his feet, and my cheeks turn red like they always do when someone references him *settling down with me*.

"Thanks." Jack dismisses. "How's everything going with the crops so far?"

"Really good. I'm sure your mom filled you in already. You're coming to the management meeting on Friday, correct?"

Jack nods. "Yeah, I plan to start attending them this month."

"That is just great. I know everyone's really excited about you stepping in."

Jack's face softens. "That's good to know."

"We're all rooting for you, Jack. I can only imagine what you will do around here with your degree and marketing experience from the big city," Edward adds. His energy is warm and kind, reminding me of someone's favorite grandpa who always has good stories and an ear to lend in times of need.

"I will be implementing some changes, but nothing we all can't handle."

Edward briefly turns to me. "So, are you moving up here to help out or—"

"She's a flight attendant," Jack interjects, gently squeezing my hand. "She'll probably want to continue that, but she'll still visit often."

Not sure of what to say or if I can add anything else to what Jack said, so I simply smile and nod.

"Oh, be careful. This place is majestic and tricky. The land will suck you in and never let you go," Edward gleefully warns, returning to his leather office chair. "Look at me. I've been here for almost thirty years."

"You never know," I tease, glancing at Jack.

Jack tilts his head in my direction with a surprised look on his face. "Good to know." Then, he turns his attention back to Edward. "Is Marybeth here?"

"Yes, she's here today. Probably running around somewhere bossing people around."

"I would expect nothing less." Jack extends his arm over the top of the desk to shake Edward's hand, but Edward stands and comes out from behind the desk to give Jack a proper handshake. "See you soon."

"It was great meeting you," I tell him as I'm ushered into the hallway.

"You too. I'm sure I'll see you sooner than you might think," he calls out.

Once Jack and I are out of earshot, he turns to me. "I appreciate you playing the part so well, but you don't have to say things you're uncomfortable with."

I turn to face him fully. Our bodies are almost flush in this narrow hallway. "What do you mean?"

Jack's eyes dart around, checking to ensure we are alone before angling his head down to mine. "Saying that, *you never know* if you could ever see yourself up here."

"How do you know if that was a true statement or not? You don't know my plans."

"Well, was it?" he retorts. Jack's breath dusts my lips, making them tingle.

I shake my head, confused by his sudden interest in such an empty statement that was only made in the heat of the moment. "I don't know. We are supposed to be pretending, right?"

"Yes, this is just an act. Let's not forget that."

"What's that supposed to mean?"

Jack backs away. "Nothing. It doesn't matter. We have more people to meet."

Confused by the sudden turn in our conversation, I try to shake it off. Why did he get defensive?

Jack leads me past an office with a sign outside the door that reads *Director of Marketing: Marybeth Hopper.* He peeks his head inside, but it's empty. "I wonder where she is."

"Should we go look for her?"

"Sure—" Jack suddenly halts, his eyes locked on the cracked double doors to our left. "My father's office," he mumbles under his breath. His palm is resting on my lower back. It feels intimate after the conversation we had a second ago. No one is around, and no need to put on a show.

With gentle pressure, he nudges me into the space. The area is larger than the other spaces, boasting large windows with clear views of the vineyards and hills. "I've only been in here once since he died." Jack runs a hand through his naturally messy blonde hair. "My mom's in the adjoining office. They both have individual entrances, but my dad insisted a door was attached between them. He wanted them to move freely between without being bothered by anyone else."

I smile. "That's really sweet. They were so much in love, weren't they?"

"Yeah," he replies. "My mom has kept his office pretty much shut off from anyone else. The plan is for me to move into this space. I'm dreading the day when I have to start cleaning it out and go through everything." Jack strolls over to the window behind his father's desk, almost like he's lost in thought, having this conversation with himself.

I can't imagine how difficult it is for him to be here. The more time I spend with him and the more I understand the weight he has on his shoulders, the more I empathize with his need not to be alone. Jack needs me in more ways than one.

I quietly move around the desk until I'm right behind him. His body stays facing the hills with his back to me. I slip my arms under his and wrap them around the front of his waist. My front is to his back, and we stand connected to one another. I lay my cheek against his shoulder blade as he tilted his head to the side, resting his face against the top of my head. I breathe him in while my lungs rise and fall in rhythm with his. They sync perfectly.

"I'm sorry this is hard for you," I keep my voice low.

I stack my hands around his stomach. He adds his on top of mine, grasping them steadily. All I can take from his gesture is that he's saying thank you.

"Jack Bradley!" A high-pitched voice from behind us slices

through the thick silence in the room.

Both of our heads jerk back simultaneously, but our bodies stay together. Once the short, gray-haired lady walks in, Jack slowly pulls from me. "Hi Marybeth, how are you?" he asks as he brings her in for a friendly hug.

"I'm good. It's nice to see you," she replies, holding a tall stack of papers.

Jack wraps an arm around my back, nudging me forward. "This is my girlfriend, Piper."

"Hello dear, it's so good to meet you. Heidi told me that you are just wonderful."

"Thank you so much. It's great meeting you, and I'm so happy to be here." Even my responses feel like a job interview or the first day at a new job, where I'm trying to make a good impression on the staff members. But since the moment we pulled up the long, windy driveway, a sense of familiarity has been overwhelming. Waves of pleasant feelings have come and gone since then.

"I'm looking forward to talking with you at the end of the week about what we've been doing with our marketing strategies and campaigns," Jack tells her.

"Of course. I have a full presentation for you. You'll be excited. But I'm also looking forward to all you're going to do." She's vigorously nodding her head.

"Great. Thanks Marybeth." Jack looks back at me with a soft smile on his face. "I'm going to finish showing Piper around. See you soon."

"Of course, of course," she quickly answers, stepping to the side and allowing a path for Jack and me to slip out of his parents' office.

"So great to meet you, Piper. I'm sure I'll see you around," she says.

"It was my pleasure." I smile, ignoring her natural comment of seeing me around. I'm unsure what Jack wants me to say now, especially after his bizarre response in the hallway earlier. We hang back by the door until Marybeth leaves, and then Jack proceeds to shut and lock the office that was once his father's, which now belongs to him.

Chapter Eighteen

JACK

"Did I handle the question better this time?" Piper's tone is soft, but I can tell there's sarcasm behind it.

"What question?" I already know what she's referring to.

"About whether I'd be around in the future. You seemed upset with my response to Edward. I assumed you would've been happier by me dismissing it from Marybeth," she replies as we make our way through the back hallway and toward the front of the tasting room.

She did exactly what she was supposed to do. Piper played her part with Edward. But I can't explain why I became defensive when I heard her response. Everything is natural with her, and I find myself getting lost in the moment and completely forgetting that none of this is real.

I stop, stepping in front of her and blocking the tasting room entrance before she has a chance to open the door. "I shouldn't have questioned you about it. You're doing exactly what I you to do. I guess I was caught up in what's real and what's not."

Piper's eyebrows pinch together. Her hazel-green eyes stared up at mine with confusion. "This is what you wanted."

"I know. You're just doing a really good job at it."

She puts her hands on her hips. "I don't know how. I'm barely even saying or doing anything."

"It's your presence. That's all. It's nice having you here." I sigh. "What do you say we continue this Bradley Family tour, huh?"

Piper lets out a dramatic exhale. "Sure."

I spend the remainder of the afternoon showing her around the rest of the property. Our winemaker, Rob, gave her a personal tour of the caves and barrel rooms. Piper wanted a taste of everything she could get her hands on—and, of course, Rob obliged by indulging her with anything she asked for. He also gave her a crash course in the chemistry and farming behind winemaking.

I looked on with pride because it all fascinated her. She was so excited and eager to learn. Whenever Rob shared an interesting fact, her eyes lit up. For a brief time, I wondered if she was playing the part or if she was genuinely interested. I hope it was the latter.

Once in a while, in the middle of one of his mini-lessons, Rob would look over at me and mouth the words "she's great" and "love her," deepening my affection toward her. After a few glasses, her giggle captivated me, reminiscent of our night in Vegas. Whenever Rob would get into the science behind growing and fermenting the fruit, Piper would purse her lips together and chew on the side of her cheek. I couldn't stop staring at the way she moved them. I made it my mission the entire afternoon to study every feature of her delicate face.

When we return to the main house, it's about dusk, and Piper's a little drunk from all the wine sampling.

"Can you stop with all the giggling?" I loop my arm around

her waist to help her walk up the stairs to the front door. *I love it.*

"I'm sorry. It's not my fault that Rob basically let me taste every varietal known to humans."

"Look at you putting your new vocabulary words into action," I smirk. "I'm so proud."

Her lavender-scented locks right into my face. "At least I'm doing what you're paying me to do, right?"

I breathe it in. "Like getting wined up?"

"No, being friendly and irresistible." She winks at me.

I run the back of my knuckles across her soft cheek. "You don't need wine for that. That's just you, my love."

"Always flirting with me."

"I can't help it."

Piper stops on the second step before reaching the door and fumbles through her purse as her phone vibrates. She holds the screen close, and then I watch as the flicks of light in her eyes go dark. Her expression and shoulders fall at the same time. I get hit with an uneasy feeling.

I bring my hand to rest on her arm. "Is everything okay?"

Piper's eyelashes flutter a few times before she answers. "Yeah, fine. It's just my mom again," she tells me, shoving her phone back into her purse.

Unsure of her response, I vaguely remember her getting a phone call in Vegas that also completely changed her demeanor. "If it's your mom, you should get it."

"No, she calls a lot. It's alright," she objects.

I wonder if it was her mom who called in Vegas too. She had almost a mirrored response and refused to answer then as well.

It's none of my business, and I don't want to pry, but this seems odd.

"Are you sure?" I press.

"Yes. This is what she does. She is fine, trust me," she gently snaps.

I nod respectfully, not pushing her again.

Piper plasters what I can now tell is a fake smile on her face. "Shall we?"

I smile back, hoping she'll tell me about these phone calls at some point. Sucking in a deep breath, before blowing it out, I slide my arm under hers and reach for the door. "Gemma, we're going to eat on the third floor," I yell toward the kitchen, assuming Gemma hasn't gone home yet.

"Of course," Gemma raises her voice as she turns the corner into the foyer.

"Gemma!" Piper shrieks, stumbling away from me and into Gemma's waiting arms.

"Oh, honey, looks like you sampled the product today, didn't you?" she says, patting Piper's head.

"She did," I say, biting my bottom lip.

Gemma's eyebrows raise. "Rob will do that to you."

Piper looks at me with the biggest grin on her face, then slips right into my arms. I pull her in close.

"Give her time. She'll learn how to hang."

"Yeah, I know. It is hilarious," I reply to Gemma while gazing down at Piper's flushed face.

"I'm fine. I had so much fun here. I love this place," she coos, rubbing her nose.

"You don't mind bringing the food up before you head out

for the day?" I ask Gemma, steering Piper toward the stairs.

"Of course not. It'll be right up." She tosses over her shoulder while walking into the kitchen.

Piper and I take the stairs to the third floor and then onto the balcony. "It's beautiful up here. Is this where we're going to have dinner?"

"Yeah, is that alright?"

"Yes!"

We both take our seats at the small bistro table. "What do you think? I know it was a busy day, and you met everyone so fast, but what did you think about the winery?"

Piper flashes me a wide, warm smile. "I love everything about this place. The smells, the stories—the people. I'm so glad you shared this part of your life with me."

Having her here has felt so natural, but is that the wine talking or Piper? "I've had a love/hate relationship with this place since childhood. Seeing it through your eyes today has been enlightening."

The sun is setting over the horizon, lighting up the hills with a low orange glow reflecting off her face. It unexpectedly causes my breath to catch.

"Good. I'm glad I could help."

I don't respond because my mind goes blank. I'm trapped in her gaze. In this light, she looks incredible—well, in every type of light, she looks incredible.

Piper sees me staring, and even though my instinct is to look away, I don't. "You are impossible to read," she complains, her forehead creasing. "And that says a lot, coming from someone like me who's good at reading people."

I hear her words, but all I can think of is the amazing day we've had. I share my childhood home with her—a place I haven't shared with any other woman. A place that I've kept to myself for more reasons than one. Does she see me for *just Jack,* even in this environment?

A light breeze brushes past us. Pushing her hair in front of her face, she whips it around and locks eyes with me. "Why are you staring at me like that?"

My heart jumps into my throat as the words I'm about to say replay in my mind before they softly come out of my mouth. "Can I kiss you?"

She inhales a sharp breath. "What did you ask me?"

I lean forward, mesmerized by her beauty in this light. "You heard me."

"If this is your way of messing with me, it's not funny. It's not like this is the first time you've seen me have a little too much to drink—" She pauses, then holds up her index finger into the air. "I guess Vegas was way different because I was plastered that night."

She's avoiding my question. But I want to kiss her. I want to feel Piper's lips on mine again without multiple drinks in me. I need that closeness right now after the day I've had. Standing in my dad's office, surrounded by her comfort, was something I hadn't felt in a long time. And maybe tomorrow I'll regret this, but right now, it's all I can think about. My whole life will be turned upside down in a matter of weeks. I'm feeling brave and want to shoot my shot.

Keeping my eyes on her, I say her name, "Piper?"

She slowly turns her head. Her pupils are large saucers. She's nervous.

I glide my hand up the side of her face, threading my fingers through her hair before hooking the back of her head. She doesn't move away. Her eyes fall to my lips. I slowly lean in, not expecting her to meet me in the middle, but she does. Then she pauses. We share a breath for a moment before Piper's mouth finds mine. My eyelids automatically close.

Her soft lips taste like a combination of watermelon lip gloss and Cabernet. At first, our mouths move slowly, massaging each other's lips. But I want a better taste. Sliding my tongue along the seam of her lips, she parts them and invites me inside.

A small whimper escapes from her, and I can't help but bite back a smile after hearing that delicious sound. I bring my other hand to her cheek, caressing her skin with my thumb. She's so tender and so—*perfect.*

I can't get enough.

"Umm," she whispers, nuzzling my nose with hers.

"Yes?"

"This is going to complicate things." Her voice is shaky and unsure, but it's enough to snap me back into reality. She's right. But I don't want to stop because she feels so goddamn good.

I draw my head back, ready to respond, when Gemma opens the balcony doors. Piper and I whip our heads around simultaneously, forgetting she'd follow us up here.

"Dinner is served, my friends," she announces, removing two flatbread pizzas and two glasses of water from a tray. We shouldn't have had to pull away when Gemma showed up. She does think Piper and I are dating. But then why did it feel like we were doing something we weren't supposed to be doing?

"You are awesome. Thanks so much." I try to catch my breath, but it's impossible, with my heart hammering inside my chest.

Piper chugs her water, looking worked up. "This food smells so good. Thanks again."

"No problem at all. You know I love doing it!" Gemma looks at me. Then, she turns to Piper. "Have a wonderful night, dear. I'll see you both soon."

The door shutting behind us is the only sound for some time. My pulse is still racing, and I'm sure hers is too. With a kiss like that, I can't imagine she didn't feel the sparks between us. Her lips are even better than I remember, if that's at all possible.

"Was that the first time you've been into your father's office since his passing?" Piper breaks our silence in an effort to push aside what happened.

Setting my napkin on my lap, I prepare to have this conversation with her. I agreed to have her as my partner, and if anything is going to cool me off, it would be this. If I had my choice, I'd love to refrain from discussing my dad altogether, but I've brought her into the fold, and the least I can do is share some of my feelings with her.

I clear my throat before responding, giving myself an extra second to formulate an answer. "I, uh," I hesitate. "Today was the second time. Believe it or not, being in his office is harder than being in this house."

"I get that. You, your mom, and your father shared the house. But his office is truly his space. I'm sure he spent a lot of time there."

I stare at the food in front of me, pushing away memories of running around his office when I was a kid, bringing food down when he was too busy to make it up for meals, and late-night brainstorming sessions with employees while I played with my toys on the floor. My chest tightens. I have to look away briefly.

Piper places her hand on mine as it rests on the table between us. All I want to do is turn it around and weave my fingers through hers. "It will get easier."

"You seem much more sober," I reply, changing the subject.

She grins, licking her lips. "Yes, that kiss definitely did the trick."

I smile at her, enjoying how the color of her cheeks always hints at her true feelings. I know I've gotten to her, and it is thoroughly satisfying.

After we finish dinner, we head back to our villa, but this time, we are leaving with different energy between us. Piper returns to Arizona the day after tomorrow, and I'm more than a little upset about it.

Chapter Nineteen

Since I got home yesterday morning, I haven't spoken to Jack. It's weird coming off the high of being with him. I can only describe it as a runner's high when all your endorphins are released, and you get that shot of dopamine—that addictive sense of well-being, energy, and euphoria. The desire to text him is intense and almost unbearable.

Why is it that everything with Jack feels accelerated? The sense of familiarity with him is off the charts. And having a connection with Bradley Wines is a whole other level of consideration as it goes beyond knowing him. I felt comfortable and safe there, with a soul-reaching, potent sense of belonging. *Am I crazy?*

I am.

Confusion swirls in my head, making me doubt my ability to think logically. I can't like him that fast. I haven't known him for that long. I'm exactly like my mother, falling for a good-looking guy who pays me attention, except she doesn't let herself develop real feelings, and I can't either. Roxy's voice echoes around me, saying that Jack is only using me to benefit his family's winery. And that his attention isn't genuine interest. It's a business deal.

I'm meeting the girls tonight for dinner and drinks. I've avoided their questions about Jack since I first mentioned him in our group chat. After I get all those out of the way, I can return to life as usual and free my mind of him—because right now, he's living in it rent free.

I stand in front of the mirror in the bathroom, fluffing my hair and adding a couple of last-minute makeup touches. My phone buzzes on the counter next to me. Thinking it's our group chat, I ignore it and head into the closet to grab my shoes. When I hear it buzz again, I poke my head out. Is it them? They will keep coming like a freight train unless I respond.

Swiping my phone from the counter, I see a picture of Jack lying on the king-sized bed in the villa. My heart drops. *He contacted me first.*

> Jack: You're right. This bed is way better than the couch.

He's lying on his back with the photo taken from above. He has a plain white T-shirt on, and his other arm is covering his face, exposing only his delicious lips. I rub my thumb along my bottom lip, remembering the sensation of his tongue gliding across it.

> Me: Don't get too comfortable. I'm coming back.

> Jack: I know, in eight days.

Is he counting? I hold my phone closer to my face to make sure I'm reading his text correctly.

Me: Yeah, I'm sure you'll enjoy the time by yourself until then.

Jack: I don't mind you here. It's been sort of lonely since you left.

Cue the butterflies. I reread that one sentence three times before writing him back.

Me: I don't believe you.

Jack: I'm serious. I started getting used to your healthy food and the smell of lavender shampoo in the shower.

He's being sarcastic, but I let myself enjoy his words anyway.

Me: If I'm being honest, it has been a little lonely for me too.

Jack: When do you fly out for work?

Me: Tomorrow is the first day of my three-day leg. Then I'm home for two and fly back out for three.

Jack: Where are you headed to first?

A quick thought of why Jack is messaging halts my happiness. He's talking to me because he's lonely, not because he wants to. I still indulge for the moment. I roll off my bed and sprint to the kitchen to grab my schedule from the calendar on the fridge.

Me: Houston, New Orleans, Miami, Bahamas, New York, Denver, Phoenix.

Jack: Busy.

Me: Yes. How was your day? Did you go to
the winery?

Jack: I did, and my day was okay. Worked
a little in my dad's office. Edward was a big
help. He told me to tell you hello.

I glance around my room, oddly feeling out of place here. I should be there with Jack. He would have needed my support. I hope it wasn't too hard for him.

Me: That's sweet. Tell him I said hello back.
How did you feel about being in your dad's
office?

Jack: That's a loaded question. It was
challenging and emotional but also
therapeutic.

I start to text him back but realize the time. I'm going to be late. I have to meet the girls at *The Poppy* restaurant in fifteen minutes. I start gathering my stuff, haphazardly shoving it all into my purse, then head out and lock the door behind me. I text Jack back on the way to my car.

Me: I'm glad. I'm meeting Bailey, Avery,
and Lina for dinner and drinks at The
Poppy tonight, so I won't be able to text
back for a while.

Jack: That restaurant project was a lot of

fun to work on. Have a good night.

Me: You too.

I hate that our conversation is cut short. I could have kept the texts going while I was on my way to the restaurant and even through dinner, but Jack deserves my attention and will get nothing less.

A short time later, the bright, illuminating letters of *The Poppy* are visible as I exit the freeway. Pulling into the parking lot, I'm so excited to see my best friends. Squeezing through the busy bar area, I head out to our favorite table in the back of the patio.

"You're here!" Bailey stands and extends her arms for a hug. Avery and Lina, sitting around the table, do the same.

"Let's get the pleasantries out of the way so that we can get into the good stuff—" Avery starts to say before Lina interrupts her. "—like, what is going on with you and Jack, and how was your visit with him in Wine Country?"

Avery nods her head. "Yeah, spill it."

I laugh and glance at Bailey to my left, and she's biting her lip and shrugging her shoulders.

"I love you guys so much," I say. "So, how's life?"

Lina frowns. "Seriously?"

A plate with different types of bruschetta is placed in front of us. "Okay, ladies, here is a compilation of our most popular bruschettas, including my favorite, brie, apple, and fig," Travis, the head chef, says, turning toward me. "Don't worry, Piper. I left off the green apple. Lina clearly said you don't like them and threatened me if I forgot."

I smile, winking at Lina. "Thanks."

"Of course, babe." She winks back.

"Enjoy." He turns around and walks back through the sea of restaurant-goers.

"I'm surprised with how obsessed Mason is with you that he isn't here tonight with us." Avery sneers, taking a bite of the salami and pesto bruschetta.

That same stupid grin Bailey always has on her face at the mention of Mason is back. "For your information, he and Luca have a fun night planned, building an oversized Hot Wheels course in the middle of our living room. Mason will probably feed him chicken nuggets and let him stay up way past his bedtime."

"Harry must be jealous that Mason stole his mini-best friend from him," I comment.

"Oh, for sure, but my brother and Mason have such a brotherly relationship that they fight one minute, and then they're inseparable the next," Bailey replies.

"Okay, okay." Avery's hands fly up in front of us. "We love hearing about your perfect little life, B, but I'm dying to know about Piper and this mystery Jack guy."

"Fair enough." Bailey rests her hands under her chin. "Tell us, Piper Moon."

My body starts to warm and even sweats a little. "Um, well, like I said on our group chat, Jack and I met a couple of weeks ago at the Las Vegas airport when Bailey and I were on a layover—"

Bailey says, "He went to college with my brother and Mason, and they hired him to do the concept marketing for this restaurant."

Lina nods her head. "Okay, so he's not brand new." Then, she turns to Bailey. "So, you've known him for a while?"

I open my mouth to speak, but Bailey interrupts again, causing a bubble in my throat. She may be more excited about Jack and me than I am—wait, there isn't a *Jack and me.*

I need to tell them.

I need to tell someone.

"Yes, and he was at Harry's wedding too," she continued excitedly.

"How you described him over text, he's Lina's twin?" Avery adds, causing the three of us to erupt into belly laughs.

"I guess you could say that." I take a sip of water.

Avery's eyes grow wide. "Lina is hot. Yeah, Piper!"

My stomach churns with the unease that I should tell my best friends the truth.

"There's something that I should tell you guys," I say before this conversation has the chance to go any further.

Lina's face softens. "What is it?"

"Jack and I aren't dating, and we're not suddenly *in love.* We're in business together." I shift a little in my seat.

Looks of confusion sweep across each of their faces.

Bailey's brows pinch together. "What does that mean?"

Nervously picking my fingernails under the table, I try to hide my apprehension. "It means that we've found ourselves in a little bit of a unique situation, and we did something," I blurt out.

The table grows quiet as it begins to register with all three of them what I've said.

"Like what? What did you do?" Avery asks.

Lina's eyes turn into saucers. 'Oh my god, are you pregnant?"

Avery cocks her head to the side.

Bailey freezes.

"Jack and I met only a couple of weeks ago. How would I even know I was pregnant that fast?" I retort.

"Okay, fine, that makes sense." She waves me off. "Tell us what it is then."

"It's pretty embarrassing and sort of why I'm in this situation with him in the first place," I begin to explain.

"Well, tell us. It can't be worse than when Bailey admitted to us that she was the fuck buddy to her archenemy and brother's best friend," Lina presses.

Bailey nods her head in agreement. "That's true. You guys freaked."

I angle my head toward the empty appetizer plate in front of me, avoiding eye contact with all three of them.

Avery leans across the table, resting her hands on top of mine. "Shit, Piper. What did you do?"

I suck in a deep breath of air, preparing to tell someone outside of me and Jack what crazy thing we did while we were in Las Vegas. "You know the day that I missed my flight and stayed the night with Jack?" Bailey nods, but the other two remain still and keep their eyes locked on me. I take a swig of some water before continuing, "We sort of got blackout drunk and—" I wince, squeezing my eyes shut. "Got married."

"What!"

"You have got to be kidding!"

"Oh fuck," Lina gasps, downing the rest of her . I slowly peel open one eye at a time. "Yes. We did that. Jack and I got married in Vegas after knowing each other less than twenty-four hours."

"Holy shit, Piper," Bailey says.

"You're not kidding, are you?" Avery squeaks.

I shake my head.

"No fucking way! You would be the only one out of all of us to do something like that. This is hilarious and kind of thrilling at the same time," Lina teases.

I crack a smile at her. "You have no idea."

"Everyone pause," Bailey says firmly. "I have a million questions. Did you get it annulled? Are you still married? How does Jack feel about this?"

"Now, that brings me to the nature of our business deal. Jack is in a bit of a predicament regarding his family's winery. His dad unexpectedly passed away over the summer, and now he's relocating back to Dupara County to take over ..." I continue slowly, waiting for one of them to interrupt me.

"So, where do you come in with all this?" Bailey interjects.

"His dad's best friend was also his business partner, and now that guy is trying to push Jack and his mom out, and from my very basic understanding, this small town is super close-knit and has a lot of influence over things. If that makes sense."

"So, the people in the community don't want Jack to run his own family's business, or do they?" Lina questions.

"I'm not sure, but from what I've picked up, they're a little apprehensive because Jack hasn't been a part of the community since he was younger," I go on.

Avery's eyebrows snap together. "That's fucked up. Why is it any of their concern in the first place?"

"And why is this your problem?" Bailey presses again, still

needing clarification.

"I'm getting to that—Jack is not married, and the town is basically looking at him as an untrustworthy flight risk of a bachelor, so he's paying me to be his fake girlfriend for the next month or so to get on their good side during all the transitions." This might be the first time I've seen all three of my very opinionated, outgoing friends speechless.

The four of them continue to pelt me with questions for the remainder of the evening, and by the time I get back to my place, all I can think about is Jack. I wonder if he's still up, but then I remember our little late-night run-in in the kitchen.

I plop down on my bed and pull my phone out of my purse.

Me: Are you still up?

Three dots immediately pop up at the bottom of my screen, sending my stomach into full somersaults.

Jack: You know that I am.

I quietly giggle and pull a pillow over, squishing it underneath me.

Me: Having a midnight snack?

Jack: As a matter of fact, I am standing in the kitchen enjoying a sandwich right now.

Jack: How was dinner?

Me: It was good. I told them about us. I hope you don't mind.

Jack: They're your best friends, I understand.

I smile, and another message comes through.

Me: Thank you. All three had interesting reactions and fired off questions at me the entire night.

Jack: I'd figured they'd do something like that.

Me: Are you sleeping in my bed?

Jack: Your bed?

Me: Yes, that's my bed.

Jack: It smells like you.

My face is on fire. Oh my god, I hope that's a good thing.

Me: I hope that's not a bad thing.

Jack: It's an irreplaceable thing.

I'm not quite sure what he meant, but the airy feeling in my chest tells me that Jack is flirting with me. I've missed him the last two days. The feeling isn't the same as traveling for work or being in a long-distance relationship. It's like being in an anxious, unsettled state.

Me: Can I call you when I'm in bed to say goodnight?

All my muscles tense as I wait for his response. My question was bold, yes, but I had to ask.

Jack: Of course.

I get a surge of energy and quickly spring off my bed to hop into the shower. When I get out, I brush my teeth and put on my pajamas. I turn off the lights and climb underneath the covers. With my heart racing, I hold my phone up in front of me, the light from the screen almost blinding in this dark room. I scroll to his name, hit call, and put it on speakerphone.

"Hello."

I mold myself into the mattress the minute Jack's calming voice washes over me. "Hi."

"Are you in bed?"

"I just got in."

"Did you want to talk about something specific?"

"No, not really." I sigh. "I didn't want to go to sleep alone."

"I don't mind staying on the phone with you until you fall asleep." I hear him smile through his words.

"I'd like that, thank you."

"You may want to put the phone somewhere safe so it doesn't fall off the bed."

"It is." I'm propping it up against another pillow next to me. "Are you going to go to sleep soon?"

"I'm in bed, but I'll be working on my laptop for a little longer."

"Alright. And you don't mind?" I ask one more time before letting my heavy eyes close.

"Absolutely not," he replies with a low voice.

The light clicking of Jack typing on his keyboard soothes me like white noise. Slipping away into twilight sleep, I also hear the faint sound of Jack's muffled breaths next to my ear. An unclear amount of time passes before his breathing turns into the distant sounds of the water turning on and back off. *He's getting ready for bed but staying on the phone with me.* Then, I hear the rustling sounds of what I believe are the moving of blankets and sheets.

"Goodnight, my love," Jack whispers barely audibly.

But I hear all three words as if they were yelled into my ears. Each one bounces off the walls of my skull and falls straight down into the pit of my stomach.

My eyelids fly open.

My heart sinks.

Chapter Twenty

Piper waves at me as I pull to the curb at passenger pickup. She's arrived back in town after being away for almost ten days. I've been anxious for her to return since I dropped her off at the airport. I didn't sleep at all last night. I've missed her more than I expected I would. We spent every single day together for six days, and then simply not having her with me any longer felt strange.

When Piper boarded that plane a week and a half ago, I knew I no longer had a claim to her. She didn't have to answer my calls or messages, and I tried to respect that space. But I missed her. We've had no contact during the day when I was working and she was flying, but every night since she asked me to stay on the phone while she fell asleep, we've continued to fall asleep on the phone together.

I've spent long days at the winery to keep my mind occupied with the other more pressing things in my already chaotic life. I've taken on more of a learning approach so far, spending time in every area of the business and getting to know the newer employees.

Our lawyer has tried many times to schedule a meeting with Steve, Preston, and their lawyers, but we've had no response. The lack of communication makes me suspicious, and I wonder if they're planning something behind the scenes. It's unsettling.

"Hello, Jack Bradley." Piper pokes her head through the rolled-down passenger window. "Long time no see."

When she landed home in Phoenix earlier this afternoon, she was finishing up from being in the air for the last three days. She had no time to go back to her apartment to change between landing and hopping on the flight out here. So, she's still wearing her uniform. Piper's tight navy blue dress and high heels make my dick jump faster than I can sprint around to the other side of the car.

"Hi. Nice to see you again," I say, remaining dry and unfazed by her return, even though it takes every bit of self-control not to kiss her glossy lips and slide my hand up the front of her dress.

I grab both of her bags and set them into the trunk, then jog back over to the passenger side before she can get to the door. Squeezing between her and the car, I open the door for her.

She gives me a side-eye. "Thanks, but I'm already your fake girlfriend. No need to try to impress me."

"I know you are. And I'm not." I flash her an exaggerated grin. "How were your flights the past couple of days?"

"Uneventful, which was nice. But I'm exhausted." Her voice is hollow as she yawns. "At least we won't have to fall asleep on the phone together this time, because you'll only be in the next room."

I grin. "Yes, that's true."

She lays her head against the passenger side window, looking exhausted and worn out.

"I got us a larger villa this time. The property manager, Faye, said a guest canceled their seven-night stay and offered it to us for the week." I glance over to her. Piper's hair is pulled back into a tight bun, but a few loose strands fly in the wind. "Still only one bed, though."

"That's fine. More space will be nice," she replies, her words not matching the tone in her voice or the look on her face.

She's silent most of the ride back to town. I hoped things would be more casual with us this time, but it seems to be business as usual.

Walking into the new villa, I can tell right away that it's more like a luxury suite than an extra-large townhome. The kitchen is better suited for cooking, there's a small office area right off the front entryway, and the living room boasts floor-to-ceiling windows with a view of the private pool in the back.

Piper and I bring our luggage into the bedroom but stop abruptly in our tracks. Red rose petals are scattered in the shape of a heart covering the king-sized bed. A small card is placed directly in the middle. I rub my chin and then dare to peer into the bathroom. A heart-shaped jacuzzi tub with Mr. and Mrs. embroidered robes hanging from the hook on the wall. I reluctantly turn toward Piper. The color had drained from her face, and her eyes bore into the love nest we'd walked into.

I chuckle. "I forgot to tell you. This is the honeymoon suite."

"Yes, you did forget to mention that important detail." She zips her necklace back and forth.

"Honestly, I thought someone would have cleaned this up after the other couple canceled."

"It's fine. Everything is fine," she repeats, unconvincingly and with a fake smile on her face. "It's going to be just fine."

Piper tries to avoid the romantic display at all costs. She starts to empty her suitcase, placing items in the dresser and hanging some in the closet. I noticed that she brought more clothes this time. I should probably be doing the same, but based on her body language, she wants some space.

As if the timing could not be better, my phone vibrates with a text alerting me that the grocery delivery has arrived and is waiting in the hotel lobby. Slipping my phone back into my pocket, I turn to Piper, buried in the closet, hanging up a semi-formal dress, presumably her choice for the Harvest Dinner this week. From what I can see, it's navy, and I have no doubt she'll look incredibly sexy in it.

"I need to head down to the lobby to grab our grocery order."

She pops her head out. "What grocery store delivery?"

"I put in an order earlier this morning, so we'd have some food around here this week. You know, in case one of us wants to cook."

"You cook?"

"I know *how* to cook."

"Hmm." She tilts her head to the side. "Alright."

I take the complimentary golf cart down the hill, eventually passing the same villa we stayed in the last time she was here. Once I get to the lobby, Faye greets me from behind the front desk with a bright yellow watering can in her hand.

"Hello, Jack!"

"Hi, Faye. Thanks again for giving us that great suite for the week."

"Oh, don't mention it. It's no problem at all." She moves from one plant to another, watering them as she goes. "I hope you and your girlfriend are settling in nicely."

I nod, looping the bags in both hands while stacking them up my arms. "Yes, it's beautiful," I declare, walking toward the door.

"Oh, and did you like the nice surprise I left there for you?" She snickers. "I figured you two would enjoy it!"

I clamp my eyes shut and slowly turn to face her. "The rose petals were lovely."

"Did she love them?"

"She was speechless. Thank you." My shoulders bounce with internal laughter. The look on Piper's face was worth the surprise. I don't care at this point, and I like us acting as a couple. I don't feel as uncomfortable about it as I did before.

"That's so great to hear. Enjoy!"

Making my way back up the hill with the groceries in the back of the golf cart, I imagine what Piper could be thinking right now. I wonder if she's upset that she had to come back because I am sure as hell not.

Seeing her this evening at the airport made my heart ache for her even more than it did when she was gone. And that short uniform skirt with legs for days. *Fuck,* I missed her legs. The urge to explore what's between them grows stronger by the minute. I've convinced myself that some time away would lessen my agony, but if anything, it's only made it worse.

Walking into the villa, I immediately feel her presence, bringing me so much relief. I'm not alone in the town I fled so many years ago. I have a partner, even if for a short time, I am learning to appreciate it.

I set the bags on the kitchen counter as Piper shuffles out of the bedroom in another pair of satin matching pajamas and fluffy white bunny slippers. How many pairs of these fancy pajamas does she own? And why do they look so fucking sexy on her? Are they meant to look like that?

But one of my white T-shirts would look even sexier on her.

"What did you get?" she asks, pulling the food out and setting it on the counter.

"I tried to get things I knew you'd like and some of the foods I saw you eat last time you were out here," I say, placing a gallon of almond milk on the shelf in the fridge. "I also know you like fruit. As you can see, I ordered a lot of it."

She holds up a bag filled with different types of apples with a wide grin. "Midnight snacks?"

"Yes." I laugh. "And no green ones. I know you hate green apples."

She slowly shakes her head and places the apples in a large bowl on the counter. "I can't believe you remembered that."

"How could I not? You were so dramatic about that fucking green apple martini," I tease.

"I was a little over the top, wasn't I?"

"You were very passionate about it."

"I'm sure."

Piper and I continue silently putting away the groceries for a few minutes. The interactions between us are more relaxed and comfortable this time.

"Thanks for doing this. I really appreciate it," she says in a small voice.

"No problem. Next time we can go together. I thought I should at least get some things in the meantime." I glance down at the empty counter now that all the items have been put away.

"I had a jam-packed few days of traveling, and I need to get some sleep." Piper's head is down while she plays with the drawstrings on her shorts. She always fidgets when she's nervous.

"Of course. I'll be on the couch if you need me."

She nods but doesn't walk away. A beat passes before she speaks, "I think you should sleep with me."

My breath stops.

Laying in the bed, under the same blankets, knowing that her half-dressed smooth body was within inches of mine would be too much to handle. How would I keep myself from touching her? She's trying to be considerate, but I don't think I can do what she's suggesting. Just imagining it, I can almost feel the sensation of her naturally tucked into my arm. I'd hold her close and sleep soundly, knowing she was safe. I would caress her face and her neck and eventually let my fingertips roam all over her body, claiming each part as my own. It would be impossible, and I'm not about to cross the line.

I can't fucking do it.

"I still don't think that's a good idea. I'm fine sleeping on the couch. You don't have to feel bad about it." I try to keep my tone firm, but she can hear the slight cracks of uncertainty.

Piper frowns. "Look, in the beginning, the thought of sleeping in the same bed with a man who's a little more than a stranger was a little unnerving, but things are different now. We know each other better, and it's not like we haven't been sort of sleeping together every night on the phone since I left," she points out.

I rub the back of my neck. "Thank you. Let's see how I feel later, okay?"

I watch as her face falls, hearing me push back. "Okay." Then, she turns around and heads into the bedroom.

Trying to pass the time, I turn on the TV and flip through a few channels. When that doesn't work, I pop in my AirPods and play whatever was on my most recent playlist. Blink 182's "I Miss You" immediately starts—*nope*. I have to go in there to get ready for bed. After what feels like a lifetime of sitting alone in the living room, I decide to face the internal conflict that ensues within me.

I carefully crack the door to the bedroom and feel my way around the dark space. Tapping the flashlight on my phone, I head for the dresser in the corner. I take care to remove my boxers and T-shirt. Then, I quietly creep across the room and into the bathroom.

A few minutes later, I find Piper tucked beneath the covers and curled into one side of the bed. Her hair is fanned out across two bright white pillows. I cautiously approach the edge to get a closer look at her. She's gorgeous. Right now, she's all mine. Listening to the faint sounds of her deep breathing lights me up and tugs at my insides. I stay for a moment, watching her sleep. She's so blissfully unaware of how beautiful she is.

I bend to my knees and hang my head. Exhaling in frustration, I shouldn't crawl in with her because the temptation to have her would be too powerful. My dick is already fighting with the inside of my boxers, and with one wrong move, I'd pop right out of the thin fabric.

I grit my teeth, then head back into the living room with every intention of making this sectional my bed for the night. But all that changes when my eyes find the pile of folded blankets and the empty space before me—*Fuck this*. I turn on my heels and confidently walk away.

I've spent almost two weeks missing Piper, craving to touch her once again, and now that she's back, I won't give up the chance to be close to her. Who knows, she might not mind me holding her while she sleeps.

I quietly walk over to the opposite side of the bed, carefully pull back the thick down comforter, and slip myself in. I get a quick look at her ass peeking out from where the sheets are pulled low. As always, her shorts are riding high, giving me a delicious view from the creases of her smooth cheeks.

My dick is already hard, and I have to adjust myself. Lying beside her, I'm aware of every movement she makes. My heart is hammering inside my chest. Afraid to move, even though she'll realize by morning that I've slept next to her, I remain perfectly still focused on controlling my labored breathing. I'd rather she catch me after I've already sneaked into her bed than during. Would she mind if I pulled her into me? I'm not crossing any lines, right?

The desire to have her close is overpowering.

Bringing one arm up to bend under my head, I cautiously outstretch the other, resting it on the backside of one of her pillows. My body stills again as Piper stirs. She rolls toward me, her face less than a foot from mine. I make a bold move, knowing that this could end one of two ways, but the need is too strong. If I have a chance of getting any sleep tonight, I need to hold her.

I slowly lower my arm from the top of the pillow to directly above her head, placing my hand on her back. My skin tingles when it makes contact with her. I feel the hollow vibrations of her breath. They travel through my veins like we're connected. With gentle pressure, I nudge her a little closer.

Piper's eyes flicker open briefly to meet mine before they fall closed again. My muscles lock in place, my heart pounds, and my lungs swell as I watch in slow motion as she scoots herself into the space under my arm. Panic sets in when she rests her cheek on my chest for fear she'll hear my thundering heartbeats.

"You changed your mind." She curls into me, her body molding to mine. The scent of lavender from her hair enters my nose, and I instantly feel at ease.

"I did. Couches are never that comfortable anyway." I take her cheeky comment as an opportunity to wrap my other arm around her and squeeze tight.

"I'm glad you did," she mumbles through sleepy eyes.

"Besides, I've gotten used to hearing the sound of your breath while I sleep anyway." I angle my head to the side, with my lips buried in her hair. I breathe her in before pressing a gentle kiss on her head. Letting my lips linger there for some time, I fall asleep.

Chapter Twenty-One

Piper slept cuddled into my side the entire night. At one point, I woke up with her arm and leg draped across me. I smiled, brushed the hair away from her face, and went back to sleep.

This morning, I got up before her as usual. I brought back breakfast and coffee for us both. Then, we took turns getting ready for the day, where she spent most of it reading on her Kindle out by the pool while I answered emails. By the evening, we were able to make it down to a networking event that Faye was hosting on the property.

Piper and I worked the room together. I often found myself memorizing her every move. She holds herself in public with such grace and confidence. Being genuine and authentic and not overly friendly is a gift. A few times, I imagined what it would be like if she were my wife by choice and not just a drunk mistake or a business arrangement. I have no doubt that she would make an incredible partner in this new role. How would I ever find someone who floats around a room full of new people with such ease?

By the end of the night, we went on with our typical bedtime routines, crawled into bed together, she snuggled into the crook of my arm, and we both fell asleep.

I suddenly wake and I sense something is missing. I sit on the side of the bed, letting my feet rest on the soft carpet. The room is dark. I glance behind me to the other side but don't see Piper. Swiping my phone off the nightstand, I immediately notice the time. It's four in the morning and still dark outside. I scroll through to her name, press call, and hold my phone up to my ear. To my surprise, her phone vibrates on the matching nightstand on the opposite side of the bed. *Where is she?* Sometimes, she has trouble sleeping.

I adjust the ties on my pajama pants, open the drawer to the left, and pull out a black hoodie. I use my phone flashlight to cross the hallway and head directly into the kitchen. But a quick look around tells me she's not here either. Dragging my eyes across the room, I expect to see her possibly having a late-night snack. I'm still learning Piper's habits, but it isn't a stretch to think she'd gotten hungry. I quietly walk through our small villa.

A tiny sliver of moonlight shines through a thin crack in the curtains and from where I stand. I see something moving around the pool in the private backyard area. We get a lot of wildlife out here, so I hope she isn't outside. I step close to the window to gain a better look. There's a slight glow from the interior pool lights, and through the thick steam that hovers over the heated water, I see a figure in what looks like a black two-piece bikini.

My breath catches when I realize it's Piper. I peer out the window, mesmerized by how her body glides through the water. Unlatching the back door, I head outside.

"You know we get a lot of wildlife out here, especially this time of night," I say in an elevated whisper, walking across the morning dew-covered grass. It's chilly. I hope she brought a towel with her.

Piper slowly swims to the pool's edge, barely moving the water with her tiny strokes. "Since it's technically morning and not nighttime anymore, I think I should be safe."

Smiling, I squat down right by the side she emerged from. She looks up at me with her hair soaked and pushed back.

"Why are you out here?"

"I couldn't sleep, so I decided to take a swim. Plus, look how beautiful it is," she says.

I stay low but lift my eyelids to look out over the hills. The sun is beginning to rise, leaving a dull hue of yellow and orange across the area. Taking in all this land and all that it entails to run the farming and business side of it is entirely overwhelming. Feelings of defeat all come rushing back.

Piper raises half her body from the warm water, leaning on folded arms. "Are you alright? You have a disturbed look on your face."

I fall back to a seated position, leaving my legs slightly raised and bent. "I don't know if I can do this." Resting my elbows on my knees, I let out a sigh of relief from finally hearing myself say those words out loud.

"What do you mean? The winery?"

"Yes. All of it. I haven't lived here for almost ten years. Despite visiting once or twice yearly for the holidays, I haven't been back," I tell her, releasing only a fraction of the apprehension I've felt for some time.

"I can see that. This is a lot to deal with, especially since it wasn't something you've ever wanted to do." She looks up at me from her long eyelashes. Piper doesn't see me as some ungrateful heir to a successful business. She shows a basic understanding of the desire to break free. To her, I'm just Jack.

"That's the thing. I do want to do this. I feel like I'm finally at a time in my life when I'm more prepared to take it on than ever." My eyes fall to her tits, which are pushed together. The tiny triangles of her bikini barely contain them. I want to run my finger along their soft skin and let my tongue explore between them. *That might make me feel better.*

Piper dips her head down, as if she can feel my eyes boring into her. I hope she knows how tempting she is. I've wanted nothing more than to taste those soft lips once again as I continue to keep her close like I have been each night. She's become essential to me in achieving adequate sleep.

"Why did you leave then? If you always knew this was your path, why avoid it?" she challenges.

I exhale deeply. "I never wanted to take over solely because everything was given to me. I wanted it to be my choice. I needed to make my own way first. Maybe proving to myself that I was capable of other things? And now that I've done that, naturally, this seems like the next step."

She nods. "I get it, but I also think it was courageous and respectable of you to want to prove your worth. You should be proud of that."

I open my mouth to speak but notice her skin breaking out in goosebumps as the top half of her body is exposed to the chilly early morning weather. I want to keep her warm, feeling her body on mine.

"Here, let's get you out. The air has got to be cold after swimming in that heated water." I reach over and grab the towel off the chair behind me.

Piper lifts herself out of the water. She walks into the open towel and my waiting arms.

"Thank you." Her teeth chatter. I hug her tighter, lowering my chin on the top of her head. There's a drumming between us, and I'm unsure if it's her heart or mine. Or both. Piper looks up at me through the water droplets that fall from her eyelashes, her long hair hanging loose and soaking down her back. The undeniable tension between us has elevated exponentially, and I don't know what to do with it.

My dick starts to harden, growing between us. I drop my arms for fear she'll feel it. "We should go back to bed."

"Okay." Her hazel-green eyes stared deep into mine.

I suck in a gulp of air and fight the urge to rip off that stupid bikini. Instead, we go back to our villa. I barely hear Piper's footfalls behind me, so I must be a few steps away, but I can feel her energy penetrating the back of my neck.

We walk through the door together, Piper aiming right for the bathroom, probably to take a shower. I collapse on the side of the bed with my head in my hands.

Fuck.

I hear the faucet turn on in the shower, and that simple sound causes my blood to pump through my body like a powerful current. I know she's naked in there. I need to go on a run. I can't be in this room anymore. I swipe a notepad and pen from the desk in the corner of the room and write her a note explaining that I'm going on a run, and I'll be back later this morning. I rip it off and slide it under the bathroom door.

The sexual chemistry between us is getting harder to deny. I see what I do to her when we're close and recognizing that only makes it all impossible to ignore.

I only get halfway down the hill before I turn around and head back. Piper brings out so many different sides of me. Sometimes, all I want to do is cuddle her, keep her, and protect her. Other times I want to defile her—fucking her so hard that she won't have enough energy ever to get off my dick. I dream about falling asleep intertwined in each other and with me nestled deep inside of her. I bet I'd get the best sleep of my life that way.

I walk up to the small door of our villa only a few minutes later. The dark windows showing no sign of light tell me she's most likely returned to bed. I intended to stay out longer, but I forgot my cell phone in my frantic rush to get away. I'm sleeping on the couch or the floor until I can get this under control.

Quietly, I slide the key into the door, slowly press down on the silver metal handle, and then push it open. I squeeze myself into the small crack I've created and gently close it behind me. The short hallway is dark, with only a tiny slice of moonlight shining in through the shutters. I remove my shoes and then turn the corner into the bedroom.

A low buzzing sound alerts me that Piper is not asleep. *Is that what I think it is?* A shot of excitement zips through me, shaking my entire body. My senses heighten as I walk right up to the side of the bed, where the dull buzz continues underneath a mound of blankets. My legs lock into place, not sure what to do. I stand back, flipping through all the ways I can handle this situation. I could walk discreetly into the bathroom and make a loud noise so she could hide what she was doing, saving her the embarrassment of knowing that I found out. Or I can pull these blankets off her and participate. My dick stiffens. Piper is my wife and my fake girlfriend, and it's obvious that I've gotten her all worked up from our proximity out in the pool.

Fuck it.

A growl forms in my throat. I'm about to do something that will significantly change the dynamics of our relationship. Nothing with Piper and me has been typical—it's all been based on gut feelings, living in the moment, and rash decisions.

In one swift motion, I jerk the covers away, letting them fall to the floor.

"Jack!" Piper screams, throwing her pink vibrator off the bed and across the room. She scrambles to cover herself with two pillows. "What the hell are you doing? I thought you went on a run!"

I smile. "I did."

Her breasts bounce up and down with the rhythm of her breath, and her face and chest are flushed pink. Damn, she's sexy.

"Did you come yet?" I ask with a stern expression. If I'm going to do this, I'm going to do it right.

"What?"

"Did you come?"

"I'm sorry. I'm a little confused about what's happening right now," she says, her pupils fully dilated.

"Did. You. Come. Yet?" I ask again, pausing between each word to keep my tone even. I plan to wait all night for her to process what I've asked because this is happening.

Piper is raised on her knees and facing the end of the bed. "I can't believe you ripped the blankets off of me!" Her tone is laced with anger as she refuses to answer my question.

I saunter over to the corner of the room and collect the pulsating vibrator from the floor. I wipe it off with my shirt, then stalk back to the bed and hand it to her. She reluctantly takes it from me. Her skin is still red, and her eyes are hooded—she definitely didn't finish.

"I want you to come for me," I tell her, then drag a chair over to the edge of the bed and take a seat.

"But I—"

"I interrupted you, and this is the least I can do, but since you are my wife, I'm going to watch." I relax back into the chair, letting my palms rest at my knees.

"You can't be serious."

"Oh, I am extremely serious. You're fucking sexy, and there is nothing more I want to do right now than to watch you get yourself off."

With an uncertain expression on her face, she slowly nods. She is giving in because she wants to come, but I won't let her unless I can watch.

Breathing heavily once again, she lowers herself and lays down on her back directly in front of me. With her head nestled into the softness of the pillow, she raises her knees and slips the vibrator into the heat between her thighs.

"Closer."

With a slight smirk, she scoots further down on the bed.

"Wider," I gently demand, craving to see all of her.

She eagerly obeys, letting her legs fall open and giving me a clear view of her swollen pussy. My mouth waters, imagining what it would be like to taste her insides.

"Is this better?" Her voice is husky and desperate.

"Yes, that's a good girl. Now show me how you make yourself come."

She places the vibrating toy on her clit, gasping as soon as it makes contact. Sliding it in and out, the rubber drips with her arousal.

My dick swells, watching her play with herself. Dying to participate, it painfully rubs the inside of my pants, so I quickly adjust myself, attempting to dull the mounting discomfort. Consumed by her, my eyes roam her naked body, appreciating her dips and curves, and I quickly become captivated by the way she arches her back, chasing the orgasm that I robbed her of earlier. A soft moan escapes from her pursed lips.

"You're so fucking sexy. I can't believe I'm married to you," I mutter under my breath.

Her neck is tilted up with her eyes toward the ceiling. "Hmm?" she purrs, then whimpers as she hits a new spot.

I can't get enough of her little noises. I give in, frantically lowering my pants, and pull out my cock. I don't care if she sees. The pit of my stomach aches, watching her slide that wet fucking massager in and out, jealous that it should be me. I spit on my hand and run it along the length of my shaft, squeezing tightly. Keeping my eyes locked on Piper, I begin to pump myself. The sounds of slapping flesh fill the room.

"I can hear you," she pants.

I grip myself harder, stroking in rhythm with the twitching of her legs. "It's all for you, my love."

"Come for me," she begs, her hips bucking into the air. "Please, I want to hear you."

She's fucking begging me to come for her. Rock hard and ready to combust. I watch tiny sweat beads fall from the corners of her thigh and down her leg.

"Oh god," I growl, moving faster. I give myself one more hard, quick stroke when I see her back arch off the bed.

"Mmm," she groans at first, then her voice elevates, turning into a high-pitched scream. "Jack!"

I unload the moment my eyes fall to her pulsing, dripping pussy, and it takes everything in me not to shove my dick in at the last minute.

I let my head fall back, breathless and cursing with heat.

From the corner of my eye, I see Piper curl into her side and face me with a smile on her face. "Thank you," she says, then wraps herself in a sheet, climbs off the bed, and sprints into the small kitchen.

When she's out of view, I quickly wipe myself off and yank up my pants. I can't believe we did that—like we actually watched each other get off. Fully aware of what I was doing before we even started, I suddenly get hit with a ping of guilt. If we start messing around outside of cuddling, everything will be much more difficult when I no longer need her. I'm paying her to be here with me. Who knows if she'd be with me if no money were involved?

If we give in to our urges again, I don't know how I could stop, and I can't let my focus falter. We need this to remain professional. We must maintain the illusion of love, or this whole plan could blow up in my face. If that happens, I'll lose so much more than a woman I have the hots for.

Piper enters the room a few minutes later with an apple in one hand and a cup of water in the other. The mental pep talk I gave myself practically out the window. Getting a taste of her is something I no longer want. It's something I need.

Unsure how we should act after what just happened, Piper and I stand uncomfortably, our eyes fixed on the floor beneath our feet.

"I don't think that should happen again," I say, being the first to break the thick silence. Then, I head into the bathroom to get ready for the day.

"I agree," I hear her mumble from behind the closed door.

I take a much-needed hot shower, replaying every one of her movements and heavenly sounds in my head. I was surprised at how little she fought with me when I told her that I was going to watch. There are so many dirty things I can do to her, and she's so ready and willing.

Chapter Twenty-Two

JACK

I walk into the large meeting room to see my mother and our lawyer, Tom, on one side of the oversized cherry wood table and my dad's best friend Steve, his son Preston, and their lawyer on the other. I forget their lawyer's name. I only know him from the horrible hair plugs haphazardly placed across the top of his bald head. After avoiding the calls and emails from Tom, the hair plug guy, who represents my parents' oldest friends, could finally schedule this meeting.

Preston and Steve stand to shake my hand. "How are you?"

"Fine, thank you." I nod, giving them a cold greeting. They don't deserve my respect after everything that's happened in the last few months. And even more now that they've been telling community members that they'll take over my dad's winery before anything is final.

I may not have wanted this when I was younger, but this is my family's legacy, and I will do everything possible to protect it. If my dad knew what these two would plan once he wasn't around, I'm sure he would have cut ties long ago.

"So, you have officially moved back?" Preston asks, only to make small talk and not genuine curiosity.

"Yeah, I have. I'll close on my house at the end of the month," I tell them.

"And your girlfriend, will she be moving here as well?" Preston presses me for information on Piper. Based on what Piper told me about the interaction she had with Sophia a few weeks ago, I know he knows more than he's letting on.

"I don't think that's any of your business, is it?"

"Is that the way this is going to be? I'm trying to be nice and ask you about your new girlfriend. Take a fucking chill," Preston barks, still standing, although his dad and lawyer have taken their seats. This is just a power struggle for him.

"Are you worried that with me being back, that I'll try to fuck Sophia? Because you can be assured, I have higher standards than that."

"Jack!" my mom exclaims at my inappropriate language in such a formal setting, but I don't care and continue to bait the asshole on the other side of the table.

"She apparently does now too," he spits back at my expense.

"You think so?" I lower my eyes. "I got rid of her once, never wanting to see her again, and yet, here we are. Did she tell you how she got all alpha female with my girlfriend at the pool a few weeks ago? Too bad for her, Piper is beautiful and a bit of a smart ass, so it didn't go so well for Sophia."

"Fuck you. You've always thought you were better than everyone in this town."

"Alright, enough!" Steve demands in a clipped tone, slamming his palm on the top of the table.

His dramatic display does nothing to faze me as I continue. "I am, since you're marrying my high school girlfriend—who was grossly obsessed with me and is now trying to help you take away my family's business. Just like when we were teenagers—get off my balls, dude."

Our lawyer has had enough of our remarks and rises from the table. "Look, there are some strong emotions and past baggage between your two families. It happens often. Now, if you two gentlemen don't mind, I would like to get down to the reason why we're conducting this meeting today. Is that alright with you?"

"Let's get started then," I say, refusing to make eye contact with them.

Preston nods, aggressively clicking the blue pen in his hand.

"Wonderful." Tom sighs, then sits back down, visibly annoyed.

"Let's cut to the chase, shall we? Bradley Wines is a large part of this community, and to be honest, Jack is a flight risk," Steve says.

I tightly ball my fists in my lap, and I have to remind myself that this is a professional setting, and I am in the presence of my mother, so I need to reign in my boiling anger. "What the hell does that even mean?"

"You left for college to pursue your own dreams, which I commend you on, but to the rest of us in this community, wine is our life and our passion," Steve starts like he's preparing some groundbreaking speech. *Fucking joke.*

Preston adds his half-baked two cents before I have the chance to speak. "I have been running one of the largest wineries in the area. I have had my hands in every aspect of this industry and know what it takes to make it run efficiently and effectively.

I am involved in our community and currently sit on many local boards. I have what it takes to keep that business alive—not you."

I start clapping. "Wonderful job. I am proud of you. Do you know that?"

"Fuck you, Jack."

My mother stays quiet, and I'm not sure what she's thinking. I can't imagine this is easy for her. She's tired, worn out, and wants to retire early. Without my father, I know she doesn't have the energy or drive to devote to it. She's still severely grieving. I push my own grievances aside and rest my hand on her shoulder, sensing her sadness.

"Preston is also marrying Sophia Dennings, who has deep family ties in this community. They will provide security for the business and our local economy. Not to mention that she's also worked in this industry for years and has many connections with vendors," Steve adds like it's going to make a difference to me.

"I could give a flying fuck about any of that, Steve." My eyes narrow. "And how would you even know if I'm qualified for this or not? You have no idea how capable I am or how I've made a name for myself in Phoenix within the restaurant industry and hospitality."

"But not in Dupara, Jack, and right now, that's all that matters." Steve shifts in his seat and softens his beady eyes like he's trying to throw me a bone.

"Again, I don't give a fuck. It's no secret that I didn't always get along with my father, but I am still his son who shares his tenacity, fuck-you attitude, and the gift of being an absolute prick," I grit out before shooting them a condescending smile.

"Here's the thing, you have been away for nearly ten years. You have no idea how to run this business. Since we all have a vested stake in the success of Bradley Wines, I think it would be best if you let Preston and I take over," Steve states, pouring himself a glass of water from the large carafe in the middle of the table.

"I still can't believe you're doing this. You were Cliff's best friend." My mother's voice is shaky as she holds back tears. She takes a softer approach than I expected, but my dad's best friend or not, I've never been fond of Steve. He's always been a wormy guy who's too focused on money and never saw eye to eye with my dad's creative vision.

"Like I've told you before, it's not personal. It's just business—" Steve tries to defend himself, but the whole situation is still shady as fuck.

"Look, the reality is that we still own seventy percent of Bradley Wines, so despite your unneeded concerns, your opinion does not matter," I interject, leaning back in my chair and resting my elbow on the armrest. "We will continue to make decisions on behalf of *our* business."

Steve glances at his lawyer to his left, and then all three sets of eyes refocus on my mother and me. "That's one of the things we'd like to discuss with you today. Preston and I are offering you a buyout."

My mother's face turns white. "A buyout?"

Steve clasps his hands together in front of the table. "Yes, that is correct, Heidi. We have drawn up the paperwork for what we're willing to offer you."

I pull my chair closer to the table. My mind flooded with

everything that a buyout would mean. I get flashes of me as a kid. My dad chasing me through the vineyards. The first time I ever crushed the grapes with my bare feet— "Wait, what?" I blurt out, interrupting my thoughts.

Steve's lawyer opens a black leather folder and removes a folded white paper. He glances at Steve again before sliding it across the table. Tom reaches out first and opens it. Straight-faced, he gives it to me. I snatch it from his hands, then open it in front of my mother.

Anger slashes at my back when I see the shameful and downright disrespectful offer. I raise my chin and flare my nostrils. "What a joke."

"This can't be a legitimate offer," my mom adds.

The three of them stand to leave. "We are willing to negotiate. When you're ready, get in touch with my lawyer and we'll see what you've come up with."

My mother, Tom, and I stay seated, neither responding as they walk out the door.

Pursing my lips together, I shake my head. "I need some time to process this. Let's talk again next week."

My mom nods in agreement, and the three of us leave the room.

"I didn't know that Sophia was awful to Piper that day at the pool. I'm so sorry," my mother offers, stepping into the hallway.

"Don't worry about it, Mom. It's not your fault."

"I didn't even know she was coming. I hope Piper wasn't too upset by it."

I shove my hands into the pockets of my dress slacks, thinking about my feisty wife I have waiting for me back at our villa.

"Honestly, it's alright. She handled it."

Tom walks out shortly after us. "I say you both think about what they're proposing, but I've known you guys for long enough to know that you won't be taking his buyout offer."

My mother glances at me with a simple look, but there's much more behind it. She waits for me to speak first, and when I don't, she starts like we're picking up a conversation that's already begun. "Look, we've talked about this. If you truly have no interest in the winery and can't see a future here for yourself, then you must make that decision soon." Her voice strains with anguish. It would be devastating for her to give up that place. She loves it so much and barely knows a life without it.

"I don't know. I honestly don't know. Yes, I want to do this—but I'm conflicted still. The entire operation is a lot to take on."

"There are other options that we can flush out. Maybe neither of you run it and instead hire a chief executive officer to handle that side of things," Tom suggests.

"That was my father's role. He had his hands in everything."

My mother turns back to me. "Since he left us three months ago, you've had a lot of space and time to figure out what you want."

I pace back and forth in the hallway, which resembles more of a hospital than an attorney's office. "I'm moving here, aren't I? I'm leaving the life I built in Arizona, my friends, a marketing job I loved, and I've already purchased a home. I don't know how much more you want me to do?" I shout. "Fuck!" My frustrations are getting the best of me.

Her eyes grow red. "I only want you to be happy. That's all I have ever wanted. I know this wasn't your dream, but your dad and I always hoped you would see its beauty."

"I know that." I blow out a heavy breath, tired of this same conversation. "I'm sorry for getting upset. It's just a lot of pressure, especially when it feels like this entire town is rooting against me. The only people I have on my side are you, Gemma, our wonderful employees—and Piper."

When I hear myself say her name grouped with others who are a part of my life, I see how much she's becoming one too. But that makes this whole situation piss me off even more because Piper lives in Arizona, and now I have another reason to resent having to move away.

I storm out of the building, feeling like the world's weight on my shoulders. That meeting didn't go as I thought it would. Steve and Preston came to play ball. I may not be passionate about wine, but I am confident to a fault, and even though a part of me is still unsure, I need to succeed. And no better way to push me to do it than this.

Fuck them both.

Getting into my car, I white knuckle the steering wheel. Adrenaline is burning through my veins. I hate being put into the position of feeling controlled. My childhood felt restrained as my path was built for me before I could even speak. I fled this life, and I'm not afraid to admit it. Now, I feel controlled once again, not only by Steve and Preston but by this community.

I'm in a haze driving along the windy highway past the wineries and vineyards. The only thing I accomplished at the meeting was proving that I have a short fuse and am still stubborn.

As I approach the entrance to the villas, my heart escalates, knowing that Piper is there waiting for me. After my morning, she's the only thing I want to see right now. The past couple of nights of falling asleep with her snuggled up to me have been peaceful and yet so simple but intimate at the same time. It was a little awkward after what we did the other night, but I'm craving more, and I believe she is, too, especially after I woke up this morning with her tangled around me again.

Chapter Twenty-Three

Low, smoky gray clouds cover the sky, keeping out the sunlight for most of the day. I've never been a girl afraid of thunderstorms and even appreciate their chaos. I'm taking full advantage of this cozy day by curling up in bed with my Kindle. I've only moved to take a quick shower, then came to lay under the thick comforter. Every few minutes, flashes of lightning light up the dark bedroom.

Jack barges in through the front door just as a loud crashing sound and vibration from the storm rattle the shutters. Startled, I yelp and inadvertently throw my Kindle across the room. Jack is standing in the door frame to the bedroom.

"Shit. You've got to stop scaring me like that."

I laugh, but his demeanor is off. When he left, he said not to expect him until later in the afternoon, and from the way he stalked toward me with a straight face, I could tell the meeting did not go as planned.

"Take off your clothes," he commands, loosening the tie around his neck. His shoulders are square, and his eyes blaze as they pin me from across the room. He stands hidden beneath the shadows in the doorway.

"Excuse me?" My eyes widen. I stare at his silhouette, slowly moving toward me and out of the blanket of the obscure darkness. *What the hell did he just say?*

"Take off your clothes, Piper," he repeats. A gentle, demanding tone in his voice makes the hairs stand up on the back of my neck, and my legs quiver with curiosity.

"Are you seriously telling me to remove my clothing?"

A look of frustration sweeps across his face, and I can tell he needs something else at the moment, and it doesn't have anything to do with our blossoming friendship.

"Yes, now take them off yourself, or I will help you take them off."

I spring out of bed and open my mouth to protest once again, but Jack steps into me, pressing a finger over my lips, halting my words and thoughts. The heat from his body pours over me like warm honey and causes my eyes to fall closed, descending into a moment of pure sensation. "I don't need you to be my *fake* girlfriend. I need you to be my *real* wife."

My lungs constrict, and I can barely suck in air. Not knowing how to respond, I'm in shock but overcome with excitement at the same time. "If that's what you want," I give in with a whisper.

I'm sensing a different Jack Bradley than the one I've been fake dating for the past few weeks. And I think I like it. Surprisingly calm, I do as I'm told and bend at my waist, reach down to pinch the hem of my T-shirt dress, and then lift it over my head.

Jack's electric blue eyes flare, turning a shade like the open ocean. He steps back and pauses, presumably waiting for me to finish undressing. Without a word, I continue to comply by unhooking my pink satin bra, then sliding the matching white and pink satin panties down my legs and off of my bare feet.

"Your favorite color is pink, isn't it?" he comments, dragging his eyes over every inch of my body. A chill breaks out behind their powerful path.

"Maybe. Why do you ask?" Uncontrolled power is coursing through my veins, standing in front of Jack, naked and completely exposed.

"Because you own so much pink. Your panties, bras, workout clothes, and even your toes,"—he shifts into me—"all pink." The roughness of his black suit rubs against my skin. "I told you I'd figure out your favorite color eventually."

"You noticed all of those things?" I ask, flinching as the heavy rain bellows at the window.

"I notice everything about you."

I inhale a sharp breath, not expecting that admission to come out of his mouth. "Jack?"

"Yes?" A lightning flash reflects across his face.

"Why are you still clothed?"

He smiles. "Do you want me to take them off?"

"Yes," I say, rising on my tippy toes. Leaning into him, I run my tongue along his bottom lip. We haven't kissed again since that night on the balcony at Bradley Wines, and it feels like I've been anxiously counting down the seconds until I'd get to touch his soft lips again. I breathe out, and he sucks in at that same time.

"I've wanted to have you ever since I ran into you at that fucking airport." He captures my tongue between his lips, sucking it into his mouth until we're fully connected. A quiet moan escapes from my mouth and into his.

Fuck, I could die now.

"Have you? And this is the first time you're doing anything about it," I say between his rough kisses.

"I won't be making that mistake again." He draws back. His smile is broad and mischievous. From the side, I see him bring both arms behind me, and then a light sting laces from the base of my scalp as Jack grips my ponytail, pulling my hair back. The sensation tingles down the back of my neck, onto my shoulders, and down to my clit, creating a throbbing need for him to do it again. A quick gasp ends with a groan filled with delight.

"I knew you'd like that," Jack whispers into the sensitive skin of my neck. My legs almost give out.

"I do," I reply with his hand still gripping my hair, my eyes facing the wooden beams of the ceiling above me. I feel helpless, and it's invigorating.

"I remember the last time you said *I do.* You think I don't remember much from the night, but I remember much more than you realize." Jack's soft lips trace my neck, along my jaw, and to the corner of my mouth, eliciting a frantic response from my nerve endings.

My brain is lost in a lust-filled fog to register what he's saying. I know I'm hearing the words, but right now, all I can think of is getting that goddamned suit and tie off him. As if anticipating my next move, Jack releases my hair, creates only an inch of space between us, and clutches his tie.

I clasp my hands over his. "I'm going to do it," I tell him, beginning to loosen the slick material. I will be the one taking his clothes off. He may think he's in control, but I will always say when—and how.

Jack lets his arms hang at his sides while I slide off his tie before moving my fingers to the buttons on his shirt. I start at the top, working my way down, until his collared shirt hangs open, giving me a full view of his six-pack. I almost cry out in desperation at the perfection of his body. I have been watching him walk around for weeks, taunting me with it as he acts like there's not this palpable surge pulsing between us.

I slide my fingers over his chest and broad shoulders, pushing off the unbuttoned shirt. Once it falls to the floor, I circle him, letting my eyes roam wherever they want. As I move onto his back, I lean in, bringing my lips to his warm skin. My fingertips follow in the line of my mouth, gliding my tongue across his body, tasting small amounts until I'm facing his front once again.

"Get on the bed," he commands as another rumble of thunder shakes the shutters.

I crawl on top of the bed. Positioning myself at the head, I lay on my back with my eyes fixed on Jack, who is still clothed from the waist down. Once I'm flat, he bends to the floor, retrieving his tie, then slides off his belt in one fluid motion.

"I have to do this. Do you trust me?" he asks. It takes a moment for me to register what he's asking, and when I do, I'm confused but also at ease. "I'm going to blindfold and bind your wrists. If it gets too much, tell me."

This is new for me. I'm a little apprehensive, but I do as he says. "Okay."

"Do you trust me?"

Biting my bottom lip, I nod. "Yes."

"Now, put your hands above your head." His voice is deep and without inflection which tells me he's confident in what he's doing.

Obeying his direction, I raise my arms above my head, linking my wrists together. Jack kneels on the bed, bends over me, and clasps my hands in one of his palms. I tilt my head up, watching his every move. Jack loops his belt around my wrists twice, then threads it through the iron bars of the bed frame before tying it and buckling the loose end.

I suck a breath of air and, by reflex, yank on the leather bounding around my wrists. They don't move. Panic creeps up my spine, but wetness pools between my legs. There is a contrast in both feeling and sensation that leaves me in utter shock.

"I knew you'd be a good girl," he praises. I bite my tongue and remain quiet, watching Jack as he towers over me. "I'm going to blindfold you now," he tells me. Again, I remain silent, entranced by his movements.

He places his black tie over my eyes, the smooth silk gliding across my skin. His two hands gently slip under my head to secure it in place. The world around me is dark. My pulse quickens, and my body involuntarily starts to tremble. Jack has taken away two of my senses, enhancing the remaining three. I hear the rustling of his pants as he lowers them to the floor.

"Jack?" I call him, my voice cracking.

"I'm right here, my love," he reassures me, possibly sensing the panic in my voice. The warm sensation from his body climbing on top of me feels like a blanket of comfort. As my sense of smell enhances, I arch my back, needing to bathe in his scent.

The mattress dips slightly on either side of my shoulders, and then I feel his breath float over my mouth. My pussy starts throbbing before he even touches my lips. Craving him, I angle my head back, and even without sight, I easily find his inviting mouth. I push my lips into him, trying to get closer, but unable to lift any farther. Jack tastes my tongue for a few moments, then sucks on my bottom lip before pulling away.

I'm out of breath, desperate for him to come back. He trails down my neck onto my chest, nibbles each breast, and they harden under his wet kisses. Then, he circles my belly button, moving on to one of the thighbrows, then switching to the other. My legs shake more aggressively the closer he gets to my core.

"Oh god," I moan in anticipation. Not based on what he's doing but where he's going.

"Every time you bent down in front of me with those little pajama shorts or that fucking bathing suit, I desperate to have you," he mutters, grazing across my slit.

"I ached to have you down there just as bad."

"Good." Jack slips his tongue in, making me melt from the waist down. The pounding rain outside has now become a faint dripping like a leaky faucet as I drift into myself. Slow and deep, he buries his lips between my legs, nibbling and kissing my most sensitive area. I feel Jack tilt his head to get a better angle like he needs more. My eyes roll back of my head, hidden behind his tie and my legs start to shake when he quickly pulls away.

"Are you ready for me?" he asks into the crease of my skin.

"Yes," I cry out, begging to feel any part of him.

Jack grips my hips and pulls them into the air. He positions himself between my widespread legs. "I'm sorry I couldn't do that longer, but I need to fuck you right now. But don't worry, I'll be coming back for more."

I moan once again, growing impatient. Without pause, he slides into me, filling me instantly. The sensation shoots from my clit, all the way up my spine, and settles with a tingling on the back of my neck.

My world is black.

I can't see.

I can't think.

I can only feel.

"Fuck." His voice is low and hoarse, an addicting tone I've never heard come from him.

I'm completely helpless, forcing me to submit to the rhythm of his thrusts. I buck back, rolling my hips up, needing to get deeper. I imagine what he looks like on top of me, his chest bare, dripping with sweat as my legs drip with juices. His muscles flex as he stiffens, and his fingers grip deeply into my hips.

I sense him bend down and cage me in. I lower my back to rest on the bed, feeling the weight of his body on top of mine. I pull on my arms that are trapped in the belt above my head, frustrated that I can't pull him close, that I can't run my fingers along his body.

"Not yet," he corrects in a low voice, thrusting harder. My ear tingles from his words. As if conducting a symphony made up of every part of my body, Jack directs me where to go while we move in sequence with one another.

As soon as I feel my body start to chase an impending orgasm, I clench my muscles, enjoying the way Jack slips in and out of me. "Jack, I'm about to come," I squeak.

He doesn't answer but picks up his pace. With every roll of his hips, my pussy vibrates harder, getting closer to my peak. My insides hum until I'm covered with a heat that consumes every inch of me.

"Oh god, Jack!" I yell, jerking my arms above my head, but they don't move. My skin stings where the leather has been rubbing against it, which I'm sure is irritated and raw by now. Riding the aftershocks with me, Jack maintains his speed and rhythm.

But suddenly, his body stiffens on top of me, and he lets out a rough groan, slamming into the sensitive bud between my legs. Air is forced from the back of my throat, making me cough. Jack's body is still twitching when he aggressively tears his tie from over my eyes and snatches the belt from around my wrists before throwing them both across the room.

My arms are sore from being held above my head for so long. Jack's flared eyes meet mine, and their energy is so overwhelming that it breaks me down.

"How do you feel?" He scoops me up and brings me into his lap.

I automatically curl into a fetal position in his arms. Blindsided by the intense emotions that hit me, my eyes swell, having never experienced that type of release. "I feel weak but euphoric."

"So do I." Jack nuzzles his nose into my hair like he always does when we fall asleep in each other's arms.

Jack and I stay in this position long enough for me to attempt to gather myself. He gazes down at me, taking two fingers to pinch my chin, raising my head to his. Then, he lowers his lips to mine, giving me a deeply intimate and overpowering kiss.

"I'm going to start a bath for you. Then, I'll go pick up something for us to eat."

I smile at him, still somewhat dizzy from overexertion. "That sounds perfect."

Jack gently lays me back down and gets off the bed.

A second later, I hear the sound of running bath water. My thoughts with excitement, apprehension, and electricity. I have given myself to Jack without understanding what we are or what we're doing. The other night, when we both watched each other get off, he said he was doing it all for me after I begged him to do it. I succumbed to the temptation of having Jack, only for him to reiterate the complications, stating that it couldn't happen again. And yes, I agreed with him—I truly did, but it's impossible to deny our connection.

Now, what happened today? I would have put up more of a fight when he came home demanding that I give myself to him, but I didn't want to. I wanted him. I wanted to have all of him, and even though my first instinct is to regret what we did with each other, I don't.

I wrap a bedsheet around myself as Jack walks out with a white towel around his waist. When our eyes meet, we stand silently in front of each other, both of us hiding our bodies when there is no need to anymore. I take in a heavy inhale before blurting out the first thing on my mind. "I don't regret it."

Jack straightens his stance. "I don't either."

I'm glad he doesn't because if he did, that would wipe out every positive emotion still buzzing within me.

Later on that evening, Jack and I are lying in bed watching a movie together. We've both been relatively quiet since he returned with takeout earlier. I wanted to ask him about his meeting while we ate, but this is a better time. He's calm and more likely to share with me what caused him to get upset.

I sit up, resting my back against two stacked pillows. Jack's arm falls from where it was around my shoulder.

He glances down at me tucked into his side. "Is something the matter?"

"What happened at the meeting?"

Jack brings his hands together in front of his face. A brief moment passes before he begins to speak. "My dad's best friend Steve and his son Preston basically told me that I didn't deserve the winery and that they would be more successful with it."

"Oh shit, I'd be pissed too. What assholes they are." No wonder Jack was so upset. What a messed up situation he's in. No wonder he convinced himself that he needed my help. Who's on his side?

"Yeah. They also explained that the winegrowers association and the community would be more comfortable with keeping it as a family-run business—and since Preston and Sophia are getting married and will most likely have kids, it's better for optics."

I tuck my legs to my chest. "That's such bullshit."

Jack's mouth is set in a hard line as he nods, sharing my frustration. "I know. It's fucked up that we live in an age where having a family shouldn't matter in an overall sense, but it does. Especially in this small community."

"This isn't fair."

"I know. I told you all this before. That's why you're here, to make me look more wholesome," he says.

"Yeah, you did, but I guess I didn't fully understand in the beginning, and now that I'm living in it with you, I realize how stressful it really is." I rest my chin on my knees.

"They offered to buy us out. And honestly, for a split second, I considered it. But then I saw the look on my mom's face. She turned white as a ghost. She misses my dad so much, and the winery is all she has left of him."

"She has you. And from what you've told me, there was nothing more your parents wanted in the world than for it to be yours." I refute his assumption.

Jack frowns. "I want that, too, and even though I'm grateful to have had these years to experience a life on my own, I wonder if it was all worth it."

I can't imagine the weight and pressure that Jack is under, and the more I chip away at that hard exterior that he's built around himself, the more I want to be the one with him when it's gone.

I cup the side of his face. He leans into it. "Don't regret anything. You made the best decision with the knowledge you had at the time. If anything, I feel like it was self-preservation. If you never would have broken free, you wouldn't have become the person you are today."

Jack gently reaches for my arm and slowly guides my hand to his lips, leaving a tender kiss on the hollow of my wrist. It's one of the most intimate gestures someone has ever given me. My eyes stay trapped in the softness of his expression even after he pulls his lips away. I wiggle myself into the safety under his arm, and he tightens around me.

"You're right. Thanks," he says in a low voice.

Chapter Twenty-Four

J ack and I have spent the last three days holed up in our villa, exploring each other's bodies and watching movies, only leaving to run out and grab takeout. When we're not chasing our orgasms, we laugh and talk about the most random things. I'm still uncertain how to ask him about the blindfold and handcuffs, but oddly, I've come to enjoy them. My stomach flips whenever I see him remove them from the bottom drawer.

Jack and I have quickly become something exciting and hard to explain. We've spent every waking hour with each other, forcing us to get to know one another on a deeper level. If we didn't have to attend the Harvest Dinner tonight, we'd continue to exist only in the confines of the six-foot-long king-size bed, living in our self-made bubble.

Standing in front of the full-length mirror in the bedroom, I'm preparing for the evening ahead. I run my palms along my hips, feeling how this dress hugs my curves. My body tingles from how Jack has awakened my senses. The world is brighter, newer, and more alive. I chose a deep blue off-the-shoulder dress that landed right above my ankles.

When I saw it for the first time, I knew it was the right

one for tonight. The color reminds me of the vibrant shade of bottomless blue Jack's eyes turn when his body pains for mine. I can tell when he's full of desire based on how his eyes flare like they're strong enough to hit the bottom of my soul.

I flip my long hair behind my back to add the last finishing touches to my makeup. My heart skips a beat when I think about the new direction that our relationship has taken. I can't tell what to make of it—instead, I've decided to live in the present.

I glance back at myself in the mirror and immediately notice my cheeks redden with the flashbacks of the past week. My legs shake slightly, remembering waking up with him between them last night.

Already pantyless, Jack had an easy time slipping under the covers. By the time I woke up, my orgasm was already breaching. With every slow lick, a bolt of electricity hit my back while warmth settled into my core. When my body started to tremble, he held me still, kept his mouth locked in place, and sucked every bit of my arousal. By the time he resurfaced with a mischievous smile on his face, I was feral and begging for his cock. After he came—and then I did for a second time, I fell back asleep on top of him. It's been animal-like and sexy as fuck.

I woke up this morning with fresh coffee on my nightstand. I smiled at Jack's thoughtfulness, but the ache in my stomach was already craving relief from the only person I knew could provide it. So, we fucked again.

I nibble on my bottom lip, suck in a heavy breath, and reach down to retrieve my heels from the floor. My fingers hook around the straps while I reach for the doorknob with my other hand, but I pause before opening it.

With purpose, I walk back over to the top dresser drawer and take out a white lacy lingerie set. The top is a strapless bra, and the bottom is a silk and lace thong. I swallow hard, knowing exactly what I'm doing, submitting to my need for him. Lifting my dress, I slide the cotton thong off my feet one at a time and replace it with want and desire. Then, I unhook my light pink bra and throw it back into the drawer, replacing it with the white one.

I'm his now.

Taking one last quick look at myself, I retrieve my shoes and leave the bedroom. Turning the corner down the hallway, I'm met with Jack's back as he faces the open doors to our private backyard and pool.

I'm overcome at the sight of his broad shoulders, dark blue collared shirt, and dress pants that hug every inch of his perfect ass. Then, my eyes fall to his brown belt, wondering how quickly I can rip that off him.

"Hi," I say, holding myself up on the counter, slipping my heel on with the other hand.

Jack slowly turns around with a smirk on his face. "My wife."

A smile pulls at the corners of my mouth. He takes a few steps toward me, closing the distance between us. With each step, my breath becomes more difficult until our bodies flush, shutting off my oxygen completely. The intensity of his stare reminds me of the first time I met him at the airport.

Still struggling with the straps on my shoes with one hand, I bend to get a better grip.

"Let me help you with that." Jack bends to his knee. I feel his warm palm gliding down my calf and across the bottom of my foot.

"Thank you." Goosebumps break out along the length of my leg. I rub my lips together, dragging my eyes around the room, searching for an escape because I already know where this is headed.

But there isn't one.

There is no more escaping him.

Jack fastens the buckle on one foot, then moves to the other side, sliding his hands along my legs, heightening my nerves before cupping my heels back. He reaches for the other shoe on the floor next to us and slips it onto my foot.

My arms bend behind me with my palms molded into the granite countertop, supporting my entire weight as gravity fights with my existence. I battle against falling to the ground and floating up into space because, at this moment, I don't know whether I want to succumb to his touch or drift away. We can't go even a few hours without fucking each other. At this rate, we'll never be able to leave.

"You look beautiful," Jack's voice is smooth. His hands run up my sides and over my curves as he raises to a standing position. "Mrs. Bradley."

I bathe in his words. My self-pride falls victim to them as it crumbles at his feet. I part my lips to speak. "I want—"

I want to taste him finally, and I can't wait any longer.

"What do you want?"

"I want to taste you," I say, facing away.

Silence.

"Yeah? Get on your knees."

Eagerly, I twist and kneel in front of him. Glancing through my eyelashes, I ask him again, "Can I taste you?"

His eyes flare. "If that's what you want."

I watch as he unbuckles his belt, slides his zipper down, and removes his pants. Every time Jack and I have had sex, I have the blindfold on, and even though I've seen his impressive length when we were lying naked in bed together, there's something about seeing his hard cock from this angle that makes me needy and desperate.

"Open for me and stick your tongue out," he instructs.

I comply, opening up for him and keeping my eyes locked on his, Jack slides himself along my warm tongue. Wetness coats my panties as I let him go deeper. Thrusting a few times, he lets out a groan. I fist the base of his cock, giving it a squeeze. He tastes so good. I let my tongue glide along him, cloaking him with saliva.

"That's so good," he grunts, gripping my hair. He guides my mouth back and forth. Hearing him call out my name in such raw pleasure urges me to suck harder, taking more of him. A desperate hunger within me needs to have all of him. It feels so real, so natural, to make his insides a part of mine.

"Mmm," I moan, enjoying his hands that are threaded tightly on the back of my head while his body curls around me. I continue sucking, lapping up the small beads of precome that drip from him.

"You're so needy," he grits out. "I love it."

I continue to pump his base with one hand while the other finds the softness of his balls. Massaging them, I coax his orgasm out. When his legs stiffen, I know he's at his peak. He's expecting me to let go so we can have sex, but this isn't about us—this is about him. I suck harder on the head, then slide down one more time before salty warm squirts hit the back of my throat. He cries out as his legs shudder. I swallow him down, sucking harder and craving for more.

I finally release, tipping back on my feet.

Panting, Jack looks down at me. His jaw clenches, and his chest heaves, chasing a full breath. "You didn't have to do that."

"I wanted to."

"You didn't have to swallow either." He bends to kiss my forehead lightly. A kiss of approval that I'd die to feel again. "I mean, it was fucking amazing, but that's not my expectation."

I start rising to my feet, taking care not to wrinkle my dress even more than it already is. "I wanted to do that too."

"Wait. Let me help you," he says while buttoning his dress pants.

"Thank you."

A smirk suddenly appears on his face. "We should probably brush your teeth before you have to be my arm candy for the night."

I giggle. "But do I have to? It would be a fun little joke knowing I'm smiling with a mouth full of your come."

"As much as I know you're not serious, that would still be fucking hot."

"Or am I?"

"Now you're messing with me."

I arch an eyebrow. "Maybe."

"Piper," he growls like a warning. "In the bathroom."

"Fine," I say, shuffling my feet with Jack on my heels.

I grab my bubblegum pink toothbrush from the holder and squeeze a dash of minty fresh toothpaste on it, but right before it hits my mouth, I see Jack's arm come around from the back. His tall frame towers over me in our reflection in the mirror. A couple of loose strands of blond hair hang over the scar above his right eye.

"Let me do it," he says, gently taking the toothbrush from my hand.

I nod, slowly opening my mouth for him again, but for a different reason this time.

Jack slips the toothbrush in, sweeping softly back and forth on the bottom back teeth before flipping to the top. I never imagined someone brushing my teeth could be such an intimate experience. But I think that's because I've never had Jack do it.

Jack and I exchange intense looks in the mirror, weakening my knees. He removes the brush from my mouth when it fills with white bubbles. "Spit."

I cup both hands around my mouth before spitting into the sink. Then, he runs the toothbrush under the water. He's still flush with my back, and even when I bend, he does the same, moving with me.

When I straighten, my eyes bounce over to the scar above his eyebrow. "Tell me the story about how you got that scar."

Looking at me through the mirror, he brings the toothbrush up one more time. Because I now respond to his every move, I open for him again.

Jack clears his throat. "I think I was about seven years old when it happened." He softly brushes in a circular motion while I stand almost limp, letting him take care of me. "I played outside all day, but it was time for dinner. I remember my mom calling me in, and as a typical kid, I wasn't ready to come yet, so I took off into the vineyards." Jack rinses the brush and hands me a cup to rinse. "I thought it was funny until I heard the inflection in her voice change, and it seemed like she was getting worried. I turned around too quickly, slipped on some rocks and dirt, and fell forward into the wires and vines. I was so hysterical that I think every staff member on the entire property came running."

I turn to face him. He runs his hands through my hair and leans down to kiss the tip of my nose. I clutch the lapels of his collared shirt. "I bet your mom was upset."

"She was." Jack glances at himself in the mirror. "We should get going."

"Okay," I reply, flattening the subtle wrinkles in the fabric of my dress.

Jack gives me another once over. "I don't know how I'll keep my hands off you tonight."

I fluff my hair a few times while he heads into the living room. "You're going to have to try. We have a show to put on."

"We do."

I walk out of the bedroom to see him leaning against the corner of the wall with that same look on his face from earlier.

"Oh no, not again!" I laugh.

He pushes himself off and stalks toward me. "It's tempting," he whispers, swiping his wallet and keys from the counter behind me.

"Yes, I know, but we have somewhere to be!"

He chuckles without a response, then intertwines his fingers through mine, like it has become so natural, and then ushers me out of the door.

The short car ride to the winery hosting the event this year is not made in silence like so many other car rides before. Jack talks to me about his family's annual crush event. He explains that in Dupara, the harvest season events are as big for the winery owners and the community as they are for the tourists that flock here each year.

"People who aren't in this community don't understand how close and loyal they are to the authenticity of winemaking and its lifestyle. Most of the families have been here for generations, some settling in Wine Country as early as the late 1800s," Jack tells me.

While he explains the brief history of this region, I study the features of his face, taking in his sharp jawline and lips—the ones that have now touched every inch of my body.

"That's interesting. No wonder they're wary of outsiders. They take so much pride in being involved in all aspects of their community," I say.

"But to a fault sometimes," he responds while parking the car in front of what appears to be a gothic Victorian-style manor.

Peering out the window and through the ominous blanket of night, the overpowering building and endless rows of cars suddenly awaken my nerves.

I feel Jack's eyes on me before I hear him speak. "You okay?"

I pull my bottom lip between my teeth. "Yes. A little nervous, that's all."

"You look beautiful, and remember, you're not the one being judged here. I am. You're only here to make me look good, and I know without a doubt that you'll be successful at it." Jack palms my cheek with one hand, then runs his fingers through my freshly blown hair. "Your job is to show up, drink wine, and be pretty."

I smile up at him, leaning into his satisfying comfort. "That sounds like the perfect job for me. I will be the best fake girlfriend you've ever had."

His expression briefly falls, then his eyes lower before darting back up to mine. "I don't doubt that."

Once Jack drops his hand from my face and opens the door to exit the car, I am empty and alone. It's not until he's on the other side, opening my door, and extending his arm for me to take—that I feel whole again. It's an unnerving feeling, and this conflicting emotion is unfamiliar to me. Forced to grow up too soon by being the unexpected caregiver of my mother's emotional well-being, I've grown accustomed to only having myself to rely on to meet my own basic needs. Has my guard dropped already?

We link arms as he guides us to the dark wood double doors with the intricately designed brass doorknobs. I suck in one more breath of precious air to calm my nerves right as the heavy doors swing open. With my hand firmly placed in Jack's, he leads me through a small crowd, waiting at a small bar area to my left. I glance to the right to see another group waiting to take tastings directly from an oak barrel.

"It's absolutely magical in here," I say, my heels clicking on the floor as I follow behind him.

Jack takes us down the stairs and through the propped open iron gates, leading us into a dimly lit space where thousands of candles are lit, welcoming guests into what seems to be a step back in time two centuries. It's romantic and almost dreamlike.

"Glad you like it. Should we find our seats or sample some wine first?"

"Sample the wine first!"

He laughs, shifting us toward the barrel room. "I knew you'd say that."

"Jack!" a female voice from behind us calls out.

We both turn around to find Sophia, Jack's ex-girlfriend, standing only a few feet away. Her long brown hair is pulled into a tight bun, making her oversized dark eyes look like they're bulging out of her head. *Okay, that was mean*—but she's a bitch.

Standing to her side is a man that I assume is her fiancé. He's wider than Jack, with fiery red hair, a goatee, and extremely good-looking. Although Jack could not be more opposite, it's hard not to appreciate Sophia's impeccable taste in men. My nose arches on one side the moment those beady eyes land on Jack.

Mine.

"Sophia," he snarls, squeezing my hand.

She smiles, flashing awkwardly straight teeth. I hold in bubbling laughter when I see a faint spot of red lipstick on her front tooth. *Could this have gone any better for me at the moment?*

"Long time no see, Jack Bradley," her voice creaks.

When his name leaves her lips, the hairs on my neck stand

up—and not in a good way, like when Jack's hitting all the right spots while railing me. It's a gross, uncomfortable, and territorial reaction.

"Yes," he says. Then, I feel the warmth of his palm on my lower back. "You remember my girlfriend, Piper?"

Sophia gives me another smile, this time looking more fake than the last. "Yes, we met a few weeks ago."

"We did. It was a pleasant encounter, wasn't it? What was it that we talked about?" I bring a finger into the air. "Oh yes, you talked about Jack the whole time that I actually questioned whether you had a financé or not," I spat, turning to the man to her left. "Nice to see that you are, in fact, *real*."

Jack tilts his head with a smug look on his face. "She's a spitfire, isn't she?" he comments to them but keeps his adoring look on me. His gaze tells me that he wants to rip this dress off me or burst into laughter. Either way, I revel in how we've learned to communicate with simple facial expressions.

"You are a sassy one, aren't you?" Preston insults.

"Don't patronize me." I sneer. From the corner of my eye, Sophia and Preston exchange glances before Jack takes his focus away from me and turns to Preston.

"Preston," Jack says, extending his arm to shake his hand in a polite gesture, but I can tell by the way Jack's shoulders are tense that he's struggling to be cordial around this man after their last interaction. Based on what Jack has told me, his hatred toward Preston goes deeper than their previous meeting.

"Hi, sorry our last meeting ended the way it did. I'm sure you know that I'd be a better fit. It's not personal," he says with a condescending tone.

I don't like him already.

"It's my family's winery, so that does make it personal," Jack quips, roughly patting Preston on the shoulder.

He jerks his shoulder away. "It's business, my friend."

"We're not friends."

I lean into Jack, sensing the exchange between them is headed into hostile territory. Flashing Sophia a side-eye, I rise to my tip toes to whisper in his ear, letting my lips linger on his earlobe, "Let's grab a drink."

Jack glances down at me. "Wonderful."

My focus stays on Jack, but I feel the heat from Sophia's stare bore into my shoulder blades, almost like a personal branding for her future sabotage.

Chapter Twenty-Five

My chest is full of pride and satisfaction with how my wife handled the interaction with Preston and Sophia. Her sassy little comment made my dick jump. God, I can't enough of that fire in her.

Over the next hour, we tried multiple samples of wine and toured the property, where we ended up in the garden. String lights cross from each end of the tree-lined walkway. Hand in hand, we stroll down one of the secluded paths with a clear night sky hovering above us.

"This garden is beautiful. I'm surprised we're the only people out here." Piper swings my arm in hers as we walk.

"I don't mind it."

"Of course you don't. You're introverted and rather be left alone." She playfully twists on one foot.

"There's nothing wrong with wanting my own space."

She squints her eyes. "You must love having me around twenty-four-seven then."

I hear Piper's words hit the air, but a different thought occupies my mind. I slowly stop and turn to face her. The moonlight shines between us, adding shadows and definition to the landscape of her face.

She's breathtaking.

My eyes roll over her petite nose, large hazel-green eyes, and naturally puckered lips. Taking one hand, I caress her cheek with the back of my knuckles. "I don't think I formally thanked you for doing this for me."

"Of course. But you are paying me to be here."

"Oh yes, the money." I rub my lips together. "That's true."

"And the divorce free and clear," she adds.

I nod, frowning. "Yes, that too."

With a gentle grab of my shoulders, she pulls me in. "I'm kidding!"

I need her to understand how much I appreciate that she's taking time out of her own life to be with me—and as she so eloquently reminded me, I am paying her. But the more I get to know Piper on the inside, her character and her heart, I believe she would've helped me anyway—with or without payment. Because that's who she is.

"I know." I laugh, looping an arm around her waist and tugging her into me.

"Besides, I have nothing else going on in my life right now." She shrugs.

Taking my free arm, I lightly grip her chin between my thumb and index finger, tilting her face up. "*You're* not looking forward to getting your own time and space back?"

"Isolation is overrated."

Crickets in the night and the faint sound of dinner guests from the event behind us are the only things I hear outside her short breaths. The hunger to taste her on my lips again pangs my insides. I dip my head, bringing my mouth to hers, but only stopping to suck in her tiny breaths like it's the only thing giving me life.

"Thank you," I whisper, then kiss her deeply. A tingling sensation slowly runs up my spine while I feel Piper shiver at the same time. I dive into her mouth, begging for more. The intimacy passing between us could light up this night sky.

Piper's nails digging into my back tell me we both need more, but not here. I reluctantly peel my lips from hers.

She slowly opens her eyelids like they have weights attached to them. "You're welcome."

"We should head back in. They'll be starting dinner and acknowledgments soon." I release my arm around her neck to slip it back into her hand.

"I'm already getting hungry," she says, intertwining her fingers in mine.

"You're always hungry." I shift on my feet and head back toward the cask room with Piper attached to my side. Her hands are safely tucked into mine while the other clutches my wrist above our embrace.

Everyone had already taken their seats by the time we got back into the event space. It looks like the President of the Wine Growers Society, also the master of ceremonies for the evening, has begun addressing the room. I peer down the long table briefly before landing on two empty chairs next to each other, presumably ours. With Piper's hand in mine, I lead her toward our place, which happens to be in the middle of the table.

Without causing a disruption, we quickly move to our seats. I quietly slide out Piper's chair.

"Jack Bradley from Bradley Wines is here with us tonight." Bending to take my place next to Piper, I hear those words blast through my ears like a megaphone.

Fuck.

Stopping mid-movement, I raise my head to give everyone a friendly wave, glancing up and down both sides of the table. Members and business owners in the community dressed in more formal wear clap as I give them a quick, polite wave of my hand.

"Why don't you come up here and say something? I'm sure everyone is eager to hear some of your thoughts and plans with Bradley Wines." The clapping gets louder, and my ears start to ring. I have nothing prepared. *What am I going to say?* Looks like I'm going to have to wing it.

Fuck.

Piper's eyes stared up at me with confusion but also empathy. Seeing the uncertainty on my face, she quickly squeezes my hand and mouths the words, "You can do this."

I reluctantly release her hand. Feeling the immense pressure from the entire room, the barrels stacked on either side of the wall close in on me. On my way to the front, I let my fingers feather Piper's hair. She gives me a comforting smile. Nerves inch up my back as I walk by the smiling faces of our community members.

"Didn't mean to put you on the spot, my friend. I thought this would be a good opportunity to get in front of the wine grower members," the president apologizes.

I extend my hand to shake his. "No worries, Tim. Next time, give me a heads-up.

He chuckles, then hands me the microphone. "For sure, Jack. Thanks for being flexible."

Sweat mists the hairline on my forehead even though there's a chill here. If I had to guess, the temperature is probably in the low sixties. I stand at the head of the long banquet-style table with close to eighty of Dupara's winery and vineyard owners, as well as influential members of the community. Ones with pride, whose families can be traced back three to four generations, all involved in the wine industry in one way or another.

But more importantly, Piper.

Her strawberry blonde hair is pulled to the side. With her hand resting on her chin, those beautiful eyes stay on me.

Rubbing my lips together, I prepare to address a room full of people who understand me only as Bradley Wines' heir and someone who abandoned his family business and the people whom he grew up with. But now they're the ones I need the most support from if I'd like to keep the winery as successful as it has been. My brain spins with anxiety and self-doubt as I scramble to prepare the appropriate words at the last minute.

"Good evening," I begin, feeling the weight lay heavy on my chest. Then, my eyes find Piper's and beyond the orange glow of the dimly lit room, I can see the encouraging smile on her face. With a quick nod of her head, I know that it's only her and I in this room.

I block out everyone else before clearing my throat to begin again. "We'd like to continue this wonderful evening filled with good food and even better wine, so I'll keep this short and sweet. I'm so grateful to be back in Dupara with all of you. During the time I've spent in Arizona, I've obtained a degree in business and marketing, which allowed me to work for one of the most successful hospitality marketing firms in Phoenix, preparing me for this exact moment. I look forward to taking over Bradley Wines and continuing my father's legacy while incorporating innovative marketing trends to enhance the business and the community. I plan to continue the local initiatives created and run with the support of Bradley Wines. I see my family's winery being directly involved in fostering and cultivating the growth of smaller businesses—"

I'm interrupted by the steady buzz of clapping throughout the room. It dawns on me that these members want to be assured that there won't be a shake-up in their small community and that things will continue to be as normal as expected. The realization washes over me, bringing a sense of peace with it. They're not looking for perfection or glaring at me through eyes of judgment. They're looking for stability.

"Thank you," I say, humbled by the surrealness of this moment. This is what Preston and Steve crave. They want to inherit the adoration and respect that my father worked so hard to maintain from his fellow business owners—whom he often referred to as his wine family. An accomplishment of his that I've always taken for granted.

In my eyes, this world has always been a burden to bear, holding me back from being myself and the ability to chase my dreams. When in reality, they could've been the anchor and support system the entire time.

"Also, I hope to support our community the best way I know how. I promise to give you all my best, coupled with the unwavering backing from the incredible staff at Bradley

Wines, some I've known since I was a child. We will continue to build and maintain the relationships needed for stable, organic growth. I look forward to immersing myself back into the people of this town, and I can't wait to get started. I don't want to take up too much of your time during this event. Again, thank you all. Cheers!"

With a round of applause and an unexpected standing ovation, I hand the microphone back to the president and stroll past the rows of chairs filled with members whose eyes follow me as I move. I stop to shake hands with almost every person I pass, and if not a handshake, I'm greeted with a smile of encouragement or nod in approval.

It feels good, and I know my dad would have been proud.

I'm halfway down the long table when I reach Piper. She starts to lift from her chair with open arms, but I don't go in for the friendly hug she's anticipating. Instead, I bring my palms to both cheeks and crash my lips into hers. A kiss not for show and not for the little thing that's been going on between us. It's a kiss for me—*us,* and who we are together.

The sound of the president speaking at the front of the cask room is drowned out by the hum of energy blasting through my veins. Piper crosses her wrists behind my neck, pulling me in closer. With her soft lips roaming over mine and a slight slip of her tongue into my mouth, I decide this night will end soon. I'm anxious to get her back to the villa where it's only the two of us.

"Wonderful job, Mr. Bradley," Piper whispers into my lips.

"Couldn't have done it without you here," I say, keeping my voice hushed that only she can hear.

"Yes, you could."

"Maybe—" I pull out the chair behind her so we can both take our seats. "Maybe not."

My eyes quickly glanced around and noticed that my hearing had returned because the string quartet had begun playing again. Piper and I are seated across from Leslie and Lyle Hockley. They're my parents' friends and come from a long line of growers. Leslie is a retired college professor and only recently started taking on more with their winery. She and Lyle both sit on several local boards.

"Such a bummer your mother couldn't make it." She frowned before sipping the starter soup. The first course in a seven-course dinner tonight, each paired with a specific wine selection.

"I know she looks forward to this event all year, but she had some things to take care of out of town," I reply, gliding my palm across Piper's leg under the table. She wiggles in her seat.

"How are you holding up after losing your father?" Lyle asks, creasing his forehead. "We all do miss him."

I rub my chin with two fingers, retrieving the canned response I've been telling people for months. "It's been tough, but I'm getting through it. It's nice to be back here again. It makes me feel closer to him, you know?"

After he passed, I took two weeks off of work to fly up here. I spent the entire time aimlessly wandering around the property. Memories from my childhood of long afternoons running wild all over the land with my dad came rushing back.

"Yes. I completely understand that," he says. "Well, we're happy you're back, and I'm sure your mom is too."

"Thanks. I appreciate that."

Leslie flashes me a quick half-smile from across the table. "I wondered why you went all the way to Arizona for school, and then I wondered even more why you didn't return once it was complete, but after meeting this lovely woman,"—she grins at Piper—"I fully understand now."

I turn to Piper, squeezing her thigh. "Yeah, you could say that."

"Thank you. It's been great meeting everyone out here. I love how warm this community is." Her eyes flicker, and her face flushes when she speaks.

Leslie dabs her face with a cloth napkin. "We do take pride in that."

The dinner conversation flows, and I could not be more grateful to have Piper here. She is a natural when speaking to people. She's unapologetically herself. I noticed that during the networking event at our villas a few nights ago. It's like she can easily read people's emotions passing through their words. It's alluring and explains how she got me to propose marriage after only speaking to her for less than twelve hours.

The wine continues to flow as the dinner courses change. The later into the night we get, Piper gets more friendly, and her voice starts to turn into this high-pitched version of her real voice. It's fucking hilarious.

We've stayed a lot later than I initially wanted to, but I catch myself alternating between cutting her off and laughing at how adorable she is. It isn't until other guests leave for the night that I take it as my cue to get out of here. The more wine she has, the more flirty she gets. And I know exactly what she wants every time she shoots me *that look*.

"Hey." Piper flips her hair around, and I'm hit with the delicious scent of lavender. "We should tell them what we did in Vegas a few weeks ago," casually mentions while in a conversation with the Dueling Hills Winery owner, who happens to be sitting on the other side of her.

Shit.

"Okay!" I urgently interrupt Piper's sentence. "It's time to go." I stand and hook an arm around her shoulders. If the other guests leaving wasn't a reason to leave—this is.

Piper gives me an over-the-top frown, pushing out her plump, glossy lips. All I can think of is slipping my cock back into that tight, wet mouth of hers.

"Oh no! But we're having so much fun."

"I can see that." I nudge her to a stand, then turn to face the few guests sitting near us. "It was wonderful to see all of you. Have a lovely evening."

"Bye—"

I whisk her away under my arm. She insists on saying goodbye to every person we pass on the way out of the building—except Preston and Sophia for obvious reasons. A little unstable on her feet, we head to my car.

I slide into the driver's seat next to her a minute later. Piper talks my ear off on the ride back to our villa. In true *drunk Piper* form, she insists on telling me who she liked and didn't like at dinner. In a passionate speech about the various food options that were served, she practices detailed descriptions of the wine's unique adjectives and metaphors people used to describe them.

I drive along the dark highway in silence, listening to her chattering. By the time we pull up to the villa, it looks like all the other guests went to sleep because there is no light except for my car's headlights. I shut off the ignition and then turn to Piper in the passenger seat. "Okay, my lovely wife, who will not stop talking. Let's get you to bed."

She pouts and crosses her arms to her chest. "But I'm not tired."

"You're going to be hurting in the morning if you don't get some sleep."

A quick movement from the passenger seat catches my eye. "What are you doing?" I chuckle while Piper crawls over the center console onto my lap.

"Fuck me."

My mouth falls open. "What?"

With her arms around my neck, she plays with the hair on the back of my head. "You heard me."

That has to be one of the hottest things a woman has ever said to me. It's so simple, yet fucking sexy. She demands to have my dick, and that's what she's going to get. "You got it." I grip her hips, moving her slightly to the side, then make quick work of unclasping my belt. While I'm unzipping my pants, Piper gathers her dress, pulling it up around her waist.

As soon as my zipper is down, my dick pops out. "I've been so fucking hard for you all night."

Piper sucks in a breath, still hovering over me. "I craved *you* all night," she croons, then moves her panties to the side and lowers herself on top of me.

My head falls back the instant I'm engulfed by the smooth, wet heat of her insides. "I can tell," I grit out.

When we start moving, a guttural groan escapes her throat.

Piper's lips are on my neck while her nails dig into the leather on the back of my seat. "Oh yes."

Tightly gripping her waist, I guide her body as she rolls back and forth. "God, Piper, ride my cock."

Her hands aren't bound with a belt or handcuffs, and they roam around my chest with excitement. I crumble under her frantic touch. Piper uses me for her own pleasure, riding my dick like that's what it was made to do. She pivots her body the way she wants while I lean back, enjoying my role of supplying her with an orgasm. "I love being in control, but I also love it when your pussy takes what it needs."

"Mm-hmm," she whimpers. I capture one of her breasts in my mouth. Flicking it with my tongue at first, then opening it wider, bringing the whole thing in. Her skin is smooth and tastes like heaven. "Goddamn, I'm going to come," she squeaks as I feel her muscle tense on top of me.

Wanting my dick to be swallowed by her, I raise my hips from the seat. I immediately straighten, on the verge of exploding myself. Piper's eyes close while her head tilts toward the ceiling. I can't take mine off of watching her while she's overcome with pleasure, demanding everything that I'm now spilling into her. Her pussy tightens around me, trapping me inside.

Once my legs stop shaking, Piper falls into me. "I can't get enough of you," she pinches out between labored breaths.

I laugh because I feel the same way about her. Wrapping my arms around her, she's tight against my chest. Still straddling me, her body curls to one side. I still manage to stay nestled inside her. "My pants are ruined now."

She lifts her head to bite my chin lightly. "Yes, they most

definitely are."

Chapter Twenty-Six

PIPER

When I peel my eyes open, I'm greeted with Jack caressing the side of my face—and a slight headache. I'm lying flat on my back, sprawled across his body, with both arms hanging over the side of the bed. A light sheet is pulled up only to my waist. The cool air pricks my nipples, reminding me that I'm still naked from last night.

"Good morning." Jack twists his fingers in a strand of my strewn hair. "Have a little too much fun last night?"

"Mm-hmm." I roll over, my bare breasts meeting the warmth of Jack's hard chest. Wiggling my body into his, he brings both of his arms around me and clutches my hips, forcing me to straddle him.

"I had a wonderful time last night with you," I purr, grinding against him slowly.

"You're ready to go again?" His hand guides my waist, rocking me back and forth.

Pressing my palms flat on his pecs, I push myself into an upright position. "With you? Always." The heavenly sensation of his heated length rubs against my clit. "Looks like you might be ready to go too," I tease, arching my hips forward, easily sliding him in before he has a chance to answer.

"Damn," he groans, dipping his head back. "You're going to kill me."

I lean forward, tucking into his chest, continuing to roll myself until I've taken in all of him. I bring my lips to his neck, trailing his delicious skin with wet kisses.

"Show me again how much your pussy needs me," Jack's voice is hoarse as he squeezes my ass.

Nibbling on his earlobe, I whisper, "It needs you to come for it."

He swiftly responds by lifting to slam his lips into mine while simultaneously picking up his pace. Jack moves my body how he wants, directing it in motion with his—and I respond without a thought. I palm the sides of his face, holding his mouth to mine and letting *him* use *me* for his pleasure. With a stroke of his tongue on mine, I groan into our connected lips. Jack's movements become rougher when he begins climbing to his climax.

After a few more rolls of our hips in rhythm with one another, I feel his entire body come to a still underneath me. My stomach flutters with tiny butterflies, knowing he's about to give me everything I now desperately crave.

"Grab the headboard," he commands, trying to hold me in place.

I do as he says, reaching up to the top of the headboard with both hands, continuing to ride him.

"Fuck," he cries out as he begins to unload. "You want it all, don't you? My good girl."

"Yes," I moan, "I need it."

With his muscles still twitching, he raises his arms and wipes the palms of his hands down his face. "I cannot stop fucking you."

"You don't have to."

Jack shifts our bodies, so I gently fall to the side. His arms are still around me while he's buried inside as we both lie facing each other on the bed.

"How do you feel?" he asks.

Now that the sex buzz is wearing off, I'm starting to feel slightly hungover again. "I have a headache," I complain.

"I'm sure." He laughs. "I hope you had a good time last night, despite the hangover."

"I had a wonderful time. Your speech was perfect, and I felt so proud to be with you." I squint my eyes from the daylight. That's aggravating my headache. "I hope you know that you can alter the universe with that smile and charisma."

Jack places two fingers under my chin and lifts it to meet his thoughtful blue eyes. "What can I do for you?"

"Food?" I say, shoving my hand under the pillow.

"You got it." He slides out of me and swings his legs over the edge of the bed. "I'll be right back."

I reach for the blankets and yank them up, covering my naked body. "Where are you going?"

Jack slips on his boxers and grabs his phone. "I'm going to get you some breakfast."

My heart melts.

By midmorning, Jack and I are sitting on the back patio eating breakfast burritos from the little cafe down the street. Even though there's a mild chill in the air, I feel cozy wearing

Jack's shorts and a white T-shirt with a blanket wrapped around me. It smells like him. If I could bottle his scent and bath in it, I would.

"As I laid in bed staring at the ceiling last night, I had an idea," he begins.

My eyebrows furrow as I catch the fact that he had a hard time sleeping. "I didn't even know you were awake last night. Did you get enough sleep?"

Steam seeps from the hot coffee in his hand. "I'm not surprised. You were passed the fuck out."

"I know." My cheeks redden, slightly embarrassed. "So, what was your idea?"

"Why can't my mom and I buy out Preston and his dad?" he exclaims, his eyes wide as if in mid-thought. Jack's face is bright. I'm sure the rush he got from the overwhelming support at the harvest dinner played a part in this epiphany. And I am so happy for him.

"That's a great idea. Is it possible? Do you think your mom would be into it?"

Jack sets his cup down on the table and opens his arms. "Come here."

I rub my lips together. Does he want to hug me or be close to me? Either way, I waste no time responding to his sweet gesture. Pinching the blanket's edges, I hold it together and approach his chair. When I squeeze between his legs, his strong arms come around from the back and pull me onto his lap.

"I think she'll be thrilled with the idea as long as she knows it's something I want," he says, resting his chin on my shoulder.

"Is it something you want?"

He lets out a weighted sigh. "I think I'm starting to realize that this is my path, and the sooner I embrace it, the more successful I can be."

"When we went out to dinner with your mom, she mentioned that she wanted to step away, which is understandable after losing your dad. Do you think that will fit into her plan?"

"I'm not sure. I'll need to speak with her about it first, but I'd be willing to take everything over if it meant her being happy and having some much-needed time away. It's honestly the least I can do." Jack slides his hand into mine. He forces my fingers to open and softly traces the lines inside my palm.

"That's very considerate and kind. She's lucky to have you," I say, partially distracted by the tickle of his fingertips.

"Sometimes I forget that even though I lost my dad, she lost her husband—her best friend and partner." Tilting my head to the side, I run my lips across his forehead as he speaks. "I could have been there for her more the last few months, but I was stuck in my own world of self-loathing. She's been holding everything together while I've been complaining about what I wanted."

"Trauma hits us unexpectedly, and no one really knows the right way to handle it, but look at what you're doing now. You're not only stepping into your family business, you're fighting for it." In our short time together, he has come a long way with acceptance. I smile, knowing that I've been a part of that.

"Thank you." Jack's arms hold me close around the waist with his hands folded on my stomach. "To offer a buyout is the right thing to do."

Forget about pretending or the faking—or whatever the hell

that we're doing. This moment is real, and I won't convince myself otherwise. I stay comfortably planted on his lap with my head resting on his shoulder for some time before Jack speaks. "Not having siblings never phased me growing up, but right now, I wish I had one to do this with."

"Like losing your dad and someone to partner with on the winery?"

Jack nods.

"I know. It was hard for me growing up alone. I always wanted a sister when I was young. Now I have Lina, Bailey, and Avery, and I'm grateful for them, but it would have been nice to have a confidant and friend as a kid." Would a sibling have helped? Or would it just have given Roxy two children to bully?

"Did you have any family around when you were growing up?"

"My grandmother." She and I were very close. She and my grandfather helped Roxy for years. They had written her out of their will by the time they passed. I replaced her. When Roxy found that out, she demanded I give her the money, but there were very strict instructions in the will stating that I would receive the money when I turned thirty. I assume that my grandparents thought I'd be strong enough to stand up to my mother by that time. I still have a long way to go.

"Are you still close with her?"

I fiddle with the loose pieces of fabric on the blanket. "I was. She died not too long ago.

His posture shrinks. "I'm sorry. When was that?"

"Uh, it's been about two years. I felt like she was the only person who understood me and the only other person who knew what my mother was like. It's been hard since she's been gone."

"It's difficult to walk through life without someone who understands you, especially when you feel like a part of you is missing or you can't be who you want to be," Jack adds, not truly understanding the depth of the relationship with Roxy.

"Yes, I know what that's like." I rise from his lap, deciding it's time to get myself together for the day. I love this moment with him, but I'm also self-conscious about how I look and probably smell. "I'm going to hop in the shower."

"I need to get in soon too. I have a few meetings this afternoon at the winery," he says, rubbing the back of his neck.

My stomach flutters when a surprising thought pops into my brain. Should I invite Jack to shower with me? He probably won't want to. That might be crossing the line. Just because we're sleeping together, we're not a couple.

"Do you, uh, want to join me?" I stammer.

Jack bends forward in the chair, looking like he's trying to hold back a smile. "I'd love to join you in the shower."

I take a sharp breath. We've had sex multiple times now and slept in the same bed, but I don't know why showering together sounds more personal.

I grin at him over my shoulder as I walk through the back door and into the villa. Jack is quick behind me, and by the time we get into the bathroom, he's already removing his shorts and T-shirt. I yank his shirt off my back, then slide down my shorts—which are also his, piling them on the floor. Jack leans into the shower to turn on the water.

His hard body is flush with mine, and the heat radiating off his skin is grazing my nipples. They harden. Jack must have felt it because he dips his head down and sucks one into his mouth. I shudder from the sensation of the wet smoothness of his mouth.

After a few playful licks, he turns and steps into the shower. I quickly follow, closing the door behind me. The scorching water rains over our bodies as we stand facing one another. I take my time creating random patterns on the curves of his chest.

My nerves come alive with his hands exploring every inch of my skin. "We actually *need* to shower," he mumbles into the space behind my ear.

"I know."

We're facing each other, surrounded by the thick steam that wraps around us. Jack twists his body around to grab the body wash and my loofah. I do the same, grabbing his soap off the holder built into the wall. While I'm turned away, I feel him begin to wash my back. He starts fast, scrubbing at a measured pace but then slows as he gets to the top of my thighs. The warm water from the shower head hits my pussy, making it throb.

I hear the loofah hit the ground. "I can't fucking take it," he growls before I feel him spread my ass cheeks, and with only enough time for me to suck in a gulp of air, the smooth, warm texture of his tongue licks at my puckered hole.

"Damn," I whimper, losing my balance.

"Sit down," he says, nudging me onto the marble bench inside the walk-in shower. Like always, I do as he tells me, backing into the heated tile. "Put one foot on the soap holder and the other on the shower door handle," he tells me, reaching up and aiming the shower head directly at my open legs.

"Alright," I comply, getting into position. He lowers to his knees between my spread legs. The water pressure hits my sensitive bud, forcing it to burn with pleasure. My clit is throbbing. I feel the slick moisture in between my thighs despite the water cascading over me. With a hungry need, I watch as Jack leaves lingering kisses on both sides of my legs until he reaches my core.

Trembling, I struggle to keep my legs in place. He hooks his arms behind my knees, bracing them. Jack's mouth reaches the seam at my apex, but he doesn't taste me yet. He waits with his mouth closed, letting the small puffs of hot air from his breath tickle me until my body takes over and opens for him. Without moving, he teases me, forcing me to beg for it. "Please," I squeak out, my hips gently bucking at his face.

"What do you want me to do?" he murmurs, running his tongue along the outside of my pussy. This is fucking torture, but I can't tell him what I want.

He senses my apprehension. "Tell me, or I'm going to get out of the shower."

I wriggle in place, frustrated with him. Fuck. "Fine. I want you to fuck me with your mouth!" I call out, gripping the back of his head and pushing him into me.

"Yes!" He shoots his tongue out, sending it deep inside of me. Jack lets me guide his head where I want him to go, and with both hands threaded through his hair, he stays licking and sucking. With his head almost completely still, except for the purposeful movements of his tongue, he feeds on me like he's starving and I'm the only one who can satisfy his hunger.

My legs are raised and securely pushed into the soap holder and the handle of the door as Jack continues to devour me. My body hums, my pussy tingles, and I keep Jack in place with both hands, demanding this powerful orgasm. My body begins to stiffen, and my breathing shallows. I curve myself around him, closing my legs with him comfortably tucked between them.

The heat and steam from the hot shower surround us, so I can barely see our bodies anymore. Like the darkness from the blindfold, I feel everything. Right as my stomach clenches, an explosive orgasm shudders through me. I desperately attempt to grab anything on the wall, but his hands are glued to me, and he stays through the aftershocks.

When he releases, Jack uses the flat part of his tongue to lick from the inside of my pussy to the outside of my clit. I stay slumped into the corner of the shower with my legs spread wide while Jack presses slow kisses on my skin from my belly button to my breasts and over the hollow of my collarbone. "I want to fucking die down there," he says darkly into my lips.

Panting and laughing uncontrollably, I kiss his lips, the ones that still have me on them. "I think I can arrange that."

His laugh rumbles inside his chest and mine. "Now I can focus on getting ready for my meetings."

I stand on shaky legs as Jack and I finish showering together.

We were both getting dressed when he asked me about my grandmother again. "Tell me about your grandmother," he says, looping his leather belt through his pants.

I stand in the closet, fastening my bra. "What do you want to know?"

"Anything," he says, walking over to me shirtless. How is he so fucking sexy? Those chiseled abs and that perfectly smooth skin.

"She studied the universe and astrology for most of her life and often refused to make decisions that weren't based on the positions of the sun, moon, and other planets."

Jack finishes clasping the last button on his collared shirt. "That's fascinating."

"It is, isn't it? Her mother studied astrology as well. Most of the women in my family have celestial names."

"Like their first names?" he asks, sitting on the side of the bed.

"No, our middle names. My great-grandmother was Nova, which means *new*, my grandmother was Celeste, which means *heavenly, and* my mother is Luna."

"And what's your middle name?"

"Moon," I tell him, shuffling over in my slippers to sit beside him.

"Piper Moon." Jack rubs my cheek with the back of his knuckles. "Illuminating the dark for all who are hidden behind the shadows. Very fitting for you."

His words hit like a thick, heady emotion, growing more powerful the closer we become. My eyes bounce back and forth, searching for a sign that this could be real. Does Jack see me—*for me?* I cannot be falling for him. This is all so crazy and so fast. It's lust. That's all this is.

"Keep talking." He encourages me to open up.

"When I was younger, I hated it. I thought it was lame that we all had themed middle names." I uncomfortably chuckle. "Now, I'm incredibly grateful to have a piece of them with me."

Jack smiles.

"When I was a kid, she gave me a gold crescent moon necklace. It had a tiny diamond in the middle. I loved it."

He takes the spot next to me on the bed. "You're talking

about it in the past tense. Do you not have the necklace anymore?"

The back of my eyes sting as I slowly shake my head. I still remember the day that Roxy stole it. We had just moved into our new apartment. She had asked me for some of my grandmother's jewelry for some time, but I kept telling her I didn't have it. She knew better. One day after I returned home from school, I found her sitting on the floor in the living room, staring at four stacks of cash. When I asked her where she got it, she told me she'd sold some of Grandma's jewelry, including the moon necklace.

He lies back, propping himself up on his forearms. "What happened to it?"

I force a smile but look away, not wanting to share something utterly embarrassing and hurtful with him.

"Tell me what happened to it," his voice firmer this time.

I pull my eyes away from him and onto the light of dawn breaking over the hills.

"Roxy sold it."

"What do you mean, she *sold* it?"

"She sold it to a pawnshop. Then after, she said that I could have kept the necklace, but our electricity would be shut off."

Jack falls to his back on the soft mattress and raises his hands in frustration. "Fuck. I'm so sorry. She told you that you had to choose between electricity and your grandma's necklace. How was that even something you should have dealt with as a child?"

"That's Roxy."

From the corner of my eye, I see Jack's arm come out, hook around me, and aggressively bring me down into him. His hold is tight, almost cutting off my oxygen. My tense muscles loosen, and I melt into his skin like it's my own. "That shouldn't have been put on you. How horrible it must have felt."

"It's weird because somehow it feels like it's my fault. Like I could have no—"

He quickly shakes his head. "What? No. None of that is your fault."

Despite the alarm bells going off, I sit with these emotions, living in them fully. I drop my eyes to his lips, part mine, and lean forward, meeting him for what feels like a connection to end all connections. Jack's soft lips move slowly around mine. I slip my tongue into his mouth and expect him to devour me, but he draws back. He let his forehead rest on mine before raising his head to kiss mine—another simple gesture that crumbles my remaining walls.

"Do you want to come with me today to the winery?"

"I haven't checked in with the girls in a while. We're supposed to Facetime later." I nuzzle his nose. "But thank you. I'll be waiting here for you to get back."

Chapter Twenty-Seven

The marketing, human resources, and operations meetings went smoothly yesterday. The more time I spend on the property, the more optimistic I become about taking over full-time. My mother and I spoke extensively about my buyout plan, and she was excited about the idea. We spent time during lunch going over what it would look like and the amount we would feel comfortable offering.

I came back to the villa enthusiastic and liberated. As soon as I walked through the door, I blindfolded Piper, handcuffed her, and fucked her until I was too weak to do it anymore.

She hasn't asked about the restraints. I'm still not sure if I'm ready to tell her yet. Feeling like I have no control over my life has made me find control in other areas. When women have mentioned it in the past, I've usually scoffed it off as a typical kink that people have. But the truth is, it's all about keeping my own control. I haven't dated anyone long enough for them to get tired of it or for me to feel secure enough to stop, so it's become a habit.

After a brief afternoon run, I walk into the villa to find Piper pacing back and forth on the patio. She has one arm across her body and tucked into her armpit while her cell phone is raised in the air in front of her. Even through the thick glass of the sliding door, I notice something off with her body language.

I take a few steps in that direction, hiding my shadow behind the curtains. I'm curious to know why she looks upset, but I fear that if I ask, she won't tell me. We've grown closer recently, but she still keeps so much hidden.

I lean into the open crack in the sliding door that was left ajar. Piper's voice is muffled, but I can still make out some phrases since she has a low-volume call on speakerphone.

"I can't give you any more money, Roxy," Piper says, her voice straining.

The female voice on the other end of the call is Piper's mother, Roxy.

"Why do you always fight me on this, Piper Moon? I am your mom. What kind of daughter are you that you wouldn't even help your mother when she needs you?"

"But you always need my help, and right now, I have a lot going on, and I need to focus on me. Why can't you be supportive of me for once?" I hear Piper attempt to defend herself, but there's no absolute conviction behind her words. She sounds intimidated and unsure of herself. It's an obvious contrast from the Piper I know.

"So many people in this world don't even have a mother. Why can't you be grateful that yours is still around!"

"That has nothing to do with it. I am grateful I have you, but I also need the freedom to live my own life." Piper's back is tense.

"Why wouldn't you want me in it?" Roxy snaps.

I'm no psychologist, but this conversation sounds like

some hardcore manipulation. Suddenly, I feel uncomfortable intruding on a personal family matter. I quietly head into the bedroom, grab my laptop, and start working, pushing aside everything I've heard. Maybe if I distract myself from what I was eavesdropping on, I can also ward off the strong territorial urges to come to her defense.

I'm not alone long when I hear her enter the villa, followed by quick footsteps and a hard close of the bathroom door. I immediately jump off the bed and sprint to the bathroom to make sure she's okay. Standing in front of the closed door, I hear the sounds of the bathtub filling up. Tapping my fingers on the handle, I slowly twist, and to my surprise, the door is unlocked.

Before adding force to open it, I second-guess my actions. Am I crossing a line? Fuck it, I don't care. There's nothing private between us anymore. I slowly open the door as she turns off the faucet. "Are you alright?" I take a few cautious steps toward her.

Her glistening skin peeks out from beneath a mountain range of translucent bubbles. She rests her chin on her knees, and her legs are pulled up to her chest. Piper's hair is tied into a loose bun on her head.

"I'm fine. I don't want to talk about it." She doesn't look my way when she speaks and instead keeps her face concealed.

I've become a perpetual invader of her privacy. "I heard the conversation you were having with your mother outside. I'm sorry for eavesdropping, but I couldn't help it. You looked upset."

She squeezes her eyes shut. "How much did you hear?"

"Not a whole lot. Just enough to realize that it didn't sound healthy," I say, maintaining a low voice as if not to scare her off.

I want her to open up to me because she has already seen me at my most vulnerable. Hell, our current situation is because of my flaws in who I am.

"Like I've told you, my relationship with my mother is complicated," she alludes, trying to dismiss me.

Looking down at Piper in the heart-shaped bathtub, she looks so small and defeated. I had no idea the depths of emotional manipulation that had been inflicted on her by her mother. I thought it was strange when I heard Piper call her mom by her first name. After the story Piper shared about her grandmother's necklace, it should have been a red flag that something was wrong.

"I'm sure that it is. No one's relationship with their parents is perfect. We all have our own level of toxicity."

"You don't understand because you grew up with caring, present parents. Your mom only wants the best for you," her voice cracks and sounds weak. "She's supportive and kind."

"I wish I knew how to help you." I lean against the counter, crossing my ankles. "I hate seeing you like this."

"I appreciate it, I do, but this is none of your concern. You're not my boyfriend. We're not really dating," she hisses.

That fucking stings.

"I am your *husband*," I counter.

Piper has given me support and let me be vulnerable around her. She's cared for me unconditionally and without judgment. I don't want to push her to talk about it, but if I don't, then who will?

She scoffs at me. "We both know that means absolutely nothing. This is a business deal, remember? You're paying me to help you, not the other way around. I'm fine, and I can handle it."

That one stings too.

It sure feels like her compassion toward me is real. I know it is. She's upset and pushing me away, but I'm not letting that happen. But I am growing frustrated with her stubbornness.

"Fine. If that's what you want." I turn on my heels and head for the door with the intention of leaving her in here by herself. But then, I hear little sniffles as she starts to cry. Even the sad noises Piper makes have a way with me. I rub my lips together and decide against walking away.

I peer back over to the tub, and her face is soaked—but I can't tell if it's wet from the water or the tears that are now streaming down her face. My heart aches to see her reduced to this, and I can't take it anymore.

I aggressively pull off my socks, shoes, shirt, and pants, throwing them into a pile on the floor at my feet. I step into the warm, sudsy water while her puffy face looks up at me with confusion. I lower myself to the opposite end of the jacuzzi tub and rest my legs on either side of her body.

"Hold me, Jack," Piper says, her voice sounding desperate and small. It's almost like she's begging me to take it all away.

I drop my entire world, thoughts, and self-existence to clutch her tightly in my arms. She molds into me, and her muscles relax.

"It's okay, my love," I whisper into the soft skin of her temple. With my arms firmly wrapped around her, she releases and shakes with sobs. "Having to support your parent financially and emotionally at a young age is something no one should have to deal with."

She lets out a delicate sigh, shrinking her body further into me and the bubbles. "How do you know that?"

"I'm not completely oblivious. I've picked up on things."

Her gaze falls to the water, avoiding eye contact with me. "I've been trying to keep that part of my life private. I always have—out of fear that people will think differently of me or that somehow it makes me less lovable or worth anything. It was hard enough telling you about the necklace."

Piper's words shatter my heart. She is anything but unlovable, especially to me.

I lift her chin, rubbing my thumb over her smooth skin. "You are not unlovable. You are worth everything in this life. Anything you want can be yours."

Her eyes narrow, and she kisses me.

I kiss her back softly and run my fingertips over the slick skin of her arm. "Tell me about Roxy and your childhood," I say, hoping she opens up.

"What do you want to know?" she asks, lowering her lips on my shoulders.

"I'm sitting here naked in the bathtub with you, with absolutely no place to go, so whatever you'd like to share. However, once the water gets cold, you're on your own."

"That's fair enough." She smiles, then sniffs. "Roxy is not like normal people. My dad was thirty years older than her and married when she got pregnant with me. He refused to acknowledge my existence, and the last thing I'd heard about him was that he'd passed away when I was a teenager."

I push a loose strand of wet hair from her sticky cheek. "I'm sorry. I can't imagine what that must have been like growing up and knowing that."

"Tell me about it. I was confused for so long why my dad never wanted me and my mom, but then I realized that he'd already had a family. He didn't need another one."

"My dad had an affair once when I was nine. I can't say if that caused the irreversible rift between us, but it was around that time that our relationship started to deteriorate. My mother forgave him, but I don't think I ever did," I admit. I do believe that's where our rift started. Saying that out loud makes it real all over again. She loved my father and eventually forgave him for his actions, but no one ever knew.

"I'm sorry that happened. I'm sure you were extremely protective over her," she says.

"Yeah, I was, but I think every child is protective over their parents. We're all born with this innate belief that we should feel accountable for our parents' actions and well-being. And I believe that outcome has everything to do with how our parents interpret those emotions."

She glides her fingertips over the slickness of her wet knees. "Some parents love and appreciate their child's devotion—others, like Roxy, take full advantage of it."

"I know, but none of that is your fault," I assure her, staring deep into her beautiful hazel-green eyes.

Later that night, I lie on my side with one arm propping up my head. Piper is on her stomach with both hands tucked under her pillow while her head faces mine. The hammering sound of the sudden downpour of rain drowns out every single thought in my mind but those of Piper. With my free hand, I graze my fingertips along the velvety skin of her back. Every so often, she'll break out in goosebumps, and I can't stop the smile that pulls at the corners of my mouth, knowing that my touch elicits that reaction from her.

"I thought about going no contact with Roxy," she says as if picking up in the middle of our previous conversation.

Wow. How sad that must be for her to contemplate cutting off all communication with her mother.

"You know how society tells us that we must endure the way our parents treat us, simply because they're our *parents*?" she continues, keeping her voice at a level barely above the pelting rain outside our patio doors.

"Yes. It's a mind fuck, that's for sure."

She raises her lashes at me before speaking again, "People say things like, *but it's your mom,* or *you only get one mom*—never asking what she could have possibly done or how she treated you to push you to the extreme where you have decided that no contact was the best solution."

I clench my jaw, frustrated that no one was there to protect her all these years. She's been alone, having to navigate through all this confusion. "Not everyone is exposed to abuse from their parents. And I don't mean physical abuse like what is mostly associated with that term—I mean emotional and verbal abuse."

"Exactly. I get hit with a wave of guilt, even thinking that my mother has abused me. She put a roof over my head, she kept me from harm's way, she fed me, but I know children need more than that," Piper adds, chewing on the side of her cheek. It looks like she's fighting back tears. "They need love, compassion, security, an emotional safe space. I was denied those things growing up and into my adulthood."

I move the hand that was gliding across her back to her face. "The responsibility of the relationship should not be solely placed on the adult child. The way Roxy treated you growing up and the things that were denied to you were not your fault, and once you find that belief within yourself, you'll be free of the guilt and burden resting on your shoulders."

"Why is it so hard? I mean, my brain knows that, but my emotions are wired in a completely different way," she counters.

I roll onto my back and rest my arms beneath my head. "I don't know why. But I do know that I don't subscribe to that belief." Then I turn to meet her eyes. "I'm sure that however you react, it has been much deserved. Because you are kind, beautiful, caring, warm, and compassionate." Her face flashes me a smile, but the heaviness in her eyes tells a different story. Piper's conditioning has led her to believe she is responsible for her mother's well-being. "Let's not talk about it anymore today, okay?"

"I'd rather not. But I would like to talk about what you'll feed me for dinner."

"Why am I not surprised you're hungry again?" With a wide grin, I link my fingers with hers. "Anything you want."

My heart is racing as adrenaline pumps through my veins. I might be overstepping, but I can't deny my overwhelming desire to step in on Piper's behalf. She is everything, and it's hard for me to imagine that her mother wouldn't be able to see that as well. The things that Piper shared with me in bed last night continued to gnaw at my insides even into the early morning hours.

By the time the sun rose this morning, I convinced myself that I needed to take the bold step to reach out to Roxy. Maybe help their relationship in some way or at least understand better so that I can be the support that Piper needs.

With Piper still asleep in the bedroom, I slip out the backdoor onto the patio. Then, when I'm confident that the door is securely latched behind me, I take out my phone and type in Roxy's number, which I found in Piper's phone last night.

To my surprise, Roxy answers after the first ring. And before I could finish my introduction, she cuts me off.

"Oh, so you're Jack. How does it feel keeping my daughter away from me?" she snaps.

Okay, damn. This is how we're going to start—right out of the gate, and she's already at a ten. No shame, no pleasantries.

"It's nice to meet you too," I keep my voice level. "I wanted to give you a call to get to know you. And to tell you what an incredible person your daughter is. She's been—"

Roxy cuts me off once again. "I couldn't care less about all the wonderful things you want to say about Piper. None of it matters to me. Now, what can I do for you?"

What type of person speaks that way about their child? Her energy and her approach have me completely taken aback. Not only to me but regarding her daughter too. For all she knows, Piper and I could be dating for real.

My eyebrows snap together, and suddenly, I feel protective over her. "To be honest, I've overheard some of the conversations you've had with Piper over the last few weeks, and they have upset her, so I thought I'd take the opportunity to introduce myself to you for you to get to know me." I clear my throat. "Thought that might alleviate some of your concerns about Piper not calling or being around as much."

"It's cute that you think you're trying to help. Well, news fucking flash to you, Jack—whatever your last name is, I will always come first because I'm the only one who can love her. Whether it's you that leaves or her—she'll always come crawling back to her mother." I hear the smugness in the tone of her voice.

What the fuck? I'm not prepared to have this sort of conversation with her. From what I know, I knew it would be slightly tense but not quite this contentious.

"With all due respect, *Roxy*, Piper and I are dating, and I intended to help you get off her back," I grit out, wrangling in my growing irritation.

"I don't know what you think you have with her, but Piper doesn't have long-term relationships. She dates, then gets tired of whoever she's with and leaves. Just like I taught her. As I said, trying to step in on her behalf is very chivalrous of you, but you're making a fool of yourself."

I clench my jaw. "For your fucking information, Piper is not just anyone, she is your daughter, and I'm not going to let you treat her the way you have been. Think about how that makes her feel when you, *her mother*, speak to her the way you do."

"What makes you think that you're more special than any other guy she's been with?" She scoffs. "And what about how I feel? Her job is to support me and pay me back for everything I did for her when she was growing up." She chuckles with a sharp, high-pitched sound that alerts every territorial nerve in my body.

"Let me educate you. If it's money that you want? I have plenty of it now. I suggest you cut your shitty attitude, or you won't be seeing a dime from her ever again." An empty threat that I have no idea how I'll follow through on since I have no influence on her. But now, I have only my gut instinct to go on.

"You have money?" Her voice has changed drastically, reflecting a more timid tone. Is that what this is about? Is that all she wants? Does she not care about her daughter?

I pace back and forth on the small strip of grass by the pool while my heart squeezes with this realization that Roxy only cares about herself—and money. An idea starts to form in my head. I'm not proud of it, but one that forms from a raw impulse to protect my wife.

Squaring my shoulders, I take a seat on the patio chair. "Okay, Roxy. Let's have a conversation about money."

Chapter Twenty-Eight

I sit back confidently as Tom, our lawyer, slides a folded-up piece of paper across the table. My mother, not so smug as I am, has barricaded herself behind folded arms at her chest. We are approaching the situation differently, but we both hope they'll accept the offer so we can put this behind us and move on.

"The amount shown reflects my client's first and final offer to buy out your portion of the winery," Tom states.

I dart my eyes over to Steve and Preston as their lawyer reaches out to grab the paper with an annoyed look. He quickly angles it in view for all three of them and opens it. Steve reacts first. His eyebrows raise, and then his head bounces between his son and the lawyer. That money-hungry bastard was not expecting us to present as aggressive of an offer as we have.

After a couple of brief exchanges between them, Steve turns to me. "Jack, Heidi, would you give us a moment?"

How his tone has suddenly changed since our last meeting. *Yes, take the bait.*

"Of course," I say, placing my palms on the table and lifting from my chair.

My mother nods in their direction. We're both followed out of the conference room by Tom.

As soon as we're in the hallway and the door closes, Tom turns around and says, "They're going to take it."

My mother's optimistic eyes brighten. "How do you know?"

"I've been doing this a long time." He clasps the lower button on his blazer. "And what we've offered is more than sufficient."

"He's greedy and power-hungry. I'm sure he'll take it," I add.

A few minutes pass before their lawyer cracks the door and invites us back in. Preston's head is down, avoiding eye contact, and Steve suddenly sits up straighter. *I knew he'd succumb to all those zeros.*

The three of us return to our seats.

Steve clears his throat. "Heidi, can you and Jack even afford this amount?"

He addresses my mother, but I answer instead. "I don't think that's any of your business," I snap.

"Before this gets contentious once again, will your clients accept the offer?" Tom turns his focus across the table.

Still refusing to look in our direction, Preston gives a subtle nod, followed by Steve.

"Yes."

I open the back door to see Piper sitting by the pool on one of the patio chairs with her legs hugged tight into her chest. She's resting her chin on her knees while reading on her Kindle.

"I've got great news." I cheerfully walk across the small patch of grass.

She quickly sets down her device and gets up from the chair. "You're back!"

"Yes—"

"Hopefully, this time is better than the last—" she casually interjects. "Never mind, I take that back. Last time went extremely well for me." She runs her tongue along her front teeth.

I smile, remembering that first night we had together. "It ended pretty well for me too." She giggles. "But seriously—" I start once again.

"Is it wrong that I was secretly hoping that you'd come home pissed off? So, you'd take your anger out on me once again?" She smirks.

A smile slips, slightly annoyed but also turned on by her admission. "If you keep interrupting my good news, we will have a repeat of last time." I bring my lips into hers, and I dive my tongue down her throat, playfully silencing her.

Piper laughs, gently pushing me away. "Okay, okay. Sorry. I won't do it again. Now tell me."

"So," I pause, anticipating her interrupting again. She stands with her hands on her hips while biting back a smile. "Pending any further negotiations between our lawyers, it's official. They've agreed to the buyout," I say excitedly.

Her face lights up, and she jumps into my arms. Her legs swing around my waist, and her arms fold behind my neck. "Stop it! That's so great!"

Piper's eyes shine bright green in the sunlight, and I smile because this success is hers too. "I can't fucking believe that we did it. The winery has never been fully ours. My dad has always had Steve as an investor, but now it truly does belong to the Bradley family."

Piper sweeps her fingers through my hair. "I bet your mom is thrilled."

"Yes, she's cried several times already. I know this is what my dad would have wanted," I tell her, feeling a sense of pride.

"This is the best decision, and you'll do amazing. I'm so proud of you!"

I slide her down my body until she's on her feet. "What I would love to do is to celebrate," I dip my head to whisper into her ear. "Then, I plan on making a shrine out of you and worshiping every inch of your body."

Piper sharply inhales. "Anything you want."

"Don't move. I bought something for us." I jog back into the house to grab the 1,500-dollar bottle of champagne I picked up on the way home and two sparkling wine flutes.

With two glasses in one hand and the bottle tucked into my armpit, I head back to Piper. She's sitting in one of the chairs, her body twisted toward me and her face beaming. I love that I get to share this with her. There's no one else in the world I'd rather be enjoying this celebration or making this huge life change with.

This means that I will no longer have the need for us to be together. A landslide bowls me over as the reminder hits me. My shoulders automatically drop, and I force a weak smile. A heavy sinking feeling settles in my core. I'm not ready to let her go yet, but she'll be ready for the divorce I promised her. Until then, I will take full advantage of the rest of my time with her as my fake girlfriend—and wife.

"Mmm, what's that?" she asks as I approach the pool's edge.

"I picked it up on the way home from the meeting. I thought we could celebrate." I shift my body away and aim the bottle outward before popping off the cork and shooting across the grass.

"Yeah!" Piper laughs, grabbing the two glasses I set on the table between our chairs.

"How does it feel to be the sole owner of Bradley Wines and Vineyards?" She lifts her champagne in the air.

"Relief and excitement—and also terror." I breathe out a chuckle.

We toast, and both take a drink with a quick flash of silence.

"I bet. It's a big decision, but the correct one. Now all you have to do is get the town to accept you again"—she tilts her—"which, after what I witnessed at the Harvest Dinner during the speech you made, won't be a difficult feat."

I smile, but my sense of joy isn't from my decision. It's also about the woman I chose to bring along for this ride. "I hope you're right," I say, glancing over the rim of my glass. My eyes briefly lock with hers, and I get this bubbly, light feeling in my chest. One that Piper always brings out of me. Looking over at her with a devious half-smile on my face, she notices.

"You're always so hard to read when you get that little flicker in your eyes and that look on your face."

I purse my lips together and shake my head. "I don't have a specific look."

She squints her eyes, suspicious of my smirk.

When she's not looking in my direction, I place my glass on the table, bend down, wrap my arms around her legs, and throw her over my shoulder.

"Jack!" she shrieks, attempting to wiggle out of my arms. "What are you doing?"

I growl playfully and tighten my hold. I give her ass one hard smack, then toss her into the pool, fully clothed.

Piper yelps midair before hitting the water. Almost immediately, her head springs up from the water. She's laughing and pushing the soaked hair away from her face. "What the hell?"

I pull my shirt off from over my head. "I'd move if I were you. I'm coming in," I warn, then remove my pants.

Piper looks away, covering her face with her hands, while I leap off the side of the pool with only my boxers on, splashing her directly in the face.

I can hear her unintelligible shrieks of random words from above the water. While under, I see her legs frantically moving away from me. Four years of swimming in high school has led me to this moment as I reach Piper at the other end of the pool within seconds. When I get close enough, I grab her around the waist while still under the water.

"It's freezing out here!" she squeals. Her head falls back as she lets out a belly laugh when I break the surface. "What the hell, Jack! I still have my clothes on!"

I lower my forehead to hers, and water droplets drip from my loose strands of hair that fall into my face. "I'm sorry about that. I should probably help you take off your clothes." She rubs her nose on mine before she lowers her wet lips to kiss me. On instinct, I pull her waist closer so our cores are flush. My hard dick escapes from my boxers, but I don't care this time. I want her to feel what she does to me.

Clutching my shoulders, she sucks in her bottom lip. "That would be gentlemanly of you."

Bringing my hands from around her hips, I slide them up her back. She lifts her arms, helping me raise her undershirt and sweater from her shoulders. I toss it outside of the pool. Piper's drenched clothes slap the concrete on impact.

My heart races when I face her hard, pebbled nipples. "Cold?"

"Maybe." She plays coy, wrapping a warm palm around my sensitive length that's already standing at full attention. She pumps me a few times before leaning in to whisper in my ear, "You don't seem to be, though."

"Not since you've been around," I quip, slipping my hands under the waistband of her cotton shorts. She wiggles her hips a few times, and they come right off. I throw them out of the pool as well. My cock prods at her core, poking it a few times without sliding in. Grasping her ass, I lift her up, while she simultaneously wraps her legs around my waist.

In the water, we're weightless, and I barely have to use any strength to hold her in place. Our mouths connect. A short murmur slips through before my tongue is in her mouth, not forceful but eager. Piper responds by latching it with both lips and pulling it into her mouth. The sound of a low grunt vibrates inside my chest. Sucking my tongue in and out a few more times before she releases. A few drops of pre-come bead at the head of my throbbing dick, only feeling it for a second before it dissipates into the cool water.

Hungry for more, I leave a trail of small bites along her chin, neck, and chest. She raises slightly, giving me full access to open my mouth over her nipple. Pulling her chilled skin into my warm mouth, I suck in rhythm a few times, then flick my tongue over her sensitive small bump.

"Oh, Jack," she moans.

Breathing only when switching sides, I give her other area the love it deserves. Piper's firm grip continues to stroke me as I slide one palm down her back, over her hip, and around toward the heat between her legs. "Open up for me, love," I mumble into the soft sweetness of her skin. With the other placed on her ass, I gently push up, giving her the angle she likes.

"That's so good." Her eyes fall closed, and her grip tightens even more. "Where's my blindfold, Mr. Bradley?"

I crack a smile. She's asking me about the blindfold. Does she like it? I knew she would. "We're going to have to pass on that because if I'm not in you soon, I'm going to blow in your hand," I tell her. "Now open for me."

Piper releases her strong hold on my dick. Instantly, it's cold, twitching to be warm again and begging to be inside her. She brings her hands to my face before lowering her head to kiss my open lips. My hips thrust forward, aiming right for the slick wetness that coats the inside of her walls. The second her pussy clenches around me, I'm pulled in. It's inviting and safe, like a warm hug.

"Fuck," I murmur, my forehead dropping to her shoulder.

As I thrust in and out, small whimpers escape from her light pink lips. She feels so good—*so perfect.* Piper's body molds to mine like I'm meant to be there. Her body moves with me until we're pushed up against the side of the pool. With her arms crossed behind my neck, I extend myself around her, further caging her in and grabbing the ledge. I can pound harder with better support, raising visible small goosebumps that span her skin.

"I'm coming," she cries.

I lift my hips forward to reach the sensitivity of her clit. "That's right, come for me. I'm here for you," I say, biting her neck.

"Oh yes," she squeaks.

"I am too," I grunt, picking up my pace. "Come for me, my love." Her thickness coats my dick in slick warmth, causing me to break. Right as I start to release, her pussy clamps down on me, squeezing out everything I have. My eyes roll back, and my legs lock in place. I crash my weight into her with my muscles limp and tired. At this point, I can't tell where I begin and she ends.

Piper's body is still cloaked around me when she slows to a still after her final few tenses. She lifts her head from the crook of my neck and flutters her eyelashes. The shades of green and specks of brown mixed in have become one of my favorite things to look at. "Now I'm freezing."

"I'm sure." I straighten to a stand on unstable legs. "Let's get the fuck out of here before it gets *really* cold."

"Burrr," she says through chattering teeth when our bodies disconnect.

"I'll get out first and grab your towel." Placing both hands on the ground, I lift myself from the water. The wind picked up in the short time we were there, and now that it's late afternoon, the temperature will quickly drop.

I grab the top towel from the stack on one of the bistro tables next to the pool, give myself a quick wipe down, and then grab one for her. "Come here." I stand by the stairs.

With Piper's arms stacked across her body, she walks to the open towel and into my waiting warmth. "Thank you," her voice quakes with shivers.

The cool breeze whips at my bare back as my towel drops. "Let's get inside."

Piper nods, following close behind while we sprint the short distance back into our villa. I slam the sliding glass door, then turn to see Piper standing completely naked in the middle of the living room with her towel gone. We make eye contact, and she breaks into an explosive and unrestrained laugh. "I'm so fucking cold, but I'm so fucking alive and I love it."

"Freezing to death?" I tease.

"It wasn't my idea to swim today, was it?"

"I guess not. Oh shit, we left the champagne outside."

Piper shakes her head. "That's all you. I'm getting into the shower to warm up."

"I'll go get it." I throw on one of my sweaters that was strewn across the back of the couch. I wrap the towel around my waist, run outside, and grab the bottle.

When I get back inside, I hear the faint sound of the shower running. She has the door open. *An invitation?* I think. I can be ready for round two, but I'm also hungry, and I'm sure she is too. I peek my head around the side of the door, warm steam hitting my face.

Piper's blurry silhouette behind the misty shower door is tempting. I clear my throat, knowing that if I give in and join her, then I will barely have enough energy to get the job done.

We need sustenance. "What do you want for dinner?" I ask, elevating my voice over the rushing water.

Piper whips her hair around, then cracks the shower door, poking her head out. "Are you coming in?"

The stream pouring from inside creates an apron around her entirely delicious body. "How hot do you have that water?"

"Not hot enough." She runs her fingers through her long, wet hair. *Tempting.*

I ball one of my fists, painfully biting it. "God, I want to climb in there with you so fucking bad, but we need to eat—well, *I* definitely need to eat."

"Your choice," she says, raising an eyebrow. "I don't care what we have. Is there anything here we can cook?"

I nod, squeezing my eyes closed to get the image of her glistening, smooth curves from my mind. But it doesn't help because she's now permanently painted on the back of my eyelids. "I think we have the ingredients to make spaghetti. How does that sound?"

"Perfect." She bats her eyes at me before closing the shower door. "I'll be out in a minute."

Chapter Twenty-Nine

I lean against the tiled wall in the shower while the blazing water hits me. I feel light as a feather. Jack and I have grown close over the last month. Being forced to live together the last few weeks has accelerated that. Leaving was hard enough last time. I can only imagine how exponentially worse it will be now. *How can I say goodbye to him?*

I leave in two days, and despite knowing I'm going home, it doesn't feel like my actual *home* anymore. I don't necessarily feel like Dupara is either, but I'm starting to figure out that when people say that home isn't really a place, it's a person, I now understand what they're referring to.

But that airy feeling of lust quickly dissipates when I remember that this is all for show. Love beyond the illusion of what we've created has become more real than I could have imagined.

The hot water cascades down my body as my eyes follow in the direction the droplets fall. I bend down, grab the shampoo, and lather my hair. Jack and I haven't discussed what will happen next, and neither has mentioned another trip. I wonder if he's assuming that everything is falling into place with Bradley

Wines—he won't need me anymore. Confusion rages in my heart like a hurricane. My anxiety is growing now that the hours trickle down to when I'll have to walk away from Jack and everything that's developing between us.

With the buyout, it makes sense that he wouldn't need me anymore. I know that, but neither one of us has said it. The thought makes my stomach turn.

A delicious and savory smell floats over the top of the glass shower and right into my nose. *He's cooking.* My stomach grumbles with hunger, so I vigorously rinse out the rest of the shampoo from my hair.

I walk out of the shower with a wide grin and the anticipation of doing something normal and mundane with him. I throw on a pair of matching plaid pajamas and head out.

I round the corner from the shallow hallway and into the kitchen to find Jack standing at the stove with his back to me. He's completely naked. My eyes scan the landscape of his body from behind, enjoying the sight of his bare ass, which I've had my mouth and hands all over.

Jack doesn't notice me right away, but as I creep closer, I can faintly hear him singing the words to "I Miss You" from Blink 182 that plays in the background. I fight the urge to bite those tight cheeks and instead wrap my arms around him. "It smells good here," I say into the skin on the back of his shoulder.

Jack raises his free arm and places it on top of mine, firmly hooked around his hard ab muscles. "I hope it doesn't taste like shit. I'm not much of a cook."

Circling his body, I leave a trail of soft kisses along the warm skin of his shoulder, making my way around to his chest. At the same time, Jack steps away from the stove and twists until my body is flush with the front of him. "From the looks of that pasta sauce, I'm sure you're much better than you're letting on."

His arms come around and link behind my back. "Thanks. I really hope you like it. If not, there's always takeout."

"I'm sure it tastes fine," I tell him before moving to the side to check out the ingredients and produce on the counter. "I can make the salad."

"I thought you'd never ask." He chuckles sarcastically. "Oh, and I poured you another glass of champagne." He gestures to the glass flute on the table.

"Thanks." I lift it to my lips and take a sip. Then, I set it next to the cutting board and the salad bowl. "Tell me about the look on Steve and Preston's faces when you and your mom countered their offer with your own buyout."

Jack shoots me a side-eye. "They were surprised, to say the least. But it got better when they got their greedy eyes on the amount we were prepared to offer. Such a little prick Preston is. He wanted to turn it down right away, I know it. He wouldn't even make eye contact during the meeting."

My forehead creases. "What? Why do you think he'd want to turn it down?" I ask Jack, but I can only think of a couple of reasons why. One is that this whole thing is based on jealousy. The other is that he'd want to decline out of spite. Either way, it speaks to the type of person Preston is, and with what I've seen during our few encounters, I can say he isn't a good one.

"I have my theories, but truthfully, it wouldn't matter anyway. He's always been a shady guy. His dad—also a piece of shit—jumped at the chance to take the money. He was foaming at the mouth when he saw those dollar signs." He picks a cherry tomato from the bowl and pops it into his mouth.

I chop the celery and carrots, then add them to the salad. "What's the next step for you and your mom?" I ask. As much as I have been a part of this with him, I won't be able to experience all the excitement that comes after the buyout and as Jack settles into his role. I won't be spending endless days on his beautiful family property. I won't have Gemma, or Heidi, or this community as anchors.

And I'm never going to experience what having a family is like. I always wanted it, but it never stung until now. Being so close to what I want, but being reminded that it is not mine. A few tears slip from under my eyelid. I dip my head, wiping it on my shoulder before Jack can notice. I swallow my sadness like I always do and force a smile.

Jack plucks another tomato from the bowl and brings it to my mouth. I part my lips and suck it in, making sure to take one of his fingers with it. "The lawyers will finish drawing up the paperwork, but by the end of the month, everything should be ready to sign," he explains in an uneven voice. I wrap my tongue around Jack's index finger, then lick down the sides. His eyes flare, and he gulps in a breath. Sucking harder and drawing my head back, I release him from my lips, causing a popping sound to echo between the walls of the kitchen.

"That's good. I'm sure you're ready to put all this behind you and start your new life," I choke out.

Jack blinks a few times, his eyes staring directly into mine. "Yeah." He sighs. "I guess that's true." A heavy silence enters the room for a beat before Jack speaks, "I'm going to put some clothes on. Standing this close to the oven, I'm afraid my dick might catch on fire."

I remove two plates and bowls from the cupboard. "Probably a good idea. However, I am enjoying the show."

A few minutes later, Jack emerges from the bedroom dressed in a plain white tee and pants that always seem to ride below his waist. I wipe the drool from the side of my mouth. I wonder if people who've been married for years still fawn over their partners. Jack and I are married, and he will still be my husband for a little while longer.

Skimming my tongue over my teeth, my mind drifts from one dirty idea to another. I think of everything we can do together until I leave on Sunday. "Not as sexy." I flip my hair around. "But I'll take it."

"I'm sure these clothes won't last long—and neither will yours." He raises an eyebrow.

"So sure of yourself, Mr. Bradley."

"You're my wife." He steps into me, biting his bottom lip. "I'm looking forward to experiencing, once again, how hard you can suck."

I have to look away because my cheeks redden. Jack's eyes flicker in apparent satisfaction with witnessing his ability to command my body, which only serves to enhance them. "I love the way you taste."

Suddenly, we both startle at the sound of the noodles boiling behind us. Jack quickly turns off the flame and removes the pasta from the stove.

"I know you do. And I plan on giving you whatever you want, whenever you want," he continues, picking up our conversation.

I playfully roll my eyes in his direction, then finish the salad before bringing it over to the table, trying to hide the beaming grin inching across my face.

After we bring everything to the table, Jack and I take our seats.

"I have to say, I think we did an excellent job on this meal." He smiles.

Staring at all the items on the table, the salad bowl, pasta, meat sauce, and our two glasses of wine, I'm overcome with emotion again. I blink a few times to relieve the sting from the back of my eyelids. A lump forms in my throat.

Jack stills with the salad tongs in his hands. "What's wrong?"

I can't breathe. Tears pour down my face.

"Piper. What's wrong?" Jack repeats, a slight panic in his voice.

I want to answer him, but I can't. My muscles are stiff. The surreal moment of us cooking dinner together, setting the table, and enjoying a meal like a family. Something that I've never done before.

My eyes blur before they once again spill. Each drop represents the things I've never experienced as a child I desperately wanted and the life I desire to create as an adult. I suck in gulps of air, my stomach spasming with every breath as I try to form the words to tell him.

When Jack saw my hysterical state, he jumped out of his chair and hurried around to the table. He twists me around to face him as his knees hit the floor in front of me. "Tell me what's going on," he demands, moving a loose hair away from my eyes.

My hands tremble. I try to gather myself to form a coherent

sentence, but I'm not having much luck. Shoving my hands under my thighs, I angle my gaze toward the floor, partly ashamed of what I'm about to say. "I'm so sorry." I sniff. "I've never cooked dinner and sat down to eat at a table like this with anyone."

Jack's forehead creases. "What do you mean?"

"I mean that I never ate dinner together with my mom or her boyfriends while growing up."

"Where did you guys eat if not at the table together?" He slides his palm up my temple and runs it through my hair before leaving it there.

"I ate alone."

"Even when you were a young kid?"

"Yes."

"Really?"

I squeeze my eyes shut. "Yes."

Jack's shoulders straighten, and I feel his grip tighten on the back of my head, nudging my forehead down to meet his. "You're not alone right now."

I sniff. This is ridiculous. I've spent plenty of dinners with friends and guys I've dated—so why does this time feel unlike any other before it? "I'm sorry, this is embarrassing. It's not a big deal," I say, wiping the wetness from my skin.

With his eyebrows still furrowed, he uses the corner of a napkin to dry the moisture on both sides of my face. "It is a big deal. It's something that you needed as a child and didn't get. I wish that I could give you everything you needed—*need*."

"Thank you. I'll be okay." I give him a weak smile, but behind it is the sadness and loss of a typical childhood.

Jack nods, then rises to his feet, but not before stopping to rest his soft lips on my forehead. Giving me a kiss filled with safety and—love. My eyelids fall closed, knowing I'll never forget the emotion behind this connection.

We spent dinner discussing his ideas for the winery and what he'd like to change. He even brings out his laptop to share all the marketing plans he intends to execute. He asks me for my opinion, and I happily provide it. Like everything else that happens between Jack and me, it's natural and easy.

There were many points during the conversation where we could both tell that we were avoiding talking about our future and how to move forward. We haven't talked about the divorce either, which has been on my mind for some time. *How can we say goodbye to each other? How is none of this real?*

I'm not naive enough to believe that we could have a fulfilling long-distance relationship or that, somehow, two strangers who got married in Vegas the first day they met would magically fall in love. I wish we had more time.

Later in the evening, I'm in bed, texting away in the group message with Avery, Lina, and Bailey, when Jack walks into the bedroom with only his boxers on and carries my bright pink vibrator in one hand.

I flush. "What are you doing?"

"I'm going to make you feel good," he states with excitement in his voice while opening the dresser drawer and grabbing a pair of handcuffs and a blindfold.

My insides flood with butterflies. "You always make me feel good."

"I can't get enough of it." I barely see his mischievous smile through the dim lighting of the bedroom.

"What did you have in mind?" I cautiously ask, pulling my mouth to the side.

Jack stalks toward me, his hard length peeking out from the slit in his boxers as he crawls onto the bed. "You'll see."

Helplessly, I watch him tower over me, binding my wrists above my head and securing the blindfold over my eyes. We've done this many times, but the quick surge of panic at first still hits me. "You're not going to tell me?"

"No," he says. Then I hear the buzzing sound of my vibrator.

Oh fuck, he's going to use it on me. And from the quick pulsing, I can tell he has it on the highest mode. My breath becomes labored while my pussy throbs.

"Now relax and enjoy." Jack's hands grip the inside of my thighs, spreading them apart. My legs start shaking.

"Relax," he tells me before his wet tongue shoots right into my core.

"Oh god," I groan.

"Of course, you're already ready for me. You always are, my love," he whispers. I feel a slight movement around the foot of the bed. I can't tell what he's doing, but I don't care. I trust him completely.

Like being struck by a powerful lightning rod, Jack slides his hard cock into my waiting heat while simultaneously pressing the aggressive pulse of my vibrator on top of my swollen clit. The moment he enters me is as good as my climax, because right then, Jack is owning me. He's taking me, and I'm utterly powerless to stop it.

My back arches, and my head lifts. "Oh god!"

As he thrusts in and out, holding the vibration in place, the intense sensation pulls the muscles from my stomach downward, a freefall from a roller coaster. My entire body trembles. I can't see him, but I can tell he's raised to his knees because I need to buck my hips into the air, lifting the bottom half of my body off the bed, desperately trying to get him deeper.

"Yes, come and get it," his voice is almost unrecognizable, and I fucking love it.

I hear Jack grunt on top of me, causing me to chase his hardness frantically. It's been mere minutes, and my body is ready to explode. A tingling sensation that begins at the top of my head rolls down to my shoulders, pings my nipples, clenches my stomach, and unleashes at my core.

"Fuck, Jack!" I yell, starting to shiver.

"That's right, it's me who's fucking you right now." His voice is sultry and spicy, moving through me like an aged whiskey. "It's me who makes your pussy throb. And it's me that makes you come harder than you've ever come before."

I completely black out, falling below the endless darkness from behind my eyelids, but then a slight burn of smooth silk blindfold whips across my face and jerks me back into reality. My eyes are blurry, my heart pounds, and I have to rapidly blink a few times to adjust to the low light of the bedside lamp.

Jack is hovering over me, his broad shoulders caging me in.

"Goddammit, that was the most intense orgasm I've ever felt!" I pant. My body is buzzing with desire. Staring into his eyes, I notice that they're a deep ocean blue. "Are you alright?"

"We're going to keep this off." Jack's words come out sharp. He starts thrusting back into me once again.

I stop breathing momentarily, searching his eyes for clarity and reason for this sudden change. "You sure?" I moan, my head dipping back into the pillow.

"Yes." From the corner of my eye, I see Jack's arm reach above my head. "These can go too," he growls, furiously unlocking the handcuffs. He tosses them across the room.

My heavy arms fall to the bed. I have not bonded with the unforgiving metal as much as the blindfold, and I'm happy to see them go.

Jack bends to kiss the hollow of my collarbone, then reaches for one of my sore hands and brings it to his warm lips, kissing the red ring that circles my wrist. "My wife," he mumbles, setting fire to my heart. "You are so unequivocally perfect."

I am entirely his. I let out a pleased hum, existing only in a world between his sounds and my sensations.

Jack Bradley is like a dream in motion, and I am undeniably in love with him.

Chapter Thirty

I am in love with Jack.

Over the next two days, we spend all our time at the villa once again. We had groceries delivered and cooked all three meals a day, so we didn't have to leave. I've become thoroughly infatuated with him.

Jack is always on me or in me, and I have never felt so complete. If gravity wasn't tying me to the ground and reality wasn't pounding on the backdoor of my thoughts, I'd have already floated away in my weightless and lustrous state. I can't go anywhere in this villa without Jack, and showers have become something we do together.

If I try to slip in without him, within no time, I hear the creaking sound of the glass door opening. I turn to see his deep blue eyes and soft smile standing before me. Jack will snuggle me under the hot water, leaving trails of kisses on my forehead, nose, and neck while washing my hair and refusing to get out before me.

My flight back to Phoenix is this morning, and we still haven't discussed what is happening between us. While standing under a rainfall shower head, I hear the subtle but familiar creak of the shower door. Smiling to myself, I turn to find Jack standing behind me.

"You were going to take a shower without me on our last day together?" he tsks, sliding his hands along the smooth skin of my curves.

I plaster a fake smile on my face, masking the pain I'm feeling inside. "Sorry."

"I forgive you," he says, cupping my elbows and swinging my arms around his neck. I interlace my fingers behind him and step into his familiar skin. I get a little lightheaded as our bodies are flush. Jack's hands clutch my hips, rubbing my core against his growing cock. He dips his head down and brings his sweet, wet lips to mine. My eyes fill with tears, savoring the taste and feel of his mouth on mine. But my uncertainty doesn't stop the way he makes me feel. The wholeness and completion that I've never known.

"I'm going to miss you," he mutters, sucking my bottom lip into his mouth. He's making this so fucking difficult. *How can this not be real for him?*

"I'm going to miss you too." My voice comes out unstable and filled with raw emotion. I tuck my arms, curl into him, and turn my face to the side against his chest.

Jack exhales a heavy sigh and wraps his arms around me. "Goddammit."

At this point, I don't know how much I will miss him or how I'm supposed to return to my life after what has developed between us over the last month and a half. My entire life has gone from vertical to horizontal and back again.

Jack takes the tips of his fingers and glides them slowly over the skin on my lower back, sending a shiver up my spine. Then, he brings the other hand and repeats the movement, allowing both hands to land on my shoulder blades, tugging me further into his embrace.

I feel like I can't breathe, and our cuddling is becoming too much. It's fucking torture. I pull back, looking deeply into his eyes.

"This is going to hurt like a motherfucker, isn't it?" He drops his lips to the top of my shoulder.

"Yes," I tell him, tracing the path of the water droplets with my mouth as they roll down his neck.

"Can I wash your hair?" He reaches down to grab the shampoo with one hand.

I clamp my eyes shut, breathing in his scent—of us. Searing it into my mind, scared that I'll forget it. *But how could I?*

After a couple of minutes, we finished up, and as always, I got out first, followed by Jack. Except this time, once I walked into the bedroom, he didn't follow me. He stays in the bathroom and puts his clothes on behind a closed door.

Fear and panic rush me with a vengeance. My nerves already sense the stark difference in his energy. I put on a pair of jeans, sneakers, and a long-sleeved white shirt.

When Jack walks out fully clothed, he glances at me and gestures toward the living room. "I'm going to get some work done, and I'm sure you want to start packing."

My mouth lifts with a smile, acknowledging him, but my eyes remain low and heavy.

I keep my distance for the rest of the morning while Jack works in the other room. I feel like we're back at the beginning—barely speaking, an impenetrable space between us, and the uncomfortableness of the nature of our relationship. We've shared an intense connection, showed our raw and vulnerable sides, and we've been exposed to each other. Now, it's being ripped away.

I need to talk with my best friends, and even though I'm not in the mood for dinner and drinks tonight, I will go anyway. Avery, Lina, and Bailey are my sisters. They'll know how to help me through this gut-wrenching situation I've knowingly gotten myself into.

"You've been quiet all morning." He walks into the bedroom, clutching two mugs of coffee. "This is going to be hard, I know."

I climb to my feet from kneeling on the floor in front of my half-packed suitcase. He hands me one of the cups. The smell is warm and comforting, providing temporary relief to the uneasiness that I've been feeling.

"I'm not trying to be," I reply, but I know I have. I've been stuck in my head.

Jack sits at the end of the bed and stares at the piles of my clothes that scatter the floor. "I didn't realize how many clothes you have."

"Because they were hanging in the closet or folded in the dresser drawers," I reply, setting the coffee on the nightstand.

"It will be weird not having you here with me." Jack avoids my eye contact.

"It'll be weird *not* being here."

A heavy silence fills the room.

"Um." Jack rubs the back of his neck. "Should we talk about what happens next?"

My breath halts. We need to address the next steps, our

business deal, and whether he needs me anymore. "Yes, that's probably a good idea." I take the spot next to him on the bed, taking care to maintain at least a foot between us which fucking slices me.

"I appreciate your help. In more ways than one." He leans forward, resting his elbows on his bent knees. "When I first thought of you helping me, I never thought it would go this far. I honestly thought you'd come out a few times to make me look good, help my image, and maybe take some of the heat off my back." He lowers his head toward me. "But you did so much more than that—"

My nose pricks and my eyes water with an impending waterfall of tears that are on the verge of breaking through. "You never *needed* me. You may have thought you did, but you don't need anyone. You're incredible all on your own," I interrupt him in a whisper.

"Thank you." He wipes a single tear from the side of his eye. "You have been so much more to me, and I want you to know how grateful I am."

"I'm happy to have helped." I wrestle with my hair and push it to the side of my shoulder as heat builds on the nape of my neck. "There's no need for me to come back, is there?"

Jack drops his head in his hands. "I was able to handle the money situation this morning," he states without answering the question. His avoidance gives me everything I need to know. And it shatters my fragile, bleeding heart. He doesn't know how to have this conversation with me.

The payment completely slipped my mind. "Ah yes, I forgot about that."

Jack leans back, removes a folded piece of paper from his pocket, and holds it out before us. "It's a check for the exact amount we agreed on."

My payment.

The payment I get for devoting myself to him. A simple transaction that sums up our entire relationship. My payment for cuddling him, caring for him, supporting him, comforting him, and letting him claim me. My payment for falling in love with him and the hurt it will cause.

"Thank you," I say, without taking it.

Jack sets it on the thick comforter on top of the bed. The one that we've made love on multiple times. It's the same one that we've laughed on. It's the same one we've played on.

Snuggled on.

Slept on.

Talked on.

Fuck, I can't breathe. I quickly rise from the bed, placing one hand on my stomach while keeping my back to him.

"Also," he continues, "I have my lawyer, Tom, working on our divorce. You should be receiving the official papers in the next few weeks. All you should have to do is sign."

I rub my lips together and swallow hard, trying to keep down the bile that's creeping up my throat. "Alright. Thank you."

"I know, this is uncomfortable," he says, picking up the check from the bed. "I'll put it in here." He gets up and slips the check into the front pocket of my travel bag. Rocking back and forth on his heels, he shoves his hands into the front pockets of his jeans. "I guess I'll give you some space to finish packing. We might hit some traffic, so we'll have to get on the road soon."

The minute Jack walks out of the bedroom, I slump against the side of the bed. Taking a minute to gather myself, I return to the floor and continue packing. It doesn't take me long before all my belongings are cleared from the bedroom, closet, and bathroom. What a whirlwind this has been.

Rolling my luggage behind me, I walk out of the room to find Jack sitting at his usual spot, typing away on his laptop. He has his square-frame black glasses on with one piece of hair falling onto his face. *Fuck.*

"I'm all set," my voice is pinched and distant.

He glances up at me, then slowly closes his computer. "Okay."

A short time later, Jack and I arrive at the airport. We haven't spoken since we left the villa.

"Can I walk you in?" he turns to me as he shuts off the engine.

I nod with a half-smile.

He helped me with my luggage as we entered the elevator. The distance between us is unbearable, but it will make things easier when I say goodbye. The elevator doors open, and Jack lets me exit first.

Suddenly, he stops walking. "This is as far as I should go."

Turning toward him, I fight back an emotional breakdown. "Probably a good idea."

"Uh, so I hope you have a safe flight." He crosses his arms at his chest.

"Thanks," I reply, keeping my eyes on the ground.

I expect him to get back into the elevator, but he continues standing before me. "Can I kiss you one last time?"

A breath forces itself from my lungs just as my eyes leak. "Yes."

He takes a single step toward me, eyebrows furrowed, and his expression has fallen. With my arms hanging at my sides, I give myself to him one last time.

Jack's warm palm glides against my cheek. I lean into it, the heavenly sensation of his thumb caressing my skin. He takes another step closer, bringing his body flush with mine. His other hand threads through my hair and hooks the back of my head.

I bring my mouth toward his. He dips down, feathering my lip with his breath. "I'm going to miss you," he whispers before we connect. His kiss is tender and soft. I press my lips into him to deepen our kiss, but Jack pulls back. With my eyes closed, I remain still, wishing it would last longer. Then, I feel him pepper my bottom and the top lip with delicate kisses, and all I can do is stand here and receive it.

My heart is breaking, my insides tremble, but I can't find the words to tell him how I truly feel.

Jack steps away and lets his hands fall to his sides, leaving me empty and cold. "Thank you."

Unable to form words, I give him a weak smile, letting him know I'll be okay. Then, he quickly gives me his back and begins walking in the opposite direction—as do I.

The reality I've come to know is being ripped from me, along with the Jack who has become intricately woven into the fibers of my existence. I immediately turn on my heels. "Jack!"

He looks back.

"Wait."

"Yes?"

I hurry toward him with my heart pounding, unsure what to say. "Wait."

We both eat the distance between each other and soon, we're back at arm's length once again. He stares at me with red, swollen eyes. *I don't want to leave him yet.* "I have a few more days left before I report back to work," I blurt out, assuming he would pick up on what I'm implying.

"Are you saying you want to stay with me longer?"

"Maybe, yeah," I admit, slight uncertainty in my voice.

His expression drops. "I don't think that's a good idea. The more time we spend together, the harder it will be."

The muscles in my throat constrict, cutting off my air supply. I hang my head, focusing on the specks of white and silver in the dark tile of the airport floor. "It's already hard."

"I know." He pains, wrapping an arm around my shoulder and pulling me in. I bury my nose in his clothes. I take a deep inhale one more time before I no longer can. "What have we done ..." he trails off, resting his chin on my head.

The tightening in my stomach caused my words to pinch. "I don't know."

"This was all for show, wasn't it?"

Jack's question vibrates through my bones, making me doubt everything. It started that way, but is it still for show? Was it fake when he comforted me? When we laughed together when we made love? "I don't know."

"What does that mean you *don't know*?" he asks with an

infliction in his tone.

My arms are tightly around his torso. "It means exactly what it's supposed to mean, that I don't know!" I squeeze harder, nuzzling myself into the fabric of his hoodie, desperately shielding myself from the world.

"We both knew this was coming," he reassures me, but it doesn't help because it feels impossible to be away from him right now.

"It doesn't make it any easier."

Jack's shoulders straighten, and he lifts his chin from the top of my head. "We've spent a lot of time together, and naturally, it will feel lonely for a while. But you'll go back to your regular life, and everything will return to normal."

I nod, agreeing on the outside but shouting with disagreement on the inside.

"You're going to miss your flight." He gently releases me. His arms fall to his sides before he quickly shoves them into the front pocket of his sweatshirt.

As panic pricks at my skin, the hair on the back of my neck stands straight up. I don't want to say goodbye. The mere action of separating myself from him feels unimaginable. The independent life I once coveted is shattered because nothing is as important as being with him.

I scour the airport in a panic, hunting for the strength to admit what I'm feeling, to acknowledge it, and give it the breath of life.

"You're right." I take a few steps back despite the energy tethering me to him and despite my heart screaming for something else. If he wanted more, wouldn't he admit it?

Wouldn't he want to spend a few more days with me?

Jack rubs his lips together and begins building an entire universe between us. "Goodbye. I'm sure we'll be in touch."

My leg bounces in place a few times before I reluctantly turn away and head toward the elevator. I fight the temptation to turn around again, refusing to inflict more pain on myself.

As I enter the small, suffocating space, my heart is in my throat, and my stomach twists in knots.

Awkwardly facing the wall, I wait until I hear the clang of the automatic doors close before I let all the air leave my lungs. Uncontrollably, my body lunges forward, and I fall to my knees. As soon as I meet the hard, unforgiving floor, a desperate wail forces itself from the back of my throat. Crying harder than I have in longer than I can remember, I let the tears plummet downward while my brain scrambles to put together the puzzle of emotions. *How do I move on?*

The bell dings, indicating that I've arrived on the correct floor. I quickly lift off the ground, wipe the tears from my eyes, and inhale deeply. Clutching the handle of my suitcase, a hard lump forms in my throat, and I force myself to begin the long walk to my terminal.

Chapter Thirty-One

I punch the gas, racing to get onto the freeway and as far away from the airport as I can. It was fucking impossible to let Piper go.

When I woke up in the morning, I felt sick to my stomach. I knew we'd either have to acknowledge or avoid what was happening between us, and we chose to do the latter. Despite the palpable sadness and hopelessness, Piper and I said goodbye to each other.

How can I have a future with a woman who lives in another state? Her career and life are in Arizona—where mine used to be. *Fuck!* Without realizing it, we were both working toward creating a permanent space between us. I'm bound to Dupara County, and I can do nothing about it. Even if we were to approach the idea of long distance, when would it end? What would we be working toward?

I could never ask her to give up her career to move to Dupara with me. The thought of that is terrifying. What if she hates it? Or if she wants to move back but has already given up her career? These questions kept me up the entire night.

When I joined Piper in the shower this morning, fully

aware that this would be our last together, it was painful and heartbreaking. I shut down and reverted to myself and created a painful distance. I got into my head, trying to sort through my emotions while not wanting to face hers. I know it hurt her, and it hurt me even more knowing I was doing it. There was a part of me that hoped if I acted withdrawn, it might also help her with our goodbye.

I white knuckle the steering wheel, frustrated with this entire situation.

Piper thinks I was at my laptop working while she packed, but I was emailing Tom to let him know to move forward with the divorce papers. If I didn't do it then, I may never have. And the check I had with me since I came home after Vegas. I wanted to ensure I had it ready in case things became too much for her or if she changed her mind about the whole thing. I had every intention of still paying her no matter how long she stayed.

I wish I had the chance to tell Piper about my conversation with Roxy and how I agreed to give her mother a large amount of money so she wouldn't have to ask Piper anymore. I also made sure Roxy knew that if she needed anything else financially in the future, she would come to me before asking her daughter whether we were together or not. I still feel uneasy about my choice to do this without Piper's knowledge. Still, I would do anything for her. If this can alleviate the emotional stress that Roxy causes, possibly improving the relationship with her mother, then I'd do it again in a fucking heartbeat.

While driving back to Wine Country at full speed, my stomach twists as a memory bombards me.

I'm leaning against the counter with my credit card in hand.

"Piper?" I repeat her name to grab her attention.

She flips her hair around to face me. "Hmm?"

Even under my semi-blurry gaze, she's absolutely stunning. "Would we like to write our own vows or use theirs?"

"Write our own!" she excitedly replies. We've only just met and barely know each other—so this seems like an obvious choice.

"You got it," I say, smiling at her from across the outdated lobby of the Tiny White Wedding House.

I should be second-guessing this decision or even getting hit with an immediate sense of fear about marrying a woman who I've only spent less than twenty-four hours with, but I don't. Strangely, there are no signs of doubt, only assurance.

While waiting, I see a couple emerge from behind a set of double doors. The man, dressed in a cowboy hat and boots, could barely keep his hands off the tall brunette in a sequined black dress and clear high heels. They laugh together as they hurry right for the chapel, slamming the doors behind them.

A laugh bubbles in my throat as I take the spot next to Piper on the velvet couch. "This small piece of paper is all we get to declare our love and undying devotion to each other," I say, handing her a clipboard with a lined paper on it that looks no bigger than an index card. "So, try to keep it short."

She gives a smooth and adorable giggle as she reaches her arm out to grab one of the blue pens from the diamond-covered holder in front of us. "I'll try."

Piper and I lay back on either side of the couch. We periodically smirked at each other from over the top of our clipboards.

I blink away a small tear as it drops from my eye. I look down to see the wet droplet, which has made a wet circle on the denim of my pants.

Fuck, this hurts.

I take my finger and aggressively tap the touch screen to the right of the steering wheel. As music seeps through the speakers, I flick the volume up. Blasting "Days Go By" by Dirty Vegas, I drown out the memories of our wedding night. A night that changed my entire life. A night that made me rethink so many things that I believed up until then.

"I understand you two have opted to write your own vows." The officiant turns away from the fiercely beautiful woman standing before me. "Jack, would you like to go first?"

I don't have to bring up my notecard to remember what I've written, because even in my inebriated state, I know it by heart.

I nod, then clear my throat. "You are captivating and utterly beautiful."

"So, vows are more like a promise. They usually begin with words 'I promise to'—" The other person in the room with absolutely no meaning to me begins to say, but my eyes remain locked on Piper and hers on mine.

Both of us ignore his comments. Piper begins to recite the vow she wrote.

"You are magnetic and addicting," she tells me without glancing at her notecard and without hesitation.

"Okay, those are fine too." He rests his hands on his oversized belt buckle. "Here at the Tiny White Wedding House, we believe that all unions should reflect the couple's own personal tastes," he drags on, sounding more like muffled noises than real words.

I can't stop staring at the woman standing in front of me, and I can't wait to get her upstairs and into the penthouse suite I booked.

My mind is slightly foggy about what tower it's in, but I'm sure we'll find it.

I affectionately smile at this flashback, even though my heart shatters into a million pieces. Piper and I had no idea what we wrote down wasn't vows. But it didn't matter and still doesn't matter because she is captivating and beautiful.

My dick was fighting with the zipper of my pants the entire ceremony. Too bad, I barely remembered getting back to the room that night. And if it hadn't been for us both waking up the next morning fully dressed with the bed still made, I would have been convinced that we had fucked.

Looking back now, I'm grateful we didn't. I would have wanted to remember every moment of it now that I know what it's like to be with her.

Before I realize it, I'm already pulling up to the outside of our villa. I turn the car off and stare at the brown door in front of me. Letting my head fall against the back of the seat, I rub my hands down my face. *I need to get my shit together.* I sit in the driver's seat for a few minutes before summoning the courage to leave.

"Piper, you are going to hurt yourself. Get down!" I call her as she dances on top of a small table to "Rock the Casbah," the remix from the Solar Twins. An industrial lamp hangs low and slowly sways under the breeze from the air vent above.

"Excuse me, miss, you can't stand on the tables here," a man in a tan uniform tells Piper. "If you're looking for a club, try the third level."

"I'm so sorry," I apologize on Piper's behalf, then lift my arms toward her, and she lowers herself into them.

Then she smiles at the man. "I really like that version of the song, though."

I laugh, still holding her against me. "I will play it on my phone later for you. How does that sound?"

Her eyes glow brightly. "I would love that. Thank you."

I lumber up the two small steps to the front door. Opening it, I'm hit with the powerful scent of lavender.

Piper.

My wife.

I never really thought about getting married. I thought I would one day, but having a wife has been one of the furthest things from my mind.

I walk down the hallway, past the kitchen, and into the bedroom. Everything is exactly where we left it. Other than her smell, it's almost like she was never here. Like all of this was a dream, she vanished as quickly as she came.

I glance over to the side of the bed she slept on and remember lying awake last night, staring at the rotating ceiling fan and listening to the delicate hums of her sleep. Another tear falls, and I quickly swipe it away, lowering myself onto the bed.

I love watching her while she sleeps. She's so blissfully unaware of how beautiful she is, and it guts me knowing I will no longer be experiencing it.

What the fuck am I doing?

Popping back up to a stand, it suddenly hits me like a wave crashing into my existence. Since I met her, it's felt like she's been the only thing in my life that I understand—*that understands me.* I want to be with her. I don't want to live without her. I'm entirely in love with her. I'm in love with every single fucking thing about that woman.

Why am I letting her go? I can't let her go.

The hairs on my neck stand up as I move around this space without Piper here. Pacing back and forth, my mind is frantic with the possibilities of what to do with this information when a small piece of white folded-up paper on the nightstand catches my eye. I snatch the paper and immediately open it. To my surprise, it's the check I gave her this morning. The money I owed her for being my *fake* girlfriend. She didn't take it.

My legs buckle underneath me, and I fall back to a sitting position on the edge of the bed. *She didn't take the goddamn money.*

She loves me too.

I'm not going to let her go.

It's abundantly clear what I must do. I need to tell Piper how I feel. I need to tell her I'm in love with her and that I'm sorry for letting her go. I never should have allowed her to get on that plane without telling her how I felt first. There are so many things left unsaid.

I bolt out of the room and down the hall, ultimately leaving the check floating in midair from the abrupt mad dash out of the villa and to my car.

I'm going to get my wife.

Chapter Thirty-Two

The longest, most excruciating flight I've ever been on—and that says a lot, considering I fly for a living. I pulled my hoodie over my head, tucked myself into the window seat, and refused to make eye contact with anyone on the flight. Once the plane landed and I grabbed my luggage, I made a beeline out of the airport, fearing running into someone I knew.

Now I stand here, eyes glossed over and a lump in my throat. Scanning every inch of my high-rise downtown Scottsdale apartment, the place I was so proud to afford and call my own. I'm unsure of who the woman who used to live here was.

I've never let a guy get to me this bad, but something about Jack is different from anyone I've ever met. This undeniable intensity and chemistry that I have with him almost act as an invisible rope pulling me in.

I glance at my plants, grateful they haven't withered away yet. Lina has been stopping by to water them while I've been in California. I drag my feet along the hardwood floors, feeling weighted and lethargic. Rolling my luggage away from the door and still with my backpack on, I head into the kitchen and crack open a bottle of white wine that's been on my counter for weeks.

Deciding not to make an effort to grab a glass from the cupboard above my head, I lift the bottle to my lips and gulp down a big swig. I'm not fazed by its barely tolerable lukewarm temperature.

The door buzzer goes off, breaking my spiral of sadness.

I flip on the intercom. "Hello."

"I have a package here for a—Piper Bradley. It requires a signature."

Of course. I rest my forehead on the wall next to the speaker and let out a heavy sigh. "Be right down."

I see a man standing in a brown uniform when I get to the main lobby.

"I have a package for a—Piper Bradley," he repeats, glancing down at the box in his hand.

I shouldn't get used to hearing that name because soon it won't be mine anymore. "Yes, that's me."

Without looking up, he hands me an electronic clipboard. "Sign here."

I blankly stare at the signature line in front of me, thinking about how to sign a name that I've never written before. That's not completely true. I had to write Piper Bradley on our marriage certificate. I squeeze my eyes shut, remembering what the penmanship looked like, and then I grip the stylus for a moment before signing.

"Thanks. Have a good day." He hands me the small box and then quickly leaves the building.

Staring down at the brown square package no larger than the palm of my hand, I already know that Jack is the only person who would address me with his last name. My pulse races the entire way back up to my apartment.

As soon as the door latches behind me, I head right for the kitchen to grab a pair of scissors from the drawer. Placing the box on top of the counter, I cut along the tape line until the two flaps pop up. Inside, I find a mound of packing peanuts, but only when I push them aside do I find what's hidden beneath.

I carefully remove a small, black velvet box. I hold my breath in anticipation of what's concealed inside. It sends my mind into a frenzy. Pinching it between my thumbs, I lift the lid to find a yellow-gold crescent moon necklace with a tiny diamond embedded directly in the middle.

"Goddammit, Jack!" I scream at the top of my lungs, tears pouring from my eyes. This necklace is the same one my grandmother gave me before she died. Through blurred vision, my fingers pry the jewelry from the box. *What the actual fuck?*

"How the hell am I supposed to believe this was all just pretend at this point!" I shout into space. From the side of my eye, I catch sight of a tiny piece of pink stationery. I lift it off the table and hold it up to read it.

Mrs. Bradley,

I know this isn't the original piece from your grandmother, and if I could replace it for you, I would, but I do hope this one brings you some joy anyway.

Love,

Mr. Bradley

It had been all a fever dream that I was never meant to wake up from. But I did. The vibrant colors and aliveness that came with it are now erased—vanished into my mind's hidden crevices, which now only live in my memory. A man who has taught me to live, breathe, and love.

I need some time to myself. I don't have the energy to leave my apartment. I swipe my phone from the table next to me and bring up our group chat.

> Me: Hey ladies, I'm not feeling up to going out tonight. Have fun, and I'll see you all in the air.

Bailey texts back almost immediately.

> Bailey: What? Is everything okay?

Always the mom in the group.

> Me: I'm fine. I think I need some time by myself. Don't worry, everything is fine.

> Lina: Obviously, we're going to worry. You always talk to us. Are you sure you're alright?

My brain is swirling. I need time alone to clear it. Figure out how I'm feeling, why I'm feeling this way, and how I'm going to move past it.

> Avery: I haven't gotten to the restaurant yet, be at your apartment in 5.

> Bailey: You can't bail on us and not tell us what's wrong.

> Lina: Bailey and I are leaving The Poppy now, will be over there in less than ten.

I decide not to respond. I'll speak with my friends when they get here. I'm grateful for them, but how am I supposed to explain what has happened between Jack and me? They won't understand. I can barely make sense of it all.

Heading back into the kitchen, I grab the bottle of wine, put it up to my lips, and take another big gulp.

While I wait for the three of them to arrive, I start to unpack my suitcase. As soon as I lift the top, my eyes fall to Jack's dark gray hoodie. A wave of nausea hits, clenching my stomach. I instantly climb to my feet and bolt into the other room. *I can't do this.* It's not like we're a long-distance couple with the hope that someday I'll get used to the back and forth.

Jack and I are over, and the finality of it rips at my soul.

The building buzzer goes off once again. Bailey, Lina, and Avery must be here. I buzz them in without answering and then wait by the door until they reach my floor.

"What's going on?" Avery storms in before I have a chance to open the door all the way.

Bailey and Lina are following quickly behind her.

"Are you alright?" Lina opens her arms. I sink into them. Feeling a soft hand rubbing my back, my eyes start to fill with tears.

"What happened?" Bailey asks, taking a seat on my couch next to Avery.

I pull back from Lina. She keeps her arm around me and leads me to the soft chair in the corner of the room. When she releases me, she squeezes herself between Bailey and Avery on the couch.

I bury my head in my hands and begin to speak. "Jack and I are done with everything we needed to do." I lift my face upward, avoiding eye contact with them. "He—um, gave me a check this morning for the amount he promised, but I couldn't take it."

"You don't want it to be over?" Lina asks.

I shake my head.

Avery rests her chin in her palm. "Did you tell him that?"

Frowning, I shake my head again.

"You're having a hard time with this. Do you know how he is feeling?" Bailey asks, keeping her voice low.

"It seemed like he was struggling too. How we were and what we were—you can't fake that."

"Wow." Bailey's eyes are wide. "How much happened between the two of you?"

I tuck a tear-soaked piece of hair behind my ear. "A lot."

Avery nibbles on her bottom lip. "Was it fake to you?"

"It was, I think," I say.

Lina clasps her hands in her lap. "But you did marry him the first time you met him, so there has to be something said about that."

My chin quivers as I pick up where I left off. "You guys didn't see how he looked at me. And when we made love, how intimate and perfect it was doesn't feel like something that can be faked."

"Maybe it wasn't?" Lina suggests, her eyebrows pinched together.

"But it was because why would he let me go?" I plead with her, but the question is more for myself.

"I'm not sure." Bailey sighs, shaking her head. "Maybe the same reason *you* got on that plane this morning?"

"I agree with Bailey. He could be just as conflicted as you are," Avery says.

I nod. "Maybe. I could tell he was getting emotional when he was in the shower with me this morning, but he suddenly shut down."

"Shit, babe, I had no idea how intimate it got between you guys. Sleeping together—showering together. Sex is just sex, but you used the words *making love.*" Lina crosses her arms at her chest. "Damn, this sucks."

"There's nothing left of us. It was all a lie. The snuggling, the laughing, the forehead kisses, the conversations we shared—" I suck in a breath. "And now it's all gone." My lower lip trembles as I speak. Lina gets off the couch and wraps her arms around me while my head hangs low between my legs. "Why does being away from him make my soul feel so bad?"

Bailey tilts her head toward me, her face suddenly softening. "Are you in love with him?"

I rub my lips together, biting back the sobs that bang on my chest. I haven't heard it said out loud, and until this moment, it's been an abstract thought that keeps resurfacing. "Yes. I'm so in love with Jack with every single part of me."

Avery's mouth drops with a gasp. "Sweetie. Oh my god."

Lina stares up at me from bent knees next to my chair. Her eyes gloss over. "Piper Moon."

Tears sting the back of my eyes. "I don't want to be without him."

Avery sniffs, places her hand over mine, and squeezes gently. "Oh, honey. Does he know?"

I shake my head. "I don't think so."

"You need to tell him." Bailey's nasally tone is firm.

"I know, but how would we even work? He's there, and I'm

here," I stammer.

"That's just geography, babe." Lina smiles, her eyes shiny with moisture. "If he feels the same, you guys will make it work."

Bailey rubs her hand over my leg in a soothing motion. "Lina's right, you have to make that shit happen."

"True love is not fleeting. It's concrete," Avery whispers, wiping my sticky face. "You said it yourself that you were drawn to him the minute you saw him at that airport in Vegas."

Lina gives me a half-smile. "Our combined experience with men has shown us that feelings like this don't happen often, if ever."

Avery nods in agreement. "Yeah, if the four of us were to add up the number of m—"

"Okay, okay." Lina's hand flies into the air. "Let's not start adding up the men we've been with."

Avery turns back to me, rolling her eyes at Lina. "The point I was trying to make is even though we all know Lina as had more experience than all of us"—she lowers her eyes in Lina's direction—"we can confidently say that this type of undeniable bond literally never happens." She sticks her finger in the air at Bailey's direction. "We don't need your two cents and your soulmate lecture about your brother's best friend. My point remains."

They're right. Everything that my best friends are saying is correct. This level of feeling doesn't happen often. I can't let this go without telling him how I feel. "How fast can we get me on a flight?" My voice comes out rough as I pop up from my chair.

Bailey quickly looks at Avery, but Avery's eyes are on Lina. "Just because my dad is a captain doesn't mean he can perform miracles," she says, "Just kidding. Of course, he can! I'll call him right now." Lina hopped off the floor and headed into my bedroom with her phone in her hands.

"Yes!" Bailey cheers with her eyes wide.

"You're going to do this, and you're going to be brave. Now where is your suitcase? Do we need to pack anything for you?" Avery adds.

I blink rapidly. "Yes, everything is dirty. I need all new clean clothes."

Lina comes barreling out of the bedroom. "We don't have time for that, ladies. She's going to be on a flight in forty-five minutes."

My heart is pounding in my chest. With the help of my best friends, I'm going after the man I love—who hopefully loves me too.

"Bring it in, ladies." Avery hooks me around the neck with one hand and Bailey with the other. Lina squeezes into our group, hugging us between Bailey and me. I take a moment to feel all the love that radiates off these three women.

"Okay, enough with the mushy stuff, we got to get you on that plane!" Lina exclaims, pulling away from our embrace.

"Let me run to the restroom quickly," I say.

Bailey exhales with annoyance. "Fine. Just hurry."

Taking a minute to collect myself and my thoughts, I turn on the sink and splash cold water on my face. It instantly calms me, practically resetting my nerves. I wipe my face with a hand towel before finding my reflection in the mirror. "You can do this," I whisper to myself.

I briskly walk out of the bathroom and into the hallway

to find Avery shoving clothes into my luggage. "What are you doing?"

"Oh, I switched out some of your dirty clothes for clean ones and slipped in a few pieces of hot pink lingerie," she says with a devious smile, visibly proud of herself.

Shoving me out the door, I quickly turn around. "Who's going to water my plants?"

"I will," Lina says, shoving her key into the lock. "We're all driving together. Then, after we drop you off, we'll take Avery back here to get her car." She turns to Bailey. "Finally, I'll drop you off at *The Poppy*."

"Fabulous. Now, let's get this woman her man. Wait. Are you and Jack still married?"

Bailey asks, hitting the down arrow on the elevator.

I squeeze my eyes shut. "Yes."

"Only you," Avery teases, nudging my shoulder. "And that's why we love you so much."

A bashful smile crawls across me while Lina and Bailey laugh.

We get to the airport in less than twenty minutes. Lina haphazardly pulls up to the passenger drop-off. I twist my body from the front seat to see Avery and Bailey's puffy eyes in the backseat and Lina's in the driver's seat to my left.

"Tell that '90s heartthrob of a man how you really feel. And don't come back to Phoenix without a husband," Bailey's voice cracks as she fights back tears.

Avery grabs my hand, giving it a little squeeze. "Keep us updated, or we'll stalk you."

Tears fill my eyes. "Thank you, and I love the three of you so much."

Lina leans over the center console to give me a full-body hug. "I emailed you all your information. You will be good to go, babe."

Stepping out of Lina's jeep, I feel light, confident, and ready to give Jack more of myself than I already have. I stop in front of the automatic doors and wave at them as they drive away. Then, I head right for the escalators that lead to the third-floor terminals.

Chapter Thirty-Three

My shoes squeak as I run in a full sprint through the airport in Phoenix. Adrenaline is pumping through my veins, and my heart hammers against my rib cage from what I'm about to do. The embers from the fire in Piper have caught me, and now I'm burning with impulsivity. Those same flames convinced me to marry her the day I spoke with her for the first time.

From the corner of my eyes, I see strange looks from people as they quickly move to the side, clearing a path for me to slip through. "Excuse me," I quickly say as I pass them.

They assume I have poor time management and am late for a flight. But that could not be further from the truth. I need to tell Piper right now that I'm completely in love with her and that I have no intention of living my life without her. My chest is tight with anticipation and excitement as I pass the tiled pillars right out of security and into the waiting area of one of the gates.

"Excuse me!" I call out again as I run empty-handed toward the escalators that lead down to the lower level. I take a sharp left, attempting to squeeze past a family of six, each rolling large carry-ons behind them. I abruptly stop. Out of breath, I take a step back, allowing them to pass in front of me.

Anxiously standing to the side, my eyes move around the place, casually jumping from person to person. Then, at the bottom of the ascending escalator, parallel to the one I'm standing at the top of, my heart stops, forcing me to take a breath. To my surprise, my gaze lands on the only thing that matters in my world. A five foot four fiery, strawberry blonde woman dressed in the same thing I dropped her off at the airport this morning.

Piper.

The family passes, and I finally have a chance to get on, but my muscles are frozen in place while I stare down at my beautiful wife. *Why is she here?* She doesn't have to report for work until Wednesday.

I move slowly, taking a calculated step onto the escalator, feeling calm and secure. Everything around me is muted, including the intercom above, the passengers chatting in the distance, and the zipping of suitcases across the marble floor. I almost reach the bottom of the stairs when a pair of beautiful hazel-green eyes spot mine.

Piper's eyes widen, and I watch the color drain from her face. I can only smile as I descend to her.

"Jack?"

"My love," I mutter, lifting her by the hips and scooping her into my arms. Piper's body melts into mine. Her weight against my chest makes me feel completely whole once again. *Euphoria.*

"Oh my god. What are you doing here?" she asks, her legs wrapping around my waist.

I squeeze her tighter than ever, looking directly into her

hazel-green eyes. "I'm here for my wife."

"What?" her voice squeaks in disbelief.

"I'm not going to live without you. And I refuse to spend another hour of our lives without you knowing how much I'm in love with you." I cup her damp cheeks and wipe away a tear with my thumb.

"You came back for me?"

"I had to."

Caught up in the heat of the moment, I realize that running into her at the airport was completely unexpected since she doesn't start work until closer to the middle of the week.

"What are you doing here? I thought you said you didn't have to report back for a few more days."

Piper lifts her head to face me but lowers her lashes. "I was going back to my—husband."

"You were coming back to Dupara?" I heard every word, but I asked again for reassurance.

She nods. "Yes. Because you are my person and I refuse to exist without you either."

My jaw twitches in shock, and I'm speechless. I bring my lips to hers, lightly kissing them before pulling away. "You don't ever have to."

Piper tucks her face into the crook of my neck. "I can't believe you're here."

Holding her, I smile at the subtle lavender scent of her hair. "I'm glad we didn't miss each other."

"This is real, isn't it?" she asks, staring into my eyes. "All of it?"

"You asked me once if I regret leaving Dupara all those years ago, and I didn't have an answer then, but I do now." I watch another tear fall from her eye. "No, I don't regret that decision because if I'd never left, I never would have met Harry and Mason in college. And ultimately, my connection to them has led me to you. With everything I've got, every decision I've made up until this point in my life, it has put me on the path to you."

She lets out a small sigh and crinkles her eyebrows while both eyes bounce between mine.

"If I could, I would go back to that night we got married in Vegas and live inside every single second. I would listen to each one of your tiny breaths, savoring every minute of it because my entire life began at that moment, and I had no idea. You are the air that I breathe and the energy in my veins. My utter existence is you."

Piper dips her head down and nuzzles my nose before sliding down to plant her feet on the floor. Her dainty hands find mine that are hanging down between us. "I am so in love with you too. I have been since I saw you walk past me at that airport in Las Vegas. You captured my body and soul, and I refuse to take them back. They are yours, Mr. Bradley."

My heart stills, taking in every word she's saying. There was something undeniable between us, and finally, admitting it feels *liberating*. I exhale deeply, grab the back of her head, and clash my mouth into hers. My kiss isn't as sweet as it was a second ago. It's ravenous.

A tight murmur slips out before I hear her sweet voice. "I love you."

"I love you," I say into the softness of her bottom lip.

I love Piper with everything I have and hearing her feel the same is the most indescribable feeling I have ever experienced. Finding your best friend and soulmate in the same person is a rarity that I will not let slip away.

As we both stand in the middle of an airport in the city that I escaped to so many years ago, running from a life already charted for me, I will now be returning to the place I desperately ran from. But this time, I'm leaving this city eager to start a new yet familiar life back in Dupara, another thing I never thought I'd do.

She slowly pulls away, leaving me pining for more. "And you flew all the way out here to tell me this?"

"Absolutely."

She smiles brightly.

Placing two fingers under her chin, I raise my wife's face to mine and kiss her softly once again.

"Let's go back to my place," she says, threading her fingers through my hair.

"I want to do nothing else besides get buried inside you for the rest of my life." I reach into the front pocket of my jeans. "Oh, and I almost forgot," I say, carefully pulling out a rolled-up straw wrapper.

Piper covers her mouth in shock. "You still have it."

I smile, grab one of her hands, and place the delicate circular-shaped piece of paper onto her ring finger. "I promise to give you a real one very soon."

She stares down at the paper ring, then looks up at me with the flame in her eyes that I love so much. "Does this mean we won't be getting a divorce?"

I shake my head. "Not a chance."

"Good, because you'd never be able to get rid of me that easily."

"I'm never going to." I interlace my fingers through hers.

"Lina, Bailey, and Avery dropped me off, so we'll have to take a rideshare back to my apartment."

"You should probably tell them you're not getting on the flight, so they're not worried, and I'll order the ride from my phone," I tell her.

Piper pulls out her phone from the pocket of her cross bag and then peers behind my shoulder. "Where's your suitcase?"

"I didn't bring one."

"Were you not planning on staying?"

"I was. I didn't think that far ahead. When I walked back into our bedroom at the villas, I realized I didn't want to be there without you. I returned as quickly as possible and hopped on the first flight out."

"You can be quite impetuous, you know that?"

I arch an eyebrow. "Me? You're the one who married a guy on the first date—in Vegas and drunk, I might add."

Piper hangs off my shoulder as we walk. "I guess we both are."

Twenty minutes later, we're going through the door of Piper's apartment.

I glance around the space while I wheel her luggage across the hardwood floors, setting it next to the corner of the wall.

It looks exactly how I thought it would be. Natural tones of green, brown, and beige, a couple of snake and spider plants are scattered throughout the room, and a large tapestry with the moon phases printed on it hangs on the far wall behind the couch.

"This is my place," she says, opening the blinds.

"It looks like my wife."

Piper grabs the flaps of my jacket, yanking me into her. "I love it when you call me that."

"I love saying it," I reply, darting out my tongue to lick the tip of her nose. At the same time, she tilts her head up and tries to capture my tongue into her mouth but misses. I do it again, bringing out a belly laugh from us both. I wrap my arms around the back of Piper's neck, folding them over her shoulder blades.

"I see you got the necklace." I glance down to where it hangs perfectly around her neck.

"I did," she says, rolling it between her two fingers. "I can't thank you enough for it."

"I wanted to do it." I glide my lips across the outside of her ear. I spot two more plants peeking out behind the couch in the corner of the room.

She sees me staring, slowly turns toward my line of sight, and shrugs her shoulders. "They keep the air clean."

I smile, appreciating everything about her. "Whatever you say."

"I'm going to shower really quick."

"Without me?"

She playfully frowns. "Never."

"I thought so. I'll be right in. I'm going to grab a glass of water."

"Don't make me wait too long," she replies, lifting her shirt over her head and disappearing down the short hallway.

I walk into the kitchen and open two cupboards before finding the correct one with the cups. The shower runs in the background, causing excitement to flood me.

While holding my glass under the spout in the refrigerator door, my eyes scan the polaroids that hang across the stainless steel. In almost every photo is Piper with three other women. I recognize one as Bailey, and I'm assuming Avery and Lina are the other two. With what she shared about her mother and home life, I'm grateful she has such a strong support system with them.

Then, my focus lands on one with Piper, Bailey, and Bailey's son Luca. I know it's him because I remember seeing him walk down the aisle as the ring bearer at Harry's wedding. Piper and Bailey have her son sandwiched between them in a tight hug, and they all have blue party hats on. I love seeing that smile on her face—I wonder if she'd ever want kids. I mean, we're already married, so why not?

Circling over to the other side, I find a dry-erase calendar with dates and notes written in black marker. The notes include things like *Dinner with the Girls, Work Week, Pay Roxy's rent,* and *Jack's Week*—that one brings a smile to my face. When my brain catches up to the words I've read, my jaw flexes—*Pay Roxy's rent.* Has Piper been paying her mother's rent as well as giving her money?

My blood boils, even though I know I handled this for her already—which she doesn't know exactly how, and I will tell her at some point. It's time she realized that she needs to put herself first. Not her mother. She's my wife. Hopefully, the future mother of my children, and she deserves the world.

I run my thumb across the dry-erase marker, wiping the words from the calendar. Piper will not be alone when fighting this battle. And with that, I stalk into the bathroom, ready to make love to my beautiful wife. Steam seeps out from the small crack in the door. I push it open with the palm of my hand.

"Took you long enough." She smirks. That's my spunky girl.

I pull my shirt off and drop my pants and boxers. "Sorry, I got caught up looking at the pictures of you and your friends on the refrigerator."

I pull the curtain back to see Piper's wet, glistening skin under the water. *I can't believe I almost had to say goodbye to this.* Stepping in, I immediately pull her into me, savoring her warm, familiar body against me.

And she is all mine.

"I loved seeing those pictures of you." I rub my thumb across her bottom lip. "Your smile is the most perfect thing in the world, and I will do everything in my power, Piper, to make sure you smile every day for the rest of your life."

She stares up at me from her wet eyelashes, water droplets forcing her to blink a few times. "How did I get so lucky to deserve you?"

"You deserve the world, my love. All of it." I softly kiss her slippery lips. "I also saw something concerning your calendar."

"What was that?"

I clear my throat. "Do you pay Roxy's rent?"

Piper dips her head, resting her forehead on my chest without answering my question.

"You shouldn't be doing that. Your mother is perfectly capable of paying for her own bills."

"I know. But you don't know the type of guilt trips she puts on me. The things she says to me and how she makes me feel. It's difficult for me to say no to her."

"I know how she speaks to you, and it won't happen anymore. A mother's love should never be conditional. You are strong, independent, and smart. You have the power to establish boundaries with her."

"I hear you, but the bad stuff is always easier to believe."

"You will no longer have to fight this battle alone. I will be here with you, and together, we'll come up with ways that you can still have a relationship with her but with healthy boundaries." I wipe the water from Piper's face. "There's this fire in you that I love so much. And if you don't stop letting other people win, it will go out."

After the shower, Piper and I cuddle into her bed. Since I have no clothes here, we both lie naked, tangled in each other's limbs and the bed sheets. She's on her side with my body draped over hers. My cheek rests on her temple, and my lips gently glide along the sweet skin on her neck. "I want you to move to Dupara with me."

Her breath stills. "What?"

"I want you to move to Dupara with me." I keep my lips in a hard line despite my muscles fighting a smile. She needs to understand how serious I am about this. I'm not lost in lust, and I'm not making this decision without a clear head—there's no doubt in my mind that she is for me.

"You don't think this is too soon?"

I tighten the arm that's securely around her body, pulling her even closer. "No."

Piper draws her head back, capturing my mouth with hers. "Wow," she mumbles into my lips before releasing me. "This is crazy, you know that?"

"Yes, I do. But that's why I trust it."

Her shoulders rise with a deep inhale. "There are so many things I'd have to get sorted out with work—and the girls are going to freak out, but yes, of course I will!"

Chapter Thirty-Four

I sit on my balcony, enjoying the warm fall weather. I think about giving up my high-rise. I have so many memories here. It's given me more security in the past six years than my entire life. Jack will stay with me for the next few days while we organize my move to Dupara. He went out to grab a few things to wear while he was here since he had no luggage.

Waking up with Jack this morning was heaven. The feelings of optimism and excitement rolled through my entire body. *Can this be it?* Have I found someone who cares for me as much as I care for them? I smile at thoughts of a future with him. But my happiness is quickly ripped away when Roxy's words push their way in like they always do, with that gnawing reminder that no one will ever love me.

I battle with my emotions for a moment. This uneasy feeling of being content. It's foreign. I must prepare for him to leave, for the impending doom that will find me once my guard is down. But what if he doesn't go? What if my story is different from my mother's? What if those beliefs and words are not mine?

I haven't heard from Roxy in a while, and it's oddly unsettling. I glance at my phone laying on the couch next to me. Fidgeting with the strings on my hoodie, I mentally prepare to call her. She is my mother, and I should check on her. My stomach turns with apprehension, not knowing what side of her I'll get today.

"What's up?" She answers the phone with a clipped tone. After not speaking with her for the last week and a half, this isn't the reaction I was expecting.

"I haven't spoken to you in a while, and I was calling to check in," I say, a little unsure.

"I'm fine. Everything is good to go."

Something is off with her attitude, and I can't place it. I pace in the small space between the balcony doors and the couch, walking in and out through the door. "What do you mean, *good to go?*"

"I mean, ever since your husband gave me that check, I've been great." She casually lets it slip like she believes that I'm aware.

My blood runs cold. My limbs lock into place. *What did she say?* "What?"

"Ugh. I'm in the mood to talk today. The check, you know."

"My husband? What check?" I scratch the top of my head with confusion. "Are you talking about Jack?"

"Yeah, the rich guy. Great job, my little Piper Moon. But I am a little pissed you didn't tell me you got married. But when I saw the amount he gave me—" She laughs, letting out that typical high-pitched shrill every time she feels on top of the world. It takes me back to when I was younger and struggled with something. She'd laugh at me and ask why I even tried in the first place. It sends chills up my spine. "Obviously, you were forgiven."

Lost in my unsettling memory, I quickly put the pieces together. Jack gave her money. "He gave you money? For what?"

"You know I don't like being told what to do, but everyone has their price, am I right?" There's that chuckle again. "And he wanted to pay me for everything I did for you growing up. He also said in exchange for taking the money, I would have to agree never to ask you for money again."

Oh my god. I take a few steps back until my heels hit the bottom of the couch. "How much did he give you?"

"I'm not telling you. But let's just say I won't need to work for a long ass time."

Feeling lightheaded, I bend to sit but miss the side of the couch and fall to the floor. My muscles stiffen from shock over what I'm hearing. "When did this happen?"

She clicks her tongue. "He called me like a week ago—"

"A week ago?" I gasp, still sitting on the floor.

"I don't remember! Maybe two weeks ago," she snaps.

I'm speechless. All sorts of emotions flood my mind. "Okay."

"I have to go, but make sure you get your own payout when he leaves you because don't you think about coming after mine."

The tips of my ears get hot, and everything around me becomes blurry. All I see is red. Jack loves me, and I trust our relationship. I'm tired of her ruining everything good in my life. I have to fight back against her voice inside of me. The repeated voice tells me I'm not good enough and that I'm only valued based on what I can give someone. My mother has never wanted the best for me, and she's never been in my corner. She's never loved me unconditionally, and I can't take it anymore. I don't deserve to live like this.

"Fuck you! Enjoy your sudden windfall and get the hell out of my life," I shout before hitting the end button to hang up on her. Seething, I throw the phone across the room.

"Whoa. You alright?" Jack asks, walking in the door with bags in his hands.

As soon as I hear his voice, tears spill from my eyes. I quickly turn to face him. "Did you pay off my mother?"

His posture falls, and then he sets his bag on the floor. "I did."

"Why?" Wrapping my arms around myself, I create some distance between us. I'm so confused.

Jack steps forward, attempting to close the divide, but stops to give me space. "Are you upset with me for doing it?"

"I—I don't know." I shake my head, stammering.

Jack's face is soft but stern. "I didn't want her to upset you anymore."

Fuck.

I don't answer. Jack comes closer, wearily bringing me into his arms, and I let him comfort me.

"I didn't want her to harass you about money. I told her that if she took what I was offering, she was agreeing to never ask you for a dime again," he tells me. As Jack speaks, I find myself conflicted. A part of me warms at the gesture, feeling grateful to have someone who might care that deeply for me, but the other side of me is overrun with panic.

Fuck.

Jack runs his hands through my hair. "I told her that if she wanted to be in your life, then it should be to uplift and support, not hurt or bring you down."

He doesn't know that I've had no contact with Roxy since he made that phone call, and I don't anticipate hearing from her anytime soon now that she has the thing she loves most in the world—money. "I don't know what's more painful, the fact that I feel somewhat relieved or the fact that she took it without a care in the world."

"I wish I could tell you that you're wrong, but she was happy with what I was offering."

Did Jack know he loved me then? Do people who love each other do these things without anything in return? Does he love me for who I truly am? My mouth twitches, trying to hold back the tears that fill my eyes. "Did you know that you loved me when you called her?"

He leans down, brushing my forehead with his soft lips. "I think I have for a while."

"Goddammit! I want to be mad at you for doing this without telling me, but at the same time, I appreciate it. Does that make me a bad person?"

"Absolutely not."

I give Jack a weak smile, but I fall into myself with relief behind it. "You can't always solve things by paying people off!"

"What do you mean?"

"Me, Steve, and Preston." I hook my fingers between the belt loops of his pants. "Roxy."

"Point taken. But money means nothing to me. Not when it comes to the people I love. I bought the winery from Steve for my mom and dad. I paid Roxy because I love you and tried to pay you because I was completely infatuated with you." Jack leans forward, his forehead misted. "More than seven billion souls on earth, and somehow I found you.”

The essence of another human intertwined around me is a thick and grounding experience. To be present in this moment, not wanting time to pass into the next minute, hour, or day, is exhilarating and breathtaking.

Jack's slick body wraps tightly around mine, so much so that I can't tell where I end and he begins. My lungs sync into his inhale rhythm, only allowing me to exhale when he does. This is what it's like when your soul finds its match in another.

He slips himself on top of me, caging me in with his broad shoulders. “Open your legs.”

I stare into his flaring eyes. Before I have a chance to move, he shifts one of his knees between my legs, spreading at the same time.

The corner of his mouth quirks up, making my stomach flutter. When he enters the wet heat of my core, chills span my body, and a shiver zips up my back. My head falls and a husky moan releases.

“I know you didn't take the money,” he says between breaths, lowering his hard chest on top of mine.

I bring my hands up to his face, my fingers feeling the light stubble of his five o'clock shadow. “I couldn't.”

“It's a lot of money.”

“I don't care.”

He stops his slow, deep thrusts, pinning me with his blue eyes. "I would have given you any amount you'd have asked for."

"I fell in love with you, and that's not something you can pay for."

Jack and I make love in my bed for the first time. We forget about the world around us, the logistics of me moving to Dupara, the fact that his house still isn't ready, and how I will tell my best friends that I'll be leaving them.

Existing with him in my space makes everything so real. I still hear my mother's words in my head, but I have to try with Jack. Life is short, and if I don't take a chance on love, am I really alive?

Later at night, I wake from a deep sleep to a cool, gentle breeze on my shoulder. Rolling over, I notice that the covers have fallen to my waist, and Jack isn't lying beside me. I notice a small light seeping through the bottom of the door to the bedroom. He must be in the kitchen. I lean over to turn on the lamp beside my bed, alerting him that I'm awake. I'm too tired to get up.

He walks back into the bedroom with an apple in hand.

"Midnight snack?" I sit up, taking the blanket with me.

"Always." He grins, taking a bite of a bright red apple. "I was thinking—"

"It's one in the morning. Seems like a good time to have meaningful thoughts," I say.

"That's what I do. You know that." He lowers himself onto the bed and scoots his back to lean against the headboard.

I crawl to him and rest my head on his lap. "That's my husband."

"That's only the second time I've heard you call me your husband." He smiles. "You should do it more."

"I will."

"So, when my dad passed away over the summer, I was looking to buy a home in Scottsdale," he picked up from our conversation from earlier.

I prop my chin in the palm of my hand, now more interested in what he's about to share. "Okay."

"What if we bought a house out here—together?" he suggests, with optimism in his voice.

"Buy a house here?" I arch a brow. "In Phoenix?"

"Or Scottsdale." Jack hands the apple to me from over the top of my head. I sink my teeth into it, then hand it back to him. "A condo would be great too. It's up to you. This way we can visit whenever we want. Northern California gets cold during the winter. It would be nice to fly here for those few months out of the year."

"You want to be snowbirds?" I tease.

He chuckles. "Exactly. And an added bonus is that you'll get to visit your friends anytime you want and have a place to stay."

I slide myself over Jack's straightened legs, straddling him. "I love you, and I think that's a brilliant idea."

"Yeah?" He sets the apple on the nightstand and grips my bare ass. I fall forward into his chest while a giggle slips out. Jack let out a full belly laugh, and it thunders through my ears.

I love that sound.

Epilogue
JACK

Six Months Later

I fell in love with Piper in a little over a month, and to many people, that doesn't seem like long enough to be unequivocally in love with another person, but it happened. Our love story didn't start as most do, but that speaks to the type of people we are.

Sitting in my father's old office, which I've officially taken over, I glance through the conjoined doors and into the bright, airy office, now home to countless vibrant green plants. I make eye contact with the beautiful, petite woman with a barely noticeable baby bump standing by the bay window while talking on the phone. I lean back in my chair with my elbow firmly on the armrest and my chin comfortably placed in the palm of my hand. Staring at my wife has become my favorite pastime.

Since I ran into Piper at the airport in Phoenix, we haven't spent a day apart. She notified the airline and was back up with me within a week. We still couldn't move into our new house for another three weeks, so we continued to stay comfortably at our villa, barely able to leave the bedroom. Those first three days together were a blur. I couldn't get enough of everything about her.

I tried to talk Piper out of resigning from the airline, but she insisted that the winery is a family business and that she wanted to be fully involved with her being a Bradley. To say that my mother was thrilled would be an understatement. She practically fell out of her chair when we told her that Piper would be joining me full-time—and then again when we said to her that Piper was pregnant.

A month after she moved here, my mom took a permanent step back from the winery. Piper was able to slip into her new role seamlessly. Together, they redesigned my mother's old office. The earthy tones and natural light look more like her anyway.

Piper catches me staring while she's on the phone and playfully sticks her tongue out. That's my wife. She has eagerly and naturally fallen into the position of Director of Human Resources, and I could not be prouder. The staff has not only welcomed me back but her as well. I stare at her as she paces the room until she eventually ends the call.

"That was Bailey." She beams, walking into my office from hers. "She said that she and Mason would rather stay with us than in a hotel."

"That's great. They'll be here a few days before Lina and Avery, right?" I ask.

Piper moves around the back of the desk, shifting herself between my bent legs. She smiles and lowers to sit on my knee. "Yes. I'm so excited to see them. We went from seeing each other every week to me not seeing them in over four months."

We decided to buy her high-rise in Scottsdale since the owners were looking to start liquidating some of the properties they own. It was impeccable timing, as it would have hit the market once her lease was up in January. The look on her face was pure joy when she knew it was hers. For now, she's decided to keep her furniture there—maybe she's still a bit sentimental about it.

My hands automatically find the tiny baby bump I've become completely obsessed with. I lightly caress her stomach. "I know."

She's only four months along and we finally told everyone this last week.

"Mason and Bailey arrive on Wednesday, and then Avery and Lina come on Friday evening," she says, looping an arm around my neck. "I'm so excited to show everyone around this beautiful place."

"It will be nice seeing them. Mason wants a crash course in winemaking, and Rob is looking forward to getting some free help." I laugh.

"I think Bailey and I are going shopping that morning. Then, we have a spa day planned that afternoon."

"I'm glad you're getting to spend time with them. And it will be our first time entertaining guests at the new house."

"I know. I'm looking forward to it," she says, leaning into me.

I sweep the loose hair away from in front of her face. "How's your morning sickness today?"

She grimaces and sits a little straighter on my lap. "The ginger candies that your mom suggested have helped a little. But water and saltine crackers seem to work the best."

"Whatever you need, my love." I kiss her sweet lips. She's had rough morning or all-day sickness the last couple of weeks.

"Thank you," she whispers into my mouth.

"I know I said this morning in the shower that I think the baby is a boy, but I'm leaning toward a girl now."

"We'll find out next week, right?"

"Yes. I'm so excited to start decorating the nursery," she says. "Me too."

"Well, hello, Mr. and Mrs. Bradley," Erin, Piper's new assistant, greets us as she enters my office from Piper's.

"Good morning, Erin," Piper greets her new assistant with a smile.

"I grabbed you a peppermint tea on the way in," she says, handing Piper a paper cup from over the top of my desk.

"That's wonderful. Much appreciated!" she says, still sitting on my lap. "We have a busy day today. Can you grab your laptop and meet me in my office in ten minutes?"

"Of course." Erin nods, turns on her heels, and sprints out of the room.

"I can make ten minutes work," I mumble, sliding my hand under her hair and leaving soft nibbles on her neck.

"Oh, Jack," she says, sinking into my arms. "Don't you have work to do?"

"I'm supposed to meet Rob in the cellar in fifteen minutes," I murmur, using my chin and nose to push the collar of her sweater down. She giggles when my mouth and face reach the top of her breast.

"Stop it!" She's in a full belly laugh. "We have work to do."

I blow on her skin, making a bubbling noise. "Fine."

"Besides, I'm sure Gemma will be here any minute to shove my face full of food while Erin and I review our donations for the hospital's annual charity gala next month."

"Gemma is good at that, isn't she?" I joke, smacking Piper's ass as she stands up.

"Yes!" she yelps, heading back into her office. But before she closes the door, she turns to me and says, "Save that energy for tonight, Mr. Bradley."

My dick swells, knowing that I get to go home to her every single night. "Trust me, I will."

Epilogue
Continued

PIPER

When you have sex as much as Jack and I do, even with birth control, accidents are bound to happen. Avery and Lina were so happy when I told them I was pregnant. Bailey, being the mom, was thrilled but also sad that she wouldn't be around to experience this with me. I am a little sad, too, but the full-time staff at the winery has quickly become the family I've always needed.

Gemma cooks only healthy meals for me and has also come over to meal prep for us the last few weeks. Yesterday, while having breakfast with her and Jack's mom, she shared with us the wonderful news that she'll be stepping down as the main chef to become our nanny after the baby's birth. Just like she was for Jack when he was a child. My heart completely sank when I heard that, and Jack was so grateful.

Heidi is every bit as helpful and kind as I could ever want. She could not be prouder to have him back and running the winery as she and his dad had always wanted.

When we told her that I was pregnant, she cried and gave me the longest hug I think I've ever had. She's been instrumental in my transition to my new position in Human Resources, and I'm incredibly grateful to be a part of it.

I thought it would be difficult to give up flying after it took me such a long time to earn my wings, but I no longer needed to run. I finally feel like I have somewhere I belong. A place where I can truly be myself. Bradley Wines has felt like home since my feet hit the ground the first time Jack brought me here. It feels like this land has been searching for me all along.

I haven't spoken to Roxy since that phone call, where she told me to make sure I got a payment from Jack. I decided enough was enough. She texted me after that, reminding me I was a worthless daughter and not to come crying to her when my world crumbled. I remember when those words would have deeply affected me, but now they don't. I know my worth and that I'm a good person. I refuse to let her dull my flames or extinguish the burning fire.

After some coercion from Jack, I started therapy. My goal is to set up healthy boundaries or to accept that I've romanticized my relationship with my mother, never giving up hope that she'd miraculously turn into the mother I need. But that's not going to happen. Acceptance is a long, bumpy road, but I'm on the right track.

I did leave her a voicemail telling her I'm pregnant, but I have yet to hear back.

Standing in the kitchen of our finally finished home, I'm chopping some veggies for dinner tonight. Since I left Jack in his office early this morning, he's been all over the property with Edward.

I hear the door open and close in the distance, making my

heart jump into my throat. My insides warm, knowing that this is the time of day I get him all to myself.

"My wife." Jack brings his body flush to mine, sliding his arms around my waist from behind.

I breathe him in, melting into his comforting embrace. "Hi."

"I thought I was making dinner tonight?" he asks, glancing at the stove.

I twist my body in his arms and slide my hands under his sweater and over the warmth of his skin. "I wanted to surprise you."

"That's sweet, my love, but if it doesn't turn out, remember there's always take out."

"Oh my god. Stop it!" I laugh, then give his shoulder a quick shove.

Jack knows I'm not the best cook, and to be honest, neither is he. We typically order out or have Gemma cook for us. Growing up alone, I could never experience a family. I have loved cooking meals with Jack. Something about cooking together just makes me feel so complete. I did spend time at my grandparents' house, and it was only there that I had consistency and stability. I will come to peace with my mother, maybe over time. Or perhaps being a mother will help me understand why she made the decisions she did.

"I'm kidding. I'm no cook either, but being married to you, someone had to learn," he quips, lifting me by my waist and setting me on the counter.

Flutters fill my stomach, and I smile, realizing how absolutely happy I am.

Jack positions himself between my legs. "I love you."

"I love you too." I keep my voice low as he bends to rest his head on my belly.

"Now, take off your pants," he calmly commands, bringing his fingers to the button at my waist.

How did I get this lucky?

Want more Piper and Jack?

Head to the Link below to read a bonus scene!

https://dl.bookfunnel.com/mtbcsjgcxv

Acknowledgments

First, I would like to thank the readers who have taken a chance on this love story and me as a brand-new romance author. The series came to me while on a flight to Las Vegas with my husband. I knew I wanted to write a story about four flight attendants who are close friends and their very unique love stories.

To my husband, thank you for putting up with my endless conversations about plots, character ideas, and scenes that seemed to jump into my head at the most inconvenient times. Thank you for putting up with my inability to stay stationary, as I'm consistently running at full speed through life. I love you and all of the ways you show up for me every day.

To Nicki, I'm so grateful for your help with these two. Their love story was big and made me feel all the emotions. Thank you for your invaluable support of my plot ideas and, more importantly, for your friendship.

To all of my beta readers, Jillian, Melissa, Sarah, and Nicki, thank you for reading Love Beyond the Illusion and making it the story it is today.

To Melissa, thank you for loving Piper and Jack just as much as I do and ensuring their deeply personal story is ready for the world.

Thank you to the incredible indie authors who have become a network of resources, knowledge, and support.

To all of the romance authors who have shared their love and creativity with the world. Your stories inspire me and provide me with an escape from the rest of the world. Please don't ever stop writing. We all need those happily ever afters.

About the Author

M.J. Huxley is originally from Los Angeles, California, but resides in the Southwest. When she isn't jamming to 80s music, eating tacos, or hanging out with her family, she's writing about the characters she loves.

M.J. Huxley strives to tell authentic stories of imperfect love. She writes emotional romances with banter & spice. M.J.'s books will always have a happily ever after, but that doesn't mean her characters won't have to work hard to get there.

Keep in Touch with M.J.

Website: https://www.authormjhuxley.com/□
Instagram: https://www.instagram.com/authormjhuxley/
TikTok: https://www.tiktok.com/@authormjhuxley
Goodreads: https://bit.ly/4aouWSG
Pinterest: https://www.pinterest.com/authormjhuxley/

Also by M.J. Huxley

"He said he'd always be there for her, even if he weren't always around."

Check out Bailey and Mason's story in the first book of the Tangerine Sky series, a steamy brother's best friend, enemies to lovers, and single-parent romance.

www.ingramcontent.com/pod-product-compliance
Lightning Source LLC
Chambersburg PA
CBHW032005310726
48972CB00002B/275